ENHANCED

BOOK ONE OF THE TERRIAN TRILOGY

by Jenny Benjamin

ENHANCED

BOOK ONE OF THE TERRIAN TRILOGY

novel

Jenny Benjamin

ANANKE
PRESS

Enhanced: Book one of the Terrian Trilogy
Published by Ananke Press
Copyright © 2021 by Jenny Benjamin
All rights reserved

Interior and cover design by Ananke Press

ISBN: 978-1-7341720-7-2 (paperback)

ANANKE
PRESS

Ananke Press
178 Columbus Avenue, #230137, New York, NY 10023
anankepress.com
info@anankepress.com

For my NOVA family with a special tribute to Kevin Bohannon, Dorrell Williams, and Dorian Crawford—only the universe can hold your wonders.

CONTENTS

CHAPTER ONE
PRACTICE

I had love's tinder heaped within my breast;
What wonder that the flame burned furiously?
She did not walk in any mortal way,
But with angelic progress; when she spoke,
Unearthly voices sang in unison.

– "Laura" from Canzoniere,
Francesco Petrarch

Jesse knew that things in the world weren't always as they seemed. As such, he almost smelled the city in his suburb on this fall day – asphalt and wind, tinder cracks of burning in the distance, but where Jesse lived now the smell meant piles of leaves smoking, not the K2 synthetic weed he remembered smelling on his dad and uncle, a scent his six-year-old self hadn't understood, but now the teenage Jesse knew. After what had happened to the two of them, he felt relief from the pungent scent of autumn-leaf smoke. He gazed across the practice lawn, an expanse of manicured green, and then his eyes stopped on the person right in front of him: Kate. Her long hair blew in the breeze. He wondered if it smelled like strawberries and felt instantly silly for it.

Didn't smell like strawberries just because her hair was red. And tempting to touch.

"Shake hands with your partner," Mr. Allen, their drum line coach, boomed.

Kate stepped closer and put her hand out; her blue eyes locked on Jesse's for a half beat and then glanced down and up. Jesse reached his hand out, and they shook. His heart thundered in his chest. When he looked at their clasped hands, his mind flashed two words:

charcoal and chalk.

They smiled nervously, released their hands, and focused attention to Mr. Allen.

"All right, everyone, we need to nail this for Saturday's performance, so sticks ready," he shouted. Mr. Allen walked the length of the drum line, which had spread down the football field, and rubbed his bald head.

"Sharing a drum with a partner," Mr. Allen continued, "means your snare beats have to be tight, and it will exercise your restraint as well. Left side go first. Non-snares – move out to the northeast corner and practice on your own."

Jesse saw Sofia, his girlfriend of over three years. She hoisted her bass drum onto her shoulders and gave a quick wave. He nodded back.

Mr. Allen moved on down the field, spreading out the teams of two even more. He put his hands on Kate's and Jesse's shoulders and gently guided them farther away from other pairs.

"Kate, take it easy on Jesse," Mr. Allen said with a jovial shrug.

Kate gave a small smile, and Jesse felt his face grow hot.

"This all right? The position, I mean, of the drum." Jesse cringed inside. Why was he so nervous? Kate was one of the nicest people in school: quiet, but nice, very real, and beautiful.

"It's a little high. You're a good four inches taller than me," she answered.

"Not a problem." He lowered the drum on his shoulders by adjusting the straps.

"Begin when you're ready," Mr. Allen shouted to the snare partners. Then he moved over to the non-snare group where Sofia and the others were practicing their parts on bass drums, cymbals, and triangles.

Jesse started and stumbled over several riffs in his section. He looked straight ahead as he'd been taught, but Kate was in his line of vision. Her encouraging face was distracting. His hands were sweating so much he nearly dropped the sticks. Mercifully, his set ended, and it was Kate's turn.

"Man, I messed that one up," he said.

Kate squinted and considered him. "Just nerves, I'm sure. You always hit your marks, Jesse."

Jesse wished it were track practice instead of drum line; then he could have bounded up and down the field to mirror his joy.

"Doubt it," he said. "You're up. You can't do worse."

She didn't. In fact, she killed it on her section, but even if she hadn't, Jesse thought, he might not have known because he was lost in her scent of soap and something else, a flowery, earthy smell, like spring. This warmed his body in the early October wind.

His next section went better because he felt comfortable and a little flattered by her intent eyes looking only at him. At the end of his turn, he knocked his stick on the drum's rim and winked at her. She blushed red, almost the same color as her long hair.

He took a step closer to her. "Kate," he said. His voice was hoarse. He wasn't sure what he was about to say. He wanted to ask her out, but this was ridiculous. He had a girl! He and Sofia had been together since the beginning of freshman year.

Jesse glanced down the field and felt heat rise to his face. Sofia looked right at him.

Kate turned to look in the same direction and then stepped away from Jesse.

He cued Kate: "You're up."

"Yeah," she said. Kate struggled through her last section, and the rest of the practice seemed tinged with guilt for something unknown, a buried thing that neither one acknowledged.

"All right, folks," Mr. Allen shouted, "that's enough for today."

The line dispersed with Kate one of the first to flee. Jesse wanted to catch up with her, but then what? Nothing. Anyway, she was clear across the lawn, heading to the band room in the northern building with rapid steps.

Sofia waited in the northeast corner of the field. When Jesse reached her, she stretched on her tiptoes and gave him a fast kiss before Mr. Allen could see.

"What was that about?" she asked. She shook her silky black hair out. Her backside swayed rhythmically with her drum on her hip. Jesse slid his snare over one shoulder and took the drum from Sofia.

"What was what about?" he answered.

"You and Miss Irish-America."

"We were snare partners. Allen set it up. That's it." He tried to keep his voice casual.

He picked up his pace, but the drums felt like dead weight. He wanted to glance back toward Kate but didn't dare.

"Okay, whatever." Sofia had a joking tone, but Jesse knew there was more beneath it: a covered-up, worried cadence, like his mom used to use when she'd talked about where his dad was. "Anyway, you think she's still with Hayden?" Sofia pointed in Kate's direction, and Jesse turned immediately.

Hayden, another boy in the line who was known for being a player, had his arm around Kate's shoulder. Jesse felt his stomach turn, but then again, Hayden always had his arm around someone's shoulder. He was easygoing that way.

"They ever together?"

"I guess. Well, I don't know," she answered.

They unloaded their gear in the northern building band room in silence. They held hands as they walked through the gymnasium to get to the series of front doors of their sprawling suburban high school. Outside the flag that read "Home of the Wolverines" flapped on a high pole. Jesse headed to the bike rack while rubbing Sofia's palm with his index finger. He wanted to soothe away her worries, forget practice, and Kate.

She squeezed his hand back and let go. A loud group of other drummers spilled out of the doors.

"Nice helmet, Woods. What're you trying out for, Special Olympics?" Kyle said; he was a rich kid from Prescott Heights who was mainly cool, but Jesse always felt like he had to play along. He didn't want to stand out even more.

"Yeah, something like that," Jesse said and pulled Sofia to his chest; he kissed her hard so that the on-lookers ooohhed.

She gave one of her sexy half smiles back. She knew he had done that for the other guys and laughed it off; as usual she helped him belong. The guys were on to something else, many getting on the late bus or others hopping into cars. Almost all had cell phones out and were calling or texting someone because they were finally out of the school and practice.

"Remember, I won't be at school tomorrow," Sofia said.

"Why? Sorry, I forgot."

"You should remember," she said and smiled again. God, he loved that smile. "Tita is taking me to *Planning Tomorrow* for the shot."

"Right. We want to keep that up," he said and kissed her again. "Not ready to be your baby's daddy."

One of her eyebrows went up and her phone buzzed. "That's Kev. The jerk won't drive up to the school, says I have to meet him on the corner where the old schoolhouse landmark is. Sometimes I want to murder my brothers. Too much Puerto Rican macho bull." She let out a string of expletives in Spanish, pecked Jesse's cheek, and was gone.

Jesse swung himself onto his bike and was relieved to be in motion. Special Olympics? How many times had that one been used? Weak-ass rich kid, Jesse thought. He peddled around the circle at the front of the school lot. The tennis courts were on his right, neat squares of green with painted borders. Beyond that, a larger section of parking stretched almost empty. Out of the corner of Jesse's eye he saw a silver car cross the lot and crawl to a stop at the tennis court fence.

Jesse paused at the Cebar Road intersection, waiting for the light. A flash of silver caught his eye and he glanced back at the car, now parked, and saw a woman in a full headdress – *hijab* – he remembered it was called, and a shimmery silver gown that covered her neck, arms, and it trailed on the gravel in the lot. She shut the door to her car and stared right at Jesse. He turned away with a snap of his neck and cursed under his breath. He had missed the light.

Damn, now it would be another forever before he could get across the suburban wasteland.

He waited but felt a pull from the Muslim woman. She had to be Muslim with that kind of full body covering.

Don't look back, he told himself. He didn't want to cause offense. Wasn't the whole point of wearing such an outfit to avoid being noticed? Jesse pretended to adjust something on his bike and snuck another glimpse.

She was there, staring right at him, her one hand, strangely covered in a silver glove, on the handle of her car.

Jesse, I'm here to warn you. A voice sounded in Jesse's head. He shot upright on his bike, twisted his head to the woman, and blinked, hoping she would be gone.

Dang, he was tired. He was hearing things, had to be. The light changed and he pumped his legs hard. His thigh muscles pulsed with blood because he was in a sprint on his bike, trying to shake off the peculiar feeling of the voice and the Muslim woman.

Probably didn't drink enough water today, and he was as hungry as Methuselah was old. That thought brought a smile to his face because it was something his mom would say. He just needed to get home; that was all. He shot across Cebar Road, easily avoiding the traffic, and cut through the Crest Valley subdivision until he reached the bike path.

Once on the smooth pavement that wove through woods and along the multitude of the southern suburbs of Chicago, he sat back on his bike seat, let go of the bars, and breathed in the woody scent of leaf rot and dusk. He loved this time of day, when the suffocation of school and the regimentation of his tight schedule expanded. The sky stretched a calm gray behind a blazing sunset. He coasted into the hazy orange for a few more minutes and then shot off into it. He wanted to make it from the school in the Molleena suburb to his New Franklin home in twenty-two minutes. He set his watch. He thought about applying for that track scholarship to Eastern University next year and peddled even harder.

Twenty minutes and fifteen seconds later he was pulling his bike into the garage and hanging his helmet on the wall hook.

Supper smells came from the kitchen and his mouth watered.

His mom was bustling over three pots on the stove, turning once in awhile to answer a homework question for Keisha. Dorian shot across the kitchen in a cape made from an old towel. He had on a mask meant for Halloween.

"Out, Dorian. You scared the life out of me!" his mom said. "Hi, Jesse, how was practice?"

"All right," he answered. An image of Kate, not Sofia, materialized in his mind, so he shut his eyes to refocus. And then he remembered the voice, clear as a bell, *Jesse, I'm here to warn you.*

He grabbed a quart of orange juice from the fridge, started to drink from the carton, and stopped himself because his mom gave him one of those looks. He got a glass and poured himself three full ones, one after another.

"You got home fast," she said.

"Yeah, one of my best times yet."

"You wear your helmet?"

"Mom, I always do."

"Just making sure," she said while stirring a pot of spaghetti sauce. "I had a traumatic brain injury patient today. Twenty-two years old and will most likely not regain his ability to walk. God knows what else is lost to him. Makes me worry."

"You always worry," he said and kissed her cheek.

"I know. Wash up. Tonight we eat like the devil's behind us because these little ones are going to bed *early*. I have to leave at five tomorrow morning, and Michael works late tonight. You two will be in charge of getting the cherubs to school and daycare."

"I have a Friday sun-up run in the morning with Coach Nelson and the half milers."

"I know, Jess-a-peek," she said and gave a look like she used to when he was five; she even used his old nickname. "It won't take but thirty seconds to pour two bowls of cereal. I'll braid KiKi's hair tonight. Michael will get them dressed and out the door on time."

"Awright."

"Go wash the day off now, Jesse," she said. She leaned over and hugged him hard, again like it was just the two of them, like years ago. She smelled of flowers and hair oil. Jesse inhaled a long breath as if it was the start of a quarter mile sprint. Kate's face surfaced again and he got a prickly feeling all over his body. He felt oedipal and strange. He pulled away.

"You okay?" his mother asked.

"Oh yeah," he said. But something felt different. He couldn't get Kate out of his mind. His body flushed with the heat of two levels of betrayal: First he really cared for Sofia, and second, there was a part of Jesse that didn't want to fall for a white girl, at least not one as white as Kate.

And then, there was the Muslim woman. Who was she? There weren't many Muslims in Molleena or New Franklin. There wasn't much of anything but white Catholics and Protestants where he lived now. Did she have something to do with what he heard?

His mom held her hand to his cheek even though he had stepped back. She gave him a sideways look as if she saw through him. Dorian broke the moment by pulling out pots and pans from a cabinet and sliding across the floor on a cookie sheet.

"I'll get you," he yelled at Keisha.

"Be quiet," she shouted back. "I'm a first grader, Dorian, and I have a lot of homework. You're only three. You'd never understand!"

"I have to do my homework, too! It's hard as yours," Dorian shouted.

"That's it, everyone, let's eat," his mom said. "I'm ready to shut this day *down*."

Jesse couldn't agree more.

CHAPTER TWO
WARNING

*The Lady, the flash of lightning, goes along the sky,
the divinity who is the sovereign of this world.*

— Rig Veda 10:169:2

The next morning, after his early run with the cross-country team, Jesse showered and dressed in the locker room. He liked entering first period before anyone else arrived. Ms. Gamble was usually there reading at her desk with a quotation from some ancient literary masterpiece on the Smart board behind her.

Jesse's shoes squeaked on the polished floors across the empty hallway. Ms. Gamble's door was open, so he slipped in and took his assigned seat, far right row, mid-to-back desk.

"Hi, Ms. Gamble," Jesse said, already pulling his backpack open to get his books out.

"Good morning, Jesse. You're even earlier than usual. Happy reading," she said and looked down, her sandy hair circling her face.

"You too," he said and started looking over his Advanced Chemistry lab for writing errors.

Though he knew the words already, he acted like he was reading. For as long as Jesse could remember, he had had a photographic memory. If he read something once, he rarely had to read it again. Often, the pages themselves materialized in his mind like a digital book on a screen.

But today, he had to focus on his write-up of the lab he had been working on with his group for the last week. Yesterday had shaken him up. First there was the weird hijab-wearing woman in the school parking lot, and then he heard a woman's voice in his head.

Jesse, I'm here to warn you.

What did he need a warning about? That thought made him nervous. As if the voice was real and not imagined. Now, he really felt like a whack job.

He had thought he would sleep it off and today would be back to normal, but he'd slept in fits and bursts and then he'd had the mother of all nightmares. He was in the desert, suspended in air – how he didn't know – and screams, horrible, humans-dying-an-agonizing-death screams came from beneath the sand. He wanted to save who or whatever was making the sounds, but he couldn't move; the air held him in a vice grip. A figure materialized in the distance, and Jesse's stomach turned. In his dream, he felt like he knew who or what was coming, but now, he had no idea who the figure was who approached on the back of an elephant-like creature. The figure stopped right below where Jesse hovered. The man on the beast could have been one of his teachers: middle-aged, medium build and white hair, two arms, two legs. But his skin had a shimmery, silver quality to it, and his eyes were pure white. They glowed like empty stars, far away and ready to implode. Or was it that Jesse felt the eyes sucking him in. Oddly, the phrase, *winner take all,* ran through his mind, in the dream or out of it, Jesse wasn't sure.

The white-eyed man spoke. *You'll have to choose, you know. I've been watching you, Jesse Voshon Woods. You thought you could solve everything with a neatly ordered life, with regimentation.* The man dragged the last word out and punctuated each syllable like a punch to the gut. *But you have no control over anything, except maybe what you'll do next.*

He had shot awake, scared and shivering in his bed. A few short minutes later, his alarm went off at 5 a.m. for his sun-up run. He'd grabbed his bag, set out bowls and spoons for his brother and sister, threw the cereal boxes on the table, and shot into the dark on his bike, hoping the bike ride and morning run would clear his head.

It had, for a bit. But now in the florescent light of early morning, before first period, he felt scared again.

Just a dream, he told himself. Pull it together.

The bottom of his backpack vibrated, and Jesse nearly shot out of his seat. His cell phone.

Ms. Gamble's eyes didn't leave the book, but she said, "Good thing that's buzzing before school hours, Jesse, or I'd have to take it." She was known for taking phones left and right.

"Sorry," he said and found the phone.

It was a text from Sofia.

Miss you already. Don't get too lonely without me.

Jesse put the phone down and went back to the lab. The fact was without having weird dreams and hearing the voice he would have been excited to have a day to himself. He loved Sofia and all, but sometimes he liked to do his own thing. She could be so needy. Like right now. He knew she was sitting by her phone, waiting for his reply. He sighed and typed back.

Miss u 2.

Then he cut it off and started his day.

Step one, first period, just like always.

The morning flew by. Once Ms. Gamble got going, Jesse was absorbed. Then it was Chem Lab, Advanced Algebra, Media Center, and now lunch. And today, without Sofia, he could sit with the rest of the drum line or the track guys, or wherever he wanted. His heart lifted a little with excitement.

He jostled through the crowd of students, noting as he usually did, how it was a sea of white people with an occasional ethnic face, a dot of brown. Sometimes he felt so large and dark, like outer space. But today, his mind was on lunch and where to sit. He decided he'd go with the drum line. Kate Hughes always sat to the right of the group with some of the other girls from band, usually the flutes. He could position himself kiddy-corner from her if he moved fast.

His heart pumped a staccato beat while he snaked through the hot lunch line. He caught a flash of Kate's red hair out of the corner of his eye. He chanced a look while grabbing two milks. She had her lunch bag already open in front her. She sat with the flutes like he had guessed. Her smile, even though it wasn't directed at him, drew him over to her table. He sat next to Jack, cymbals, and across from Kate at a diagonal. He was in luck.

"Hey Jesse," Jack said. "No Sofia today?"

"Naw," he answered, aware of Kate looking up and away from him in an instant. "She's sick today."

Jack nodded and the two went quiet. Jack was the perfect foil. Jesse was cool with him, and they could easily sit and eat in silence, giving Jesse an opportunity to listen to Kate's voice, or even talk to her.

He worked through his chicken tacos with his ear on

Kate's conversation. She tended to listen more than lead and he wondered if he was imagining her leaning his direction. What could he say to her? They didn't have any classes together to bring up assignments. Even though they were both snares, it felt lame to ask about the weekend's competition. If she were in track he could ask what races she planned to run in the spring, but the drum line – they all did the same thing. He couldn't really get into anything deep, like how did it feel to be the only girl snare player.

Lame, lame. Double lame.

They had about five more minutes of lunch. Kate was packing her bag up; it had designs on it like a Jackson Pollack painting. Could that be a doorway to conversation?

Before Jesse had an aneurism over what to say to her, she slid an inch his way and said, "How are you?"

He almost looked over his shoulder to be sure no one stood behind him.

"Me?" Oh, please, something, anything – what could he say not to blow this? "I'm okay, how about you? Ah, what class do you have next?"

Misery. He was a total idiot.

"I have Tech Science. I usually cross to the east building outside. I like to get fresh air," she said, her voice like fresh air itself.

"I go that way, too, to get to..." He had no idea what his next class was.

"Yeah, I know, I see you go that way sometimes."

What they both left out was that Sofia was usually on his arm. They sometimes kissed against the back wall of the building because teachers hardly passed that way.

The lunch bell rang, and the room erupted in a surge of bodies moving.

Before she could get away, Jesse said, "I'll walk with you, if it's all right." He had never wanted to walk with a girl so badly in all his life. Ironically, at this very moment Sofia was getting a birth control shot as he was trying to squeeze next to another girl. He buried the thought and waited the half second for Kate's answer.

"Yeah, okay," she said, and they grabbed their books and garbage.

Jesse was quick to get rid of his tray, always keeping a peripheral eye on where Kate waited: at the back door, hugging the cement wall, her eyes expectant.

What the hell was he doing? He wanted to kiss her of all things, and was he imagining her wanting that too? He shook off the sensation of someone running a feather along his skin and made his way to Kate.

"I got the door," he said, holding it open for her to slip under his arm. She fit there so easily. He caught a whiff of her scent, intoxicating, and he had to clench his hand in a fist to keep from touching her hair.

She turned, opened her mouth to speak, and closed it. Her face turned red, but she smiled.

The gravel crunched below their feet. Jesse went at a fast clip when he walked this stretch with Sofia; she usually dragged her feet, tried to pull him back, and teased him about being late to his next class.

Jesse could tell Kate was measuring her steps, too, as if they were both trying to slow time down.

"So," she said.

They both laughed.

"Yeah, I..." There he went again, trailing off. Since when did he get so nervous?

"How about we just walk," she said. "We don't need to talk."

Jesse was about to answer when he caught a glimpse of silver out of the corner of his eye. The Muslim woman stood near the building they needed to enter, waiting. She gestured toward Jesse and Kate with a barely perceptible wave. She was in the same shimmery full body outfit as the day before.

"Do you know that woman?" Kate asked.

"Ah, no, not really. But I saw her at the school last night after drum line practice," he said. The sight of the woman made him feel fuzzy headed. The sunlight caught the sheen of her dress, and Jesse felt disoriented, like the eye doctor had just put in drops to dilate his pupils.

"I think she wants us to come over to her. Maybe she needs help." Kate picked up the pace.

"Kate, no, wait—" Jesse said, but Kate was already on her way. A buzzing started in his head, like an alarm, but despite his fear, he, too, felt compelled to find out about this woman, so he followed. It felt like the sky was doing flip flops above them.

They were next to the woman within thirty seconds, and in that time, Jesse became downright dizzy. What was happening? His head might explode if he didn't hold onto something. Kate turned to him, caught his eye, and looked worried.

"Are you all right?" She grabbed his hand and it felt like he'd stuck his fingers in an electrical outlet. Kate must have felt it too because her arm twitched, but she held his hand harder for a few seconds before she let go, moving her fingers in and out from the touch. Jesse wanted to thank the eerie, silver-eyed Muslim woman who stood still, watching with intent. Had she not been there, Kate would not have taken his hand.

"It's beginning," the woman said in an even voice, almost with a British accent, but not, just posh.

Jesse gained some focus while still warm from the memory of Kate's hand. This in itself was such a betrayal to Sofia, but he'd give anything for one more touch.

"Do I know you?" Jesse asked.

Students swarmed around them; they had about two minutes until the next period bell rang. Jesse was vaguely aware of the heavy metal door clicking open and shut.

"Not yet, but I know both of you. I don't have much time, but I'm here to warn you. And one other – Hayden Monroe."

"Wait, warn us?" Jesse said. Now his head truly spun. Maybe it was some kind of aneurism or stroke, strange things have happened to seventeen-year-olds before. Maybe he'd be the youngest stroke victim in the world.

"Warn us," Kate said. "About what?"

"You must feel it, don't you? Your minds are triggering. It's only a matter of time until you see us, and your world will come crashing down," the woman said. Her eyes flitted to the sky. Her eyelids and all around them were caked with make-up, an odd juxtaposition to the full-body dress, but the silver coloring matched and both make-up and dress had the same iridescence.

"Do you need help or something?" Kate said. "Um, we don't really know what you're talking about."

"Jesse," the woman said, "you feel it happening now. I can see it in your eyes. I know you heard me in your head yesterday, but you didn't come to me. I understand. It's a strange sensation when your mind opens to pathways it had never run along before, when the core of your genetic make-up is coded for supernatural actions, and suddenly those markers awaken. Just by being in contact with me, your body chemistry is responding. You must listen to me—" Ms. Gamble came out of the east building door, a large tote bag full of books slung over her shoulder. She caught Jesse's eye and squinted. He must have looked sweaty, dizzy, ready to vomit, because he felt all of the above and Ms. Gamble came right over to the bizarre trio.

Kate's hair kept getting in her face, which was pale, and her hands shook a little.

"Jesse, hi," Ms. Gamble said. "Is everything okay?"

"Ah, um, yeah, fine," he mumbled.

"You look like you don't feel well, and hello." Ms. Gamble put out her hand and the Muslim woman took it in her gloved one. The shake was brief. "Do you know Jesse, and um, I'm sorry, young lady, I'm not sure of your name."

"Kate. Kate Hughes."

"Do you know these students?"

The woman started speaking in a language that sounded like Arabic, and the thing that nearly sent Jesse into cardiac arrest was that he understood her.

"Jesse, there is no time," the woman said. "You must be ready. I will try to help you, but you need to be open to whatever happens. You need to stay close to Kate and Hayden."

"What are you talking about? Where's Hayden now? What do you mean be ready?" he answered. IN ARABIC!

The bell rang.

"Jesse," Ms. Gamble said. "I didn't know you spoke Arabic?"

"Ah, yeah, a little," he said.

The Muslim woman looked at Jesse and resumed her speech in Arabic, "I have to leave. You and your friends have power. Be open to the changes ahead of you."

Jesse felt every hair on his body stand at attention.

The woman continued, "Earth is in trouble. You and your friends may be the only ones who can save it." She released her gaze without another word, and as quickly as she had appeared, she turned and walked around the side of the building.

"Jesse, what did she want?" Ms. Gamble asked.

"Um, she needed directions, she's not from here. I told her how to get to Route 355."

"Wow, you never cease to amaze me, Jesse," Ms. Gamble said. "You two better get to class." She walked off in a quick clip across the drive.

"Oh my God, what was that about?" Kate said. "Do you think she's crazy?"

"She must be, right?"

"What did she say to you in Arabic?"

Jesse relayed what the woman had said. His mind was clearing a bit, but he still felt disoriented.

"Okay, she must have some sort of mental illness," Kate said. "But I have to admit, something happened with you. You looked like you might be sick, and can you really speak Arabic?"

"Yes to the sick part, and no to the Arabic, at least not until now," he said in a rush.

"Are you all right now?" Kate asked, tilting her head up to get a better look at his eyes.

"No, not really, but what are we going to do? Find Hayden in his fifth hour class and sit next to him, so we're all *ready*? We have no idea what that means?"

"But the Earth's in trouble? Who talks like that?" Kate smiled and reddened. "We better get to class."

"Yeah," Jesse said. "We need to forget it all happened." He held the door to the building open for her and she slid under again.

Looking over her shoulder, her eyes half open, she said, "Well, not *all* of it." She glanced to his hand and turned away, her red hair streaming behind her in waves.

CHAPTER THREE
TORNADO

The voice of the Lord flashes forth flames of fire.
The voice of the Lord shakes the wilderness.

— Bible, Psalms, 29: 7-8

The weird day at school had ended without more sightings from the Muslim woman. Jesse was dressing in his band uniform for the afterschool rehearsal when his cell phone buzzed in his locker. He grimaced; he made sure no teacher was looking and peeked at the text. It was from Sofia.

Done with appointment. Tita took me and called school as Mom. Subterfuge intact.

For the second time that day Jesse didn't feel like texting back, but he knew she'd be waiting and wondering why he didn't answer. An image of Kate's red hair whipping in the wind flashed in his mind. He typed a response to Sofia.

What're u doing now? I have to get to practice.

Just took a shower and chillin'. I have the house to myself, so rare.

Have fun.

Luv u, Jesse.

His fingers froze on the keys for awhile, and then he typed.

Me too. See u later?

Yeah. Gotta go. Someone's at the door.

Almost everyone in the line was moving out of the locker room. Jesse didn't care for the purple and yellow band uniforms with brass buttons and tassels, but he knew they would look impressive as a group for the competition with Davenport High the next day. He saw Hayden Monroe out of the corner of his eye. Should he say something to him? Ask if he had had any peculiar run-ins with a Muslim woman? Jesse opted not to say a thing.

"You coming?" Hayden said. "Or would you like to make love to your cell phone some more?" He and Hayden were close enough to rib each other, to a point.

"Funny," Jesse said. He tucked his phone in his bag and stowed everything in his locker.

"No hot Puerto Rican on your arm today?" Hayden asked.

"No, she was absent."

"Lucky her. These uniforms suck. We all look like we should have trumpets sticking out our asses."

Jesse laughed and followed Hayden to the football field for their practice. The line was already assembling, and Jesse's eyes immediately found Kate. He watched her slender form move beneath her uniform.

"Oh yeah," Hayden said. "I see her too. She's not hard to spot as the only chick with a snare, but man, something about her."

Did Hayden's comment mean that he and Kate weren't going out?

Kate turned to look directly at the two boys, but her stare fell on Jesse. He held her gaze long enough to feel uncomfortable. He was especially grateful for his dark skin because he knew it masked his blush.

"Dude." Hayden started to say more, but a loud warbling rattle, like a train grinding to a halt, sounded overhead just as the boys reached the field. Jesse felt the vibration in his chest. Everyone looked up, but the sky was clear except for a few puffy white clouds. *GRRRRRR*. It sounded like a truck without a muffler was barreling down from above.

"It must be a plane or something," Mr. Allen called. He made hand gestures for the drum line to form their positions. "No need to keep your faces to the heavens, good people. Let's start."

The sound lessened a little, but some kids ducked their heads lower when there was a shift in the volume.

"Okay, from the top," Mr. Allen said, but as soon as the words were out of his mouth, the sky changed from a clear blue to an ominous green-black.

The bizarre overhead noises howled more, and gray and black clouds formed whirling masses in the sky.

Jesse saw giant, scowling humanoids break through a fissure in the clouds. They streaked across the sky in streams of silver and gold rivers. Then they stopped for seconds, their bodies quivering like Jell-O not completely set. The waning autumn light danced on their forms in glistening waves. He held his drumsticks in front of his eyes, thinking this would somehow refocus the image, or make it go away. But, no, the beings were there, unless he was totally losing it.

"Whoa," someone yelled and pointed up. "What the heck — the sky is going crazy over there."

Jesse turned his head to see others' reactions, but everyone appeared to see a brewing storm. He was about to flee, but then he noticed Kate. Her hands were shaking, and her eyes were wide. Was this it? Was this what the warning had been about?

Kate's red hair tossed in the wind; it almost looked like the oncoming storm would yank her up into the sky by a wisp of her hair. She blinked, rubbed her eyes and then pointed, saying to Kyle, "Do you see those people?"

"What?" he asked. "You mean the scary storm clouds?"

"Yeah," Kate said and caught Jesse's eye.

Jesse blinked hard. This wasn't happening. But the sky told him something else: Hundreds of feet above him giant male and female forms swam in the green-black gloom. Some had silver hair and some had gold, but all had gelatinous, undulating bodies; they combed the clouds together, sealing the fissure. Within seconds their enormous rake-like hands swept the clouds in swirls, like a drum major twirling a baton.

Hayden screamed and Mr. Allen glared at him. The clanging above grew worse.

"Y'all don't see this? We need to move out," Hayden shouted.

Jesse started to run toward Hayden but stopped when a clap of thunder echoed overhead. He ducked and glanced at Hayden out of half-opened eyes. Hayden looked crazed with his spikes of hair whipping in the wind, his eyes intense and blazing with fear.

Metal crunch and broken glass sounds reverberated. Jesse couldn't help but put his hands over his head in defense.

"Hayden!" Mr. Allen yelled. "Enough! But yes, there's a storm coming. Let's head to the field house, everyone."

"Storm?" Hayden shouted. "What the hell's going on?"

Enormous elastic-like hands above them were making circular motions. All the kids were walking quickly to the field house, but Hayden shot off in a dead run. Kate and Jesse followed suit, leaving the rest of the drum line staggering behind in the increasing wind.

The wind started to whistle, high pitched and ringing. The three crouched toward the ground and covered their ears.

Hayden was about to say something to Jesse and Kate, but a swift wind pulled him back. Alarming gusts of wind knocked people off their feet. Hayden whirled somewhere to Jesse's left, but he couldn't make out where in the dust. Kate was on his right, and both bent their bodies into the wall of wind, trying to push toward the field house.

GGGRRRRR. The rumbling rocked overhead, and the ground shook beneath Jesse's feet. His ears popped and dust flew into his mouth. He could hardly see. The field house was a graying blur ahead of him, and Kate was a hunched purple and yellow form next to him.

Crack!

The sky exploded in a surge of light. Jesse chanced a look at the waves of giant figures coming closer, closer. The forms were battling, clawing, and punching at each other in furious fits.

More shouts and wails clanged from above. The huge figures were waving their monstrous arms, swirling the air. But no, some were still fighting. What the hell? This wasn't happening. Jesse didn't like to think he was losing it, but going crazy would be better than this. Then again, people didn't usually go nuts in a group. Kate and Hayden saw what he did. Ripples of sweat poured from Jesse's face and down his back. He slammed his hands to his ears to muffle the noise, but the booming continued. He had to get out. Get somewhere safe. But where? It was as if the sky was a continuous car wreck on the side of the road. Jesse couldn't help but look.

The swishing, slashing fingers in the air mesmerized him for a moment. Then the storm clouds swirled into a funnel that streamed across the earth, sucking up trees and dirt, tearing through houses and channeling itself toward the football field.

All the students scattered. The funnel cloud kept coming. It tore through the metal fence; it devoured the field house, sending bricks, bodies, and roof shingles high into the air. It churned up dirt and grass.

Mr. Allen was frantic. He was yelling something, but Jesse couldn't make it out. He signaled for students to run to the gym, and then enormous hands ripped off a piece of roof. The roof flew across the field: heading right for Mr. Allen! Jesse lunged to help him as it cut through his coach, severing the man in two.

"No!" Kate screamed, and Jesse lost her in the rising dust and turmoil.

He ran. He ran as fast as he could. His snare drum banged on his back. He slipped off the harness and crawled his way up a hill on the opposite side of the field, but something clicked in his brain, and he remembered that the best place to be in a tornado, even one tossed about by weird looking giant humans, was to be low to the ground. So he threw himself over the other side of the hill, hoping to land in the ditch.

"AHHHHH," he screamed. Horror flashed in his line of vision. Arms, hair, legs, but no people, just parts of them flew. If they were attached to whole friends, Jesse couldn't make them out. He writhed into the now dark air, expecting to hit the earth and log roll down the hill.

But something caught him midflight. It was one of the human forms that had started this chaos, a woman with silver hair and skin; her face was beautiful, enormous, but beautiful. Though she was gigantic and gel, the likeness was unmistakable, it was the Muslim woman. Her gargantuan hand cradled Jesse for a fraction of a second and then a bubble of light engulfed him. He shook and gasped for breath while floating in a protective bubble through the destruction and wind.

Kate was in the bubble with him. She struggled to climb up the slippery iridescence. Then Hayden was there too, swinging at the air and swearing.

"Try to punch through it," Hayden yelled and all three poked and jabbed at the slick sides of the bubble.

"It's useless," Kate said and slumped down.

The three of them whirled through the sky until they were above the pandemonium. The path of the tornado sliced a long trail through the field and made rings within rings as if zeroing in on a target.

"They're looking for something," Jesse said. He glanced at Kate and Hayden when suddenly a force pressed them together in the glowing bubble. Jesse felt slippery liquid on his arms. Kate's right leg was between his legs. Hayden was right along his back with his face and chin on Jesse's shoulder.

"Sorry, man," Hayden said, and Jesse could tell he was trying to keep himself from pressing in too much. But there was nothing else to do but hold each other. Finally, Jesse let himself hold Kate in his arms. Her words were muffles in his chest.

They felt even more pressure as the bubble squeezed through the gymnasium door and emerged into its peace as if they had stepped into another world. The bubble around them floated like a feather and stopped when it touched the floor. Then it popped, leaving the teens in their former positions. Kate's hands were clenched, her cheeks flushed with color, and her hair wet with sweat. Jesse still held her. She was shaking uncontrollably, then pulled away and ran to the gym doors.

It took every nerve and muscle in Jesse's body to keep control of his bowels.

Please, God, he thought. *Don't let me crap myself with Kate right here.*

Hayden instantly jumped back and marched around in a circle, throwing his fists in the air and yelling.

"What's going on here?" Hayden's voice echoed. "Where is she? I saw her at the gas station yesterday. She had on the silver gown thingy and she tried to warn me about something." He paced some more and yelled at the ceiling, "What are you?"

Kate was grabbing each door. She looked over her shoulder at Jesse, "The thing with the bubble – It's the woman, from after lunch." Her voice cracked. "These shouldn't lock on the inside."

Once Jesse got control of his gut, he tried all the doors as well. Nothing budged. They were trapped.

"What the hell is that?" Hayden asked and pointed to a silver bubble like a massive bead of mercury that squeezed through the broken roof and floated near the sports banners on the far wall. It shined and dripped down to the floor until it took the shape of a woman. She was a smaller version, but it was the same giant gel woman, also known as the Muslim woman, who had saved them. She had long silver hair and glistening silver skin and eyes. She wore blue tights, a form-fitting dress, and boots. The outfit was much different from the hijab getup. Except for the silver tint to her skin, eyes, and hair, she looked human. But how?

The woman took three small balls of liquid from a pocket on her hip. She threw the balls to the floor. They rolled a few feet and halted. They quickly oozed and began to form into backpacks. Jesse stared in amazement.

"Are you three all right?" she asked.

Hayden stepped forward, fuming.

"What just happened? What are you?"

"I know you all must recognize me from when I tried to warn you. I wore the dress I did because it was an easy way to cover my silver skin and hair. My name is Hallia, and I'm a Terrian. You must feel disoriented, your minds are already triggering. We are an alien species from a planet just beyond your solar system. I must speak quickly to all of you. There isn't much time"—

"Time for what?" Jesse asked. He was sweating profusely. His stomach was churning again. He had just seen a woman form from a liquid ball. How? Was this Armageddon? What happened to everyone else?

"Please, just listen. Our species and humans have shared a unique history. You've been witnessing the rising trouble. Let me explain."

"There are people out there who need help," Jesse blurted. "You can help them."

"There is nothing left of your drum line, I'm afraid. Please, listen, for a few minutes. You three have the ability to stop this destruction," Hallia said.

Kate screamed and charged Hallia who waved her hand, securing Kate in a bubble again. She slipped and clawed at the sides yelling, "Let me out." At least that was what Jesse thought she said; her voice sounded like she was shouting into a blanket.

"Let her out, or we're done here," Hayden said and ran toward the woman. Instantly he was in his own bubble. Jesse was smart, but it didn't take a genius to see that if he lunged at this alien Hallia, then he would have a matching bubble of his own. He concentrated and took a deep breath to get control of his body.

"We'll listen, just let them out," Jesse said.

"We really don't have time for your Earthly time-outs," Hallia said. "I have much to explain, and human life depends on it. You three can help, but you need to know what you're up against. When I let you two out, please gain control of yourselves." Hallia waved her hands again, and Hayden and Kate plopped to the floor. Kate's face was as red as her hair.

"You better have a pretty frigging good something to say, gel lady. Because we were the only ones to see your giant brethren in the sky, we were nearly killed, and now our friends and teacher are dead. What I want to hear is that this is some whacked out communal nightmare," Hayden said.

"I'm afraid it's real, Mr. Monroe," she said in a softer tone.

Jesse looked at Hayden and Kate and took it upon himself to nod at the alien Hallia to continue.

"Thank you," she said and then continued. "My species, the Terrians, have been following human evolution since there were multiple humanoid groups vying for dominance in prehistoric times. Ancient Terrians saw that *homo sapiens* would win out. They determined this both from observation and from our ability to see snippets of the future. The Ancients tracked human progress and once they saw humans begin to question what was beyond earthly reality, the Ancients began to provide guidance. Soon the Ancients became gods to your ancient ancestors. In some cases, they endowed special gifts to certain worthy humans. They even bred with them."

"What do you mean, gods?" Jesse asked. She had to be running a game. God was there; at least that was what he had been told all his life at church. He didn't know how he stood with God since his dad died, but still it was a whole other ball game to hear an alien say her species played god for humans. Maybe she was a crazy rogue alien, and she should be in a Terrian institution or whatever they had on her planet.

"That's blasphemy," Kate said.

"Yes, from your social construction, I could see where you would think so, but please listen. I would have made myself known to you earlier than the last couple of days, but there wasn't a way. My planet has laws against revealing our god status to current humanity. But now both of our planets need you," Hallia said.

"How do you do the Jell-O giant thing? And the make a bubble of energy with a wave of your hand?" Hayden asked.

Hallia sighed like they were annoying grade school kids. "We are a humanoid species like you, but the biggest difference – along with our technological advances – is that we have learned to use all parts of our brains. We can alter our genetic codes to enhance certain innate abilities or to manipulate matter. We've been working on these skills for millennia, so our superiority is evident. Our species are genetically compatible to yield offspring, but our ancestors shunned it over time."

"Get on with it. Why the hell has your species torn our school apart?" Kate asked in a shrill voice.

"Like I said, we share a unique history," Hallia said, looking away.

"You said that," Hayden yelled. He punched the air, and Jesse put a hand on his arm, trying to calm him.

"What's this really about?" Jesse said.

"The Ancients could foretell the future and saw a time in both Terrian and human futures where we would need each other to save both of our planets, so they determined that we should be linked in a specific manner for centuries, leading up to this time in history."

"You got to be kidding me? What, so the world really is going to end?" Jesse said. Heat spread through his body.

"No. Our worlds won't end. If you listen to me," Hallia said. She brushed her hair back and it glistened. "After the prediction, the Ancients put this relationship in place. Our superiority came with a responsibility. Early humans sought more beyond the natural world around them. The Ancients made it so our place in the development of human civilizations was as your gods."

Jesse's head was spinning. Hallia wasn't some delusional alien. She had a clear way of thinking, a linear mind, as his mom would say. Were all those giants in the sky fighting over being gods?

Hallia threw her hands in the air, and the noise from outside lessened. "Most of the human population prays to us on a daily basis. We have been worshipped in numerous manifestations since the earliest human civilizations – call us Ishtar, Zeus, Juno, Anu, Shiva, the Great Spirit, Allah, Yahweh, or God. We are the one and the many. We are the gods you humans seek." Hallia stared at Jesse in particular. He held her stare in defiance but said nothing. She was not his god.

"This is not real," Hayden said and stepped backward. He started running, actually doing sprints around the gym. Hallia closed her eyes in concentration.

"I don't believe you," Kate said. "Your species may think you're gods or maybe you messed with our early ancestors and made them think you're gods or something, but there is a real God out there. I know there is."

Hallia still had her eyes closed. Jesse motioned to Hayden who nodded. Kate saw they were planning to charge Hallia while her eyes were closed. Hayden dashed from across the gym and Jesse and Kate took off too.

Hallia waved her hands. They weren't in a bubble this time, but they sure as shit couldn't get to her. There was some kind of force field protecting her.

"Ms. Hughes, I will not counter your heart," Hallia said. "But please know that my species has played a role in the advent of all your early religions, and they have guided all religious reformations and changes in the last five thousand years."

"Why are you telling the three of us all this?" Jesse asked. He stood between Kate and Hayden. Two tears rolled out of Kate's eyes, but she wiped them away and clenched her fists again. What were they going to do?

"Because we, your gods, need your help. You three are one

of several Youth Triumvirates who have Terrian gifts. When I encountered you earlier, I wanted to say more, but circumstances made it so I couldn't. Jesse, think of the Arabic, you instantly were able to speak to me. That's evidence that your mind has been triggered, awakened to your dampened abilities. It's only the beginning. You all have them. We need you to use these abilities to locate a power source for us."

"First of all, you aren't my god," Hayden said, "and second, that doesn't make a whole lot of sense considering your superiority and all." Jesse liked this about Hayden. In classes he was always great for discussions and debates because he got to the crux of weakness in someone's argument.

"Yes, true," Hallia answered and began to pace the gym. Her boots clicked on the waxed wooden floor. "Haven't you three ever felt you could do more than what your human prison bodies would allow you to do? Ms. Hughes, you have deep emotions that can manifest into telekinesis." Kate flushed red.

"And you Mr. Monroe," Hallia said and stopped inches from Hayden's face. "What of your almost supernatural bursts of strength and valor. You tone it down in your human games called athletics." Hayden stared her down and she turned to Jesse.

"Mr. Woods, your test scores are off the charts because of your photographic memory. What you see in your mind of what you read is beyond human capabilities."

"So we're part alien?" Kate asked.

"We believe your ancestors were given 'gifts' from our Ancients, and they have been passed to you in your DNA."

Thunder boomed outside, and Hallia shook her head.

"We don't have much time," she said. "To speak from your cultural and religious perspective, the demons are trying to take over your planet. Demons – that's the Christian construction, of course, other human religions depict evil in other ways. But these 'demons' are simply bands of my kind who wish to destroy the present structure. I'm part of a Terrian group called the Shaaris, and we want to protect Earth. You may have seen us in the sky; we have the silver hair. The ones with gold hair are another group of Terrians, your demons. The enemy."

"Wait a minute. Drop the good versus evil pseudo-Bible stuff," Hayden said. "I'm sure these 'demons' have a name too. Maybe they need to take you down a notch."

"No," Hallia said, looking angry, "all you hold dear will perish. You just came from a display of destruction of human life, your friends. And this is only the beginning."

Hayden looked away, his face red. More tears rolled down Kate's cheek. Jesse noticed his hands were shaking so he stuffed them in his pockets. The ceiling started to turn. His head pounded with pain, but Jesse adjusted his eyes to stare at Hallia, gaining composure. Then he spoke, "So these demon-aliens, what're they called and what exactly do they want?"

"They are called Belites. They want humans to follow them instead of us, but the difference is how. They have no problem killing and causing destruction in order to strike such terror in humans' lives that they will do anything to make the horrors stop. They will dominate your planet with force instead of faith."

Hallia's long silver hair shimmered. Whatever Hallia had done to muffle the outside sounds was gone. Jesse heard the wind screaming. Explosions popped as lightning struck the earth and thunder boomed.

"You said that all of our drum line friends are dead," Kate said, "what about everyone else in the school? Where are they? The school is silent."

"I've shielded us from them. Not many were here when the storm began, and that's all they see, a tornado. People are in the basement or they have left. They can't see us now, with my shields in place. But my powers are fractured from the fight. I need to move on quickly or all of our lives are in jeopardy."

"Shields?" Kate asked, dubious.

"In the simplest terms, it's a manipulation of molecules." Hallia opened her mouth to say more, but then shut it. Was she lying?

"What about our families?" Kate's voice wavered.

"I'm glad you asked that, Ms. Hughes. We, the Shaaris, your God, are protecting them."

"What does that mean exactly?" Jesse asked.

"See for yourselves." Hallia closed her eyes and signaled for the three of them to do the same. Suddenly images filled Jesse's mind. He saw his mother, stepdad, and two younger siblings curled together on a large bed. They nestled under a downy blue blanket. His mother's strong arms were wrapped around both of his siblings. The fingers of her right hand cradled his sister Keisha's braided head. Her left arm completely swaddled Dorian.

Jesse opened his eyes and the images disappeared. Soon Kate opened her eyes and so did Hayden.

Hallia said, "See, we want to protect your families and all of humanity. From the evil of the Belites. They will try to get to you by using your families as a manipulation tool."

"Please, stop this," Kate pleaded.

"There is no stopping now. The Shaaris need you to retrieve the power source. You three could be the Triumvirate to attain it. It has been protected since Terrians have been involved in human civilizations. It's been relocated several times since the advent of our status as your gods. For safety."

The gym doors blew open. The right corner of the building was blown apart. Fire blazed through the corridor that led outside. Hallia turned quickly, moved her hands together, and Jesse, Kate, and Hayden were thrust together. This time they were slammed into a heap on the floor. Jesse saw the same bubbly light in a halo over all of them. Then Hallia turned to the explosion and thrust her hands into the air again. A similar force field kept the fire back.

She looked down at Jesse and the others, her eyes frightful, "There's no time. You must leave. I've packed your things. I'll do my best to communicate with you, but from here on out you will be hunted by Belites. They are humanoids as well, but they have beasts. Beware. You'll see us in our enhanced forms and the Belite beasts, but average humans will think they are being plagued by more natural disasters. Stay off of transportation. It will be targeted. Don't use any kind of device for communication, or you will be found—"

Fire was pushing into the gym then. Hallia looked over her shoulder and focused her concentration. When she finished she said, "Avoid human interactions – Belites could track you. Head north and read the instructions in your packs after you've cleared this group of suburbs. The fate of humanity and its faith are with the three of you."

With that Hallia became a giant gelatinous-liquid body again and filled the gym. She burst through the missing portion of the roof, sending the rest on top of the three shaking students. The shield kept hold until the dust cleared. She sprang and flew off to join the battle that lit the dark sky.

Hayden's face was white, and Kate shook. Jesse didn't want to have those gel giants on their backs again; he didn't want to think there wasn't a god; he wanted to wake up from this nightmare. Was this a game to get them to do what they wanted? Whatever the case, they had to move, or they'd be dead like the rest of the drum line. Jesse grabbed Kate's hand and shoved at Hayden to move. They snatched up the backpacks and ran into the fiery gloom that had become the new suburban Chicago landscape.

CHAPTER FOUR
RUN

Hearken to the thunder of his voice,
and the rumbling that comes from his mouth.
Under the whole heaven he lets it go,
and his lightning to the corners of the earth.
After the lightning his voice roars;
he thunders with his majestic voice.
And he does not restrain the lightning when his voice is heard.
God thunders wondrously with his voice;
he does great things which he cannot comprehend.

— Bible, Job, 37:2-5

"We have to keep moving," Jesse shouted. He, Hayden, and Kate struck out across a field of new construction.

"Oh yeah, but hell, I feel sick, like my head's going to fly off," Hayden called back. "Never mind, we have to get clear of their fight."

Raucous clashes sounded behind them. Jesse snuck a glance over his shoulder. The school building was completely obliterated now. Lightning strikes hissed momentarily and illuminated their new reality: Though the tornado had ceased, thunder clouds partially obscured a group of more luminescent aliens piled in the fray. Their massive bodies moved with unnatural rapidity; each time they connected in combat, fire sparks rained from the sky as if it were a grand finale on July Fourth. He shuddered with fear and ran faster.

Emergency vehicles blared and cut through the thunder and eerie yelps from above them. It pained Jesse to think the others in his high school were injured or killed by the wild storms. He fought the desire to turn back and help the emergency teams. Instead he pumped his legs like he did when he ran the four-hundred-meter race in track. He wasn't sure how far they went, but the ominous clashes from above no longer felt like a ceiling ready to collapse on top of them. In Jesse's mind, Hallia's words punctuated each footfall on the ground: *The fate of humanity and its faith are with the three of you.*

The field had craters from the battle, and the houses that were springing up in another uniform suburban neighborhood had holes torn out of roofs. Skeletal frames of houses in the midst of construction had beams dangling from them like partially severed limbs. Some sites crackled with fire that had spread from the tornado site and the raining fallout from the alien battle.

"I don't think that's regular fire," Hayden said. He ran next to Jesse. His chest heaved up and down as he labored to keep up. "You got some lungs, man. Good thing I have superhuman strength according to alien-bitch. But I can't say I feel like running with a furnace in my lungs."

Kate started to trail them in silence. Finally, Jesse turned to find her shape in the surreal autumn darkness. He could no longer see any of the battle above, the clouds and smoke thick in the sky. "It's a little quieter. Let's stop a minute, Kate has to catch up."

Hayden nodded in agreement and bent over at the waist with his hands on his knees. Jesse backtracked and found Kate in the same pose, but she grasped her side.

"Sorry. I have a bad cramp and my head is throbbing," she said through gasps. "I'm a drummer, not a runner." She gave a strained smile. Her hands shook.

"Take some deep breaths. And hold here," Jesse steadied her hand, put it under her nose, and pinched. "I learned this in track. It's a pressure point— it should help."

She held tightly and breathed. "Thanks," Kate said while rubbing her side, "the pressure point thing helped. But there go my hands again. They won't stop shaking. And my head. Is yours spinning at times, too? This triggering stuff she talked about." She sounded terrified.

Jesse felt it, too, but he steeled himself to be strong for Kate. "Yeah, it's going like a top, but if you focus your eyes on one thing, it stops."

She met his eyes and held them, "Thanks, that helps," she said in a soft voice.

Hayden ran up beside the two of them and put his hand on Kate's shoulder. "You okay?" he asked. She nodded in agreement. "So how far do you think we have to go before we take a break? Alien Lady said after this group of suburbs, but as a superior species doesn't she know that the Chicago suburbs go on forever?"

"We definitely need to get outside of Molleena. This is the place of the tornado strike, at least let's hope it's the only place. Get beyond New Franklin? I dunno – it's just a guess." Jesse looked at Kate and tried to assess if she was ready to move again. Her breathing had regulated. His own body was a tangle of nerves and adrenaline. "I think we really need to move again. At least it seems like the battle above the school isn't going on as strong." The pops in the atmosphere had dwindled even more.

Jesse breathed deeply to stay in control. Keeping control had always been his mantra. If he took things one step at a time, no matter the obstacle, and kept his head, things worked out. This was no different. Okay it was different with the whole aliens posing as gods thing, but he could still figure this out and help his family, and Sofia. Where was she? He just had to keep his head, as long as it didn't spin off his body with the *triggering*.

"Look I know we're all freaking out, but we need to stay together and get to safety. Things are dying down," Jesse said.

"How can we tell?" Hayden bounced up and down like Jesse had seen him do before a wrestling match. "We need to hit it."

"Ready?" Jesse asked, looking right at Kate. She nodded in affirmation, so they took off. Jesse purposely slowed his pace, and the other two followed suit. They moved through the new development that was deserted and destroyed even before anyone had had a chance to live in it.

Hayden slid closer to Jesse's right side. "Hey guys, okay, yeah, freaking out, trying not to, but what the heck – I can't get my head around all this. I mean, I never thought much about God, my family being occasional Methodists who don't ever talk about anything, but this alien stuff is weirding me out. I have to admit, though, supernatural abilities – whoa – this Hallia cornered me the other day, decked out as a heavily garbed Muslim, telling me I had kinetic abilities and she said she had to warn me about something."

"The same thing happened to us," Kate said between breaths. "My mind is racing, it's not just the running that makes me feel like passing out, it's, well, everything."

"I'm not letting myself think about it. I'm reacting, like in the line, when we perform. You know it so well, you just go. Well I'm running right now, trying to make it to a place where there isn't any fire to run through and we can open these packs and get some answers."

"Yeah, not thinking is the best way to go," Kate added. "We can't know what to believe, but I know Hallia and her species are not my God."

"I hear ya," Hayden said. "But she's one big alien when she wants to be."

"So creepy," Kate said. "My hands keep shaking. Thanks for the pressure point thing, but it's hard to keep up."

"The only time I run like this is when I have to drop weight," Hayden said.

Boom. The sky exploded with light and the tree line in front of them caught fire. All three hit the ground. Jesse lost sight of Kate, but Hayden was right next to him and swearing into the dirt.

Through the smoke Jesse saw outlines of the giant aliens as they streaked across the blackness and away from them in blurs of silver and gold light. He sighed in relief, but then coughed until he nearly choked on his own spit because the smoke had gotten so thick. His eyes burned when he tried to open them some more, so he and Hayden crawled like they were marines and yelled Kate's name.

Jesse couldn't even see his hand in front of his face, but he felt Hayden shimmying through the torn-up grass next to him. "Kate!" they yelled, but their voices didn't carry and were drowned out with the sound of sirens and cracking branches that burned and fell.

Suddenly he felt a hand on his ankle, and then another on his calf, and then the back of his thigh. His first reaction was to jerk away, and he hoped it was Kate and not a Belite pulling him into smoke and darkness. He twisted and saw her small hands.

"I'm here, Kate." He didn't recognize his voice. It was

hoarse, and there was her name again. Kate, he said it like he was pleading, or praying.

"Jesse." She breathed in relief. He had rolled onto his back and pulled her up the length of his body to roll her between himself and Hayden.

"Now what," Hayden asked and coughed. "We can't see."

"We need to get out of this field. But the good news is that I saw the aliens fly off. Looks like a cease fire for awhile."

"Yeah, fire is the operative word here, bro." Hayden squinted at Kate. "You all right?"

Hayden brushed her hair from her face and held her cheek. The gesture seemed so intimate, but then again Jesse had just felt her slimness slide up his body like a trombone.

"I don't think I'll ever be all right from here on out," she said.

"Okay, we backtrack. I know where we can pick up the bike trail. That thing goes all the way to Orley Park. I don't think we'll need to go that far before we can rest."

"Fine," Kate answered and nodded.

"Okay. On three follow me."

"How we gonna follow? We won't be able to see you. And you run so damn fast," Hayden said.

"All right, then what?" Jesse asked.

"We hold hands," Kate said and grabbed them both in her hands. "Tell us when to go and get us to the bike path."

"One, two, three – Run!" They shot up and into the smoke, coughing and panting. Jesse felt his lungs burn, but he held Kate's hand and pulled the line through suffocating smog and an acrid smell of burning rubber.

Hayden must have tripped because their whole serpentine run jostled and nearly collapsed. But Jesse saw Kate yank at

Hayden to steady him, and her grasp on Jesse tightened. He led them back toward the school and then over to where School Lane used to be. Most of it was torn up from the tornado path, and the landmark red schoolhouse was completely gone, except for some cement and bricks from the foundation. Oddly though, the historic marker still dangled from a post, so Jesse knew where he was and pulled harder on Kate's hand.

"Come on," he said. "We'll pass the old schoolhouse and then there's a ravine, or at least there used to be. We can run down it to the bike path."

Jesse glanced back and saw them nod in agreement, their pale faces like ghosts in the shadows. They had cleared the fires, but the smoke still lingered. Large pot holes dented the ground and upturned trees made them slow their pace and look warily for safe footfalls. Finally Jesse saw the earth dip, and this time it wasn't because of the bizarre alien battle. It was the ravine. He had often slipped down this way on some of his group runs during track practice. And he and Sofia had also walked the path a lot and had stopped in some isolated clearings to kiss.

Jesse wanted to make himself focus, but it was hard not to think about his family or Sofia. He had lied to Hayden when he'd said he was simply reacting. He shut his mind to this and clutched Kate's hand tighter.

They stopped at the lip of the ravine. A line of trees, some still standing, and many struck down on their sides, blocked their way.

"We climb over this group or go around?" Jesse asked.

Hayden was panting from the smoke and wiping his eyes.

"Man, this burns. I say climb. Who knows how long this goes on. You're sure this will get us to the path?"

"Yeah."

"Let's go."

Jesse clambered up the base of an uprooted evergreen tree. The needles poked his hands, but he could smell the pine like it was Christmas Eve. Once he had plucked his way through some branches, he turned to help Kate and Hayden over. They moved through the prickles in this alternating pattern where one slashed ahead, reached through for the other two, and then passed through themselves. This went on not only through the evergreen tree, but a series of fallen trees that lay like dead elephants on the sloping ground. They descended into the ravine, and soon scaling the trees became less calculated and more haphazard until all they could do was crawl through some trees, fall a couple of feet, and roll a ways down the incline. At one point Jesse heard Hayden let out a nervous whoop and then a string of profanity.

After what felt like an hour of trail blazing, they emerged on the paved bike path. The remaining trees above them made an eerie canopy. The wind was gentler as it blew through the partially bare branches making some dried leaves take flight and fall through the air and land, soundlessly, on the path.

"I hate to admit this, but I have no idea which way to go," Hayden said.

"New Franklin is that way," Kate said and pointed.

"Yeah, she's right," Jesse added.

"Do you suppose we can walk a little while? There's no fire or smoke on our backs and no alien slime balls around us."

"Yeah, let's walk for a ways, but then pick it up if we hear anything."

"Okay, track star, you're our pace car," Hayden said.

Jesse smirked, but said nothing. Their feet crunched in the fallen leaves. It wasn't long before they couldn't see anything. Jesse realized how much the fires, despite the smoke, had helped them see where they were going. He heard Hayden swing his pack from his back to his hands. Hayden jostled the zipper and said, "I'm gonna peek in here. Look for a flashlight, water, you know, those Earthly necessities. We can keep walking though."

Kate walked in silence next to Jesse. He heard her rubbing her hands up and down her arms. "You cold?" he asked.

"Just a little," she said and looked at him. The whites of her eyes were visible, and when the moon broke through the trees, the blue in her eyes gleamed. "I think all the running helped with the shaking and head pounding."

"Ah hah!" Hayden said and cracked open a bottle. "Water." He passed it to Kate, who gulped so hard she coughed and handed it to Jesse. He let the water stream down his chin a little. Then he took the moisture and smoothed it over his face.

"And here," Hayden continued, "food, I think, looks like a granola bar." He passed them to Kate and Jesse. All three walked and ate in silence for a few minutes. "Tastes like berries and tree bark."

"You eat bark?" Jesse asked.

"You know what I mean – at least it's edible," Hayden said.

"How far do you think we've gone?" Kate asked between bites.

"Not very. After we eat, it would be a good idea to jog for awhile," Jesse said and tried to study Kate's reaction with the help of moonlight.

"Okay," she said. Hayden must have nodded in agreement because he didn't say anything. Jesse could hear him crunching into another Terrian bar. Once he heard that Hayden had finished, he suggested that they start. The three started a slow trot, and Kate stayed to the side of Jesse.

Hayden broke the silence, "So can we talk about some of this now? Are your families all right? When I closed my eyes I saw my parents and my little sister Norah curled on a bed asleep."

"I saw my family, too," Jesse said.

"Me too," Kate said. "It was weird to see my parents and three brothers in the same bed."

Hayden cracked a smile. "All right, so all we can do is assume that they're okay, but now we need to find this power source for the Shaaris, but I'm not convinced it's the best thing. How can we trust Hallia? Her people have tricked humanity for centuries."

"I know," Jesse agreed, "and 'protection' could also mean 'hostage situation' to me. I hate to think about what would have happened if we'd said 'no.'"

"Yeah, I'd actually like to hear the Belite side of things. You know, to try to figure out the power play."

"You've always been good at that," Jesse said.

"Good at what?" Hayden asked, his interest piqued.

"Good at figuring out who's in a power position. It made you great at debates in class."

"Thanks, man. Means a lot coming from you – track star, drum line maestro, literature wiz."

Kate coughed. Hayden and Jesse stopped and looked at her. "Sorry," she said, "How about we stop for a bit? Just to look and see where we're going? See what else's in our packs."

"Sure," Jesse said quickly. All three squatted or sat on the isolated bike path. Clouds had moved in front of the moon, so they barely could find the zippers. Finally, Hayden found a small flashlight and made a sphere of light in the middle of their circle. They leaned into the light and started to rummage through the bags, pulling out more packs of alien food, flashlights, water, pens, and two sets of clothes for each of them.

"I am changing out of this uniform right now," Hayden said. All three agreed and found their own isolated areas to change. They returned to the path to examine the rest of their supplies.

"Okay, so we have alien 'gifts,' like Hallia talked about. Do you guys feel that, you know, like she's right?" Kate started twisting a strand of her hair. "I mean, my family has told me I have a 'sixth sense' and it sometimes feels like I can sense what someone in thinking or feeling, but I don't know."

"I do have a photographic memory, but I always thought there are a few other people like that," Jesse said.

"Well, we all know I'm an athletic marvel," Hayden said and chuckled. "But seriously, this is one big mind fuck. I hope this triggering stuff brings on more, because if those aliens come back, we can't fight them otherwise."

Hayden pulled out a long dagger from his bag and said, "Whoooaaa." His eyes were wide.

"That's crazy, dude. I'll see if I have one too." Jesse scrambled through the contents in his pack, but he didn't find a weapon, only an oil skin pouch with a draw string. He opened it and found detailed maps of Illinois. Some were only topographical; others were of the transportation lines; and another looked like the plat maps farmers used. Jesse knew this from Mr. Miller's AP History course. He scanned the papers and saw another set of the same types of maps of the city of Chicago. Different locations, such as Union Station and Millennium Park, were highlighted with the words *possible power source location* on it.

"Looks like we're walking to Chicago. I have maps in my bag."

"Chicago, huh," Hayden said, "at least it's closer than any other city."

"What about you, Kate?" Jesse asked. "What do you have in yours?"

She pulled out a lightweight sphere the size of a cantaloupe from her backpack. Hayden aimed the flashlight glow onto the orb. Kate read something etched on the side of it, *For warmth, light, and strength.* "I just don't see how you turn this on?" Kate was turning the smooth ball in her hands. Hayden leaned over her and moved the beam until they had searched every curve.

"Ya got me," he said.

"Okay, we'll have to figure that one out. Right now, let's think about this. We can't use transportation, so we need to follow the quickest path to Chicago. And Hallia mentioned not using any kind of communication. I put my cell in my locker at practice, so I don't even have one on me. How about you two?"

"Mine was in my locker too," Kate said.

"I got mine." Hayden pulled a phone from his pocket and held it up.

"Let's get rid of it," Jesse said.

"All right." Hayden gave it a good heave into the trees. The phone landed with a thud in the distance.

"Do you think we should rest here? This path is isolated, and we haven't heard anything for awhile." Jesse had settled onto his backside. It was a relief to be off of his feet.

"I definitely wouldn't mind stopping," Kate said.

Hayden seemed energized by the dagger. "I'll keep watch," he said, his knife in the air. "You two get some rest in those leaves."

"I wish I could figure this orb out; I'm freezing," Kate said.

"Here, I'll cover you up with leaves and stuff," Jesse said.

Kate curled in a ball on the side of the path. Jesse did his best to find the driest leaves. He put them all over her body and felt a surge of loss when he remembered doing the same act with friends as a kid. If only all of this alien stuff was nothing more than a childhood game. But it wasn't.

"Ya know, I don't think this is the time to be modest you two. Huddle up. Body heat is the best thing – I'm sure my man Jesse knows about this with Sofia."

Jesse tensed, but Kate looked up from beneath her leafy blanket and nodded in agreement. So Jesse put himself on the ground next to Kate and curled his frame around hers. Then he slung one arm over hers, amazed at how tiny her elbow felt, like a folded bird wing. She relaxed instantly beneath his weight and murmured "thank you" before she fell into silence.

Jesse felt alert and nervous. What were they doing? They just went through backpacks given to them by a giant alien woman. He had seen it; the packs had been liquid balls in Hallia's pocket. Now they were cloth bags with solid objects in them. He and his drum line mates were walking on a bike path to Chicago, and they spoke about it like they were planning a drill in practice. But what choice did they have? Those aliens had their families; he had to do something. Could this power source be used to save his family? He didn't realize it, but he had started to worry a place on Kate's elbow with his index finger.

"I know, I'm scared too," was all that she said.

Jesse almost recoiled, but she felt so good next to him, and she smelled like smoke from the fires, pine needles, and some fragrant flower Jesse recognized as her every day scent. He stayed in this state of dazed attention until the sky above him filled with a glowing blue and crimson light. Both he and Kate shot up. Hayden was already in the center of the path with his dagger in the air.

The light gathered and morphed into a figure. At first Jesse couldn't make out the shape, but then it was clear: A massive bull floated above them on the path. Its hoof pawed at the air; its red eyes flared and shot fire that died before it made it to the ground. The bull circled above them, and Jesse saw a human form, another alien, a man with gold hair, a flowing purple coat, and glossy golden skin. He was steering the bull in circles and homing in on their location.

"Charge!" The alien yelled and pointed right at Hayden.

CHAPTER FIVE
WARRIOR

Gilgamesh got up and came to the house. Then Enkidu stepped out, he stood in the street and blocked the way. Mighty Gilgamesh came on and Enkidu met him at the gate. He put out his foot and prevented Gilgamesh from entering the house, so they grappled, holding each other like bulls. They broke the doorposts and the walls shook, they snorted like bulls locked together. They shattered the doorposts and the walls shook.

— The Epic of Gilgamesh,
N.K. Sandars, translator

The giant bull with the Belite on its back spun in the air until it was a floating ball of liquid. Then it dripped to the ground and re-formed to smaller proportions; this meant that the Belite was a head taller than Hayden, but the bull loomed as large as an elephant. The beast and alien jumped high into the air, and when its hooves struck the earth, a crack formed. Jesse and Kate were thrown while the earth peeled back to make a crevice that stretched the length of a football field. Jesse caught a glance of the massive blue bull and Hayden, armed and pumped with energy, before he and Kate fell.

They plunged down a slide of dirt, dead leaves, and roots for about fifteen feet. Above their heads the hooves on the bike path pounded, sending more reverberations and cracks in the ground. Lights flashed above Jesse's head and he heard Hayden yell, "Come on you overgrown cow, bring it on!"

"What pluck, Mr. Monroe," the Belite said, "are you sure you know how to use that thing?"

"It's a knife, Glow Stick; I stab and cut."

"You'll do a lot more if you use your head. Circle now, Bull of Heaven, and be ready to charge."

Strangely, Jesse thought of a book he had read in AP World Literature when he heard the bull's name. What was it? He tried his photographic memory, but while trying to steady himself along the muddy wall, his mind went blank. He didn't have any more time to ponder because as the bull charged Hayden, more dirt collapsed and made them slide some more. Kate hung onto roots and rocks next to him, but he feared that if they didn't climb out immediately, they would be crushed with more earth and worse, fallen trees.

"Come on, climb!" Jesse yelled while the pounding above them was deafening. He heard Hayden yelp and more light flashed over his head, but he had no idea if the bull killed Hayden on the first charge.

Kate proved to be a better climber than Jesse. Her slight form shimmied up the fissure wall with relative ease. Her little hands and nails found tiny roots to secure her grip. Jesse felt large and leaden. Usually he carried his muscular frame with pride, knowing how to move to attract girls and make guys ask, "How much you bench press?" He could bench two hundred and fifty pounds, but now it felt like there were blocks of granite tied to his muscular body. He kept at it, fearing that he and Kate would be buried alive.

He bit down; grains crunched between his teeth. The cold dirt smelled like worms on a sidewalk after a hard rain. He breathed hard and listened for signs that Hayden was still fighting and not dead on the bike path. He pawed the dirt, hand over hand, and slowly lifted his girth up the pitiless slope. The ground shook some more, but they didn't slide farther. He strained to hear anything. Then the alien's voice bellowed like a thunderclap.

"Good pass, Mr. Monroe. But you'll have to do better than that," the Belite said. "Come now, ready yourself!"

Kate looked back at Jesse. "Come on, Jesse. We have to help Hayden."

"I know. I'm almost there."

Kate reached solid ground first and put a hand out to help Jesse over the final lip of the fissure. She yanked on his hand, her face red with exertion. Jesse slammed his feet into the muddy wall and heaved himself over the top. But they were on the wrong side to help Hayden. Kate panted, her eyes wide with worry, and pointed at Hayden who now stood at one end of the bike path and the bull and Belite at the other. The bull's flanks went up and down as it breathed in and out, sending puffs of smoke from its nostrils that made fog in the semidarkness. The glow from the bull and the alien made the entire scene visible to Jesse. The alien man sneered at Hayden and patted the bull's hide. He leaned into the bull's neck, murmuring something that sounded like an incantation.

On the other end, Hayden looked fierce and ready for battle. Jesse watched him do his pre-wrestling match bounce again. His blondish spiky hair made a jagged outline on top of his medium-sized frame. Hayden wielded the dagger above his head, swinging it in a swooping back and forth motion. Then a strange thing happened. Hayden closed his eyes and breathed in. He raised his arms above his head and flapped them downward while he took more deep breaths. Soon the flapping motion seemed to work like a pump, and though Hayden didn't grow in size like Hallia had done, he started to glow. His skin cast a shimmery ray that led right back to his opponents.

"Ah, I see you're using your mind. Charge, Bull of Heaven. Now!" The Belite held the bull's hide and hunched closer to the animal. Both alien beings' eyes were gold and flashing with light.

Hayden turned in place, as if gaining momentum, and charged back at them. He pumped his legs furiously and held his dagger in his left hand, ready to stab. When the forms collided, there was more light and a crackling sound like the *rat-ta-tat-tat* of firecrackers. Both Jesse and Kate had to shield their eyes.

When the light faded, Jesse could make out Hayden who now clung to the side of the beast with his right hand. The bull thundered on down the path until the Belite directed it to turn around and tack along the path in order to shake Hayden off. But Hayden clung to the blue shine like a steel trap. Then he thrust his dagger hand into the bull's side. The bull writhed and bucked, but still Hayden clung. Pavement broke up and flew in the air, dinging Hayden's blade, but the boy seemed to be invigorated. He climbed the bull's massive shoulder until he nearly reached the horn. Now the alien gained a better grip on the beast and started kicking at Hayden's hands. The Belite swiped his hand, and branches that had been on the ground flew in the air, their tips like spikes flying at Hayden's face. Hayden deflected them with his blade and continued up the bull's side. And then in one swift motion, he tossed his body at the Belite and side-kicked him off the bull's back. Hayden was steering then, and he didn't lose any time. He grabbed the bull's horns and thrust his knife into its neck. The bull slowed immediately, but Hayden kept stabbing in the same place. Suddenly the bull dissolved into a glimmering pool of crimson and blue.

Hayden dropped to the ground and immediately ran from the liquid. He had his dagger aimed at its stillness.

The Belite clapped mockingly and then made a stirring motion with his hands. The liquid gathered, spilled into the alien's palms, and made a balled form. The alien man stuffed the ball into the pocket of his cloak. "A fine effort, Mr. Monroe, but we aren't finished yet." Then he ate something and grew like Hallia had done in the gym and became liquidy light. A smear of gold, red, and blue whizzed across the sky in seconds.

Everything was quiet. Jesse and Kate stared at Hayden in awe. Hayden no longer glowed but stood with his dagger up and ready for the alien and beast to return. Hayden's hands shook.

"Dude," Jesse called over the gap, "that was awesome!" He laughed with relief.

Hayden bent at the waist and puked. Once he was done, he stood. "Yeah, except for the vomit at the end, I'm a beast!"

Both boys whooped. Kate laughed and clapped as she jumped up and down.

"Whoa, how'd you two get over there?" Hayden stopped suddenly, pointing across the enormous crevice.

"The bull did this," Jesse answered. "There's no crossing it, but let's keep heading north on opposite sides – hopefully this thing ends soon."

The three followed the crack in silence. Once in awhile Hayden would shout something across the gap, like "Did you see that thing's hooves!"

Jesse would nod in agreement, but it didn't matter if Hayden could see him or not; he was in his own world of triumph. Finally, the crack in the earth was coming together, and when it got to a place where they could jump across, Jesse practically threw Kate to Hayden, who caught her clumsily, but then held her tightly. Jesse hurdled the gap himself. When he reached the other side, Kate was still in Hayden's arms. Hayden beamed at her, obviously looking for praise.

Kate's face was red. Her hands clutched Hayden's neck. Jesse felt heat rush through his chest. He wanted to yell, "Put her down," but stopped himself.

"Ah, Hayden," Kate stammered, "do you mind setting me down?"

"What? Oh – yeah. Sorry. Your eyes are so blue, even if I can only see them from the moonlight." He put her down, and Jesse felt better.

"So, one Belite beast dead," Hayden said, beaming.

"Yeah, dude, great stuff." Jesse clapped him on the back, but Hayden looked at Kate.

She smiled, looked away momentarily, and said, "That was amazing, Hayden," in a soft voice Jesse wished was meant for him.

"Thanks, Kate," Hayden said quietly. The three stood in awkward silence until Kate said, "Should we move on?"

"Yeah, let's go," Jesse said. "We're lucky our packs are all right. We can't lose this stuff. I'm moving the map pouch to under my sweatshirt."

"Good, yeah, I'm keeping the dagger on me for sure."

"I can't really wear the orb." Kate chuckled.

Jesse smiled and looked at her muddy face and hands and her torn blue hoodie. "Man, we look rough. And Hayden, did you know you glowed before you charged the bull?"

"Yeah. We need to talk about that. I'm not sure how, but I did what you talked about earlier, Jesse. I lost myself in reacting. All my thoughts were gone, and it was like my body was mechanical, just moving. Then I felt this surge in my brain, like maxed-out cerebellum, and boom, I glowed and had more power, more speed – well you saw it. I obliterated that thing." Jesse and Hayden slapped hands in the air. Kate was silently studying her stride between them.

"Another thing," Jesse said, "I know that name 'Bull of Heaven' – it's from a book we read in Ms. Gamble's AP World Literature course. Do you remember, Hayden?"

"Yeah, it sounds familiar, but I don't read everything in there."

"You don't?" Jesse couldn't keep his hands off the books she assigned. *The Epic of Gilgamesh*! Jeese, that's it. Gilgamesh and Enkidu killed the Bull of Heaven. That story's from ancient Sumer."

Jesse looked to Hayden who nodded and then to Kate. She caught his eye. "I'm not in AP."

"All right, but think about this, the stories or myths we read today were sometimes not only stories of heroes, but they showed the spiritual beliefs of ancient people. This book had all the Sumerian gods in it. Ishtar wants to marry Gilgamesh, but he refuses cause she's a, well, she's loose, if you get what I'm saying, and she turns her lovers into moles and things. The gods get mad and send the Bull of Heaven, but they kill it. It's so cool because Enkidu cuts off the thigh and shakes it at her while she sends out a curse."

"I remember now, yeah, and then the gods kill Enkidu," Hayden said.

"It's so hard to take all this in, so those gods for the Sumerians were Terrians," Kate said. She looked disturbed. "They were messing with people, but I believe there is a god out there. There has to be."

"Yeah, it's a heck of a lot." Jesse tried to make his voice reassuring. He wanted to add more, like what's the difference if a supreme being is an alien species or something else, people believe what they need to, but she looked so upset, so he bit his lip. He decided to change the subject. "I also can't help but wonder what everyone else sees? Hallia said most people see natural disasters, but I wonder if some humans really saw what we just did? You know, the ones that were part alien, or the ones that were given gifts from the aliens, like she talked about."

"Maybe, man," Hayden said.

They walked in silence for awhile, each in their own thoughts. The moon had come out from behind the haze of cloud and lit the bike path. Even so, Jesse kept a flashlight beam on where their feet had to step. They were walking away from much of the destruction that had occurred in Molleena, the school's suburb, and toward the next suburb, which must have been spared. The bike path snaked along without potholes or upturned trees. The trees swayed in the autumn air without the sinister whirring that had accompanied the tornado and fires. Jesse finally relaxed a little, but his mind raced. He kept thinking about all the different myths or stories he had read about ancient religions, and then he came to modern religions. He tried to remember anything he could about Islam or Hindu. Then he thought about Christianity.

"It's hard to think about this, especially if you're religious, but so much about Christianity is just like Sumer."

"What do you mean, just like?" Kate asked.

"Well, not identical, but some people who are Christians

see the stories in the Bible as the word of God. Other religions think this too."

"Yeah, obviously not the case," Hayden said.

"These Terrians have been controlling our faith since the start of human civilizations."

"No offence, but you're kind of stating the obvious here. I mean, Alien Chick said as much back in our most bizarre gym class," Hayden said.

"I know, I know, but I'm thinking about any commonalities across belief systems. You know, like how Ms. Gamble talked about archetypes."

"What are you talking about?" Kate asked.

"Archetypes are patterns or images the recur over time and throughout different cultures, like the trickster, the hero, battle of good vs. evil—"

"Yeah, man, I feel like I just lived that one," Hayden said and slashed at the air with his sword.

"I don't know where I'm going with all of this. Just thinking out loud, trying to look for patterns and things to give us a better defense against whatever the Belites might send our way."

"Or the Sharris," Kate said. Both boys looked at her. "How do we know they won't attack us too?"

"True," Jesse said and paused. "You know, I was wondering, since we're on the whole religion thing. What are you two? I mean in terms of religion? I go to this Baptist church in the city. I haven't really believed in much of it, especially since my dad died." Jesse's throat felt tight. He had to stop talking and looking at his companions. He hoped one would speak soon so that he wouldn't have to.

"Hayden, didn't you say your family is Methodist?" Kate asked.

"Yep, but not very devout or anything."

"I'm Catholic. I don't like everything about the church, but I believe in the Holy Trinity and the saints, and I still do. No matter what Hallia said." Kate pulled at her hair and clenched her fists in and out. Soon she wiped her face with her sleeve.

Jesse wanted to say something, but he couldn't think of anything that would comfort. Hayden took her hand and rubbed her shoulder for a few seconds.

"I'm fine," Kate said, breaking away. She smoothed her hands along her jeans.

After a few silent minutes, Hayden began slashing the air again. "I think we'll be fine. We'll smash any enemy, Belite or not, that crosses our paths. We'll find this 'power source' and figure things from there."

"All right," Jesse said. He felt invigorated by Hayden's confidence.

"What could be worse than the bull? Maybe a Hydra or Harpies from ancient Greek mythology," Jesse said.

"Whatever it is, we'll be ready. We can figure out how to use more of our brains too, and the orb. We'll be unstoppable!" Hayden shoved Jesse playfully. He and Hayden began shadow-boxing in front of Kate on the path. After jabbing and dodging for several minutes, Jesse saw that Kate had stopped, so he signaled to Hayden to wait for her.

Kate gained on them. "I hate to say this, because it's clear you two feel pretty great about the bull fight and all..." Her voice trailed off and she kicked at a stone on the ground. "But I have to say this. I think our lives depend on it."

Jesse's interest was piqued. Both boys stood staring at her.

"Hayden," she blurted, "you were great and all, destroying the Bull of Heaven, but that Belite alien let you win."

CHAPTER SIX
MESSAGES

As for the unbelievers, their works are like a mirage in a desert. The thirsty traveler thinks it is water, but when he comes near he finds that it is nothing. He finds Allah there, who pays him back in full. Swift is Allah's reckoning.

Or like darkness on a bottomless ocean spread with clashing billows and overcast with clouds: darkness upon darkness. If he stretches out his hand he can scarcely see it. Indeed the man from whom Allah withholds His light shall find no light at all.

— Koran, 24:36

"What? I killed that thing, Kate," Hayden said. Jesse looked at his friend's profile. His jaw was clenched and twitching. He ran his right hand through his sandy, blonde hair. He still had the dagger in his left.

"Yeah, I know. But think back to the actual fight. He gave you a lot of time to prepare yourself. He even gave you the hint about using your mind." Kate said in a rush, took a breath, and then continued, "And the most obvious thing is why did he shrink before the fight?"

Jesse took Kate's words in. He thought Hayden had done an amazing feat, but now he wondered, did the Belite let Hayden kill the Bull of Heaven? Was the beast even dead? Its glowing remains slid right back to the alien. Maybe Kate was right.

"That was all me, Kate. I'm the one who did what those aliens do – I tapped into another part of my brain. And look at me." Hayden yanked off his jacket and t-shirt to reveal his muscular chest and stomach. "I'm cut. I worked hard to get this body, and now it's paid off." He strutted in front of Kate and walked backwards, his eyes burrowing into hers. She held his stare for a moment and looked away. Jesse wondered if they were dating. Or had they dated in the past? He wanted to ask so badly his throat burned, but now seemed like a strange time, with the three of them trying to work out this whole alien attack with a massive bull of light.

"I know you're strong," Kate said softly, "but think about what we've seen these aliens do, like back at school. They become giant gelatinous people in the sky. They make tornadoes, enormous beasts from past mythologies, and who knows what else. My point is," she paused, "my point is that if they wanted to attack us and fight us to the death, well, we'd be dead."

As soon as Kate spelled it out, it sounded so simple and true. What had they been thinking? Of course they'd be dead. But why let Hayden win?

"Okay Miss You're-a-Fool-Hayden—"

"I never said you were a fool. You did a great job. It's just—"

"It's just that I'm not good enough for you. Again," Hayden said. He turned and ran ahead.

Kate and Jesse walked at a faster pace.

"Want me to go after him?" he asked.

"No, give him some time."

Jesse found his window to get more information about the two of them. What was going on with him? His entire belief system had been turned on its head; he had witnessed the death of his coach and friends, and who knew if he could trust that his family was really alive, and here he was wondering if Kate Hughes liked Hayden Monroe. And yet, something had turned over inside of him that he couldn't explain. He could sooner stop himself from blinking than to stop wondering about her.

"What's all the 'I'm not good enough for you' stuff? You two date or something?"

"No. Yes – I don't know. It's murky," Kate said. Her breath made puffs in the air. She stuffed her hands in her sweatshirt pockets.

"How about this, have you ever gone on a date with Hayden?"

"Yeah, one time last year. He had been asking me out a lot, and I liked him, but I was nervous to say yes."

"Why?"

"I don't want to say."

"Okay."

They walked in silence then. Jesse's mind raced. She said she *liked* him. That was past tense. Did that mean she was over him? They went on a date, so what. Obviously, Hayden felt rejected by her. Did he still like her, or was this about his wounded pride? Did she still like him?

"Let's jog and try to catch up to him. None of us should be alone out here," Jesse said.

Kate nodded in agreement and then picked up the pace. It wasn't long before they met Hayden, who wore his shirt and jacket again, sitting on the path. He sat right in the middle of it with his dagger and a water bottle in front of him. He munched on more alien food from small packages. Before Jesse or Kate had to worry about what to say to him, he stood. "You're right, Kate, that Belite ran a game on me."

No one said anything else. They sat down again in the path and ate some more food in silence. Jesse felt so uncomfortable, like he had just witnessed a very private part of Hayden's inner life. Hayden was dressed and composed again, but his display couldn't be taken back, and both boys knew it. As for Kate, she didn't reveal much. What did it mean that she was nervous to go on a date with Hayden?

"I think we'll be to Hainer Park pretty soon," Jesse said, breaking the silence.

"Should we sleep there for awhile?" Kate asked.

"Naw. The police patrol there a lot," Jesse said.

"How'd you know about the police?" Hayden asked.

"Sofia and I got caught there one time. They made a big deal about it, which wasn't a surprise to me because I'm black and all."

"Does that have anything to do with it? Isn't it just that you were there when you weren't supposed to be?" Hayden asked.

"That's what most white people think, but it always has to do with me being black, in Molleena, or New Franklin, or any of these really white suburbs."

No one knew what to say. Kate was still visibly upset about her conflict with Hayden. Jesse decided to turn the conversation back to moving on.

"Let's cut through the park and head to Route 6. We could camp under a viaduct or something, to shield up from the wind," Jesse said. "Then let's figure out how to get the orb going so we won't freeze to death."

The bike path opened into the park through a patch of trees.

There was a play structure with swings moving with a ghostly creaking from the wind. Leaves stirred and nocturnal animals made rustling sounds in the woods. Jesse actually jumped when a raccoon ambled across a nearby hill and toward the parking lot where there were garbage cans.

Hayden looked toward the raccoon and snickered, "Man, you better get a thicker skin than that if a raccoon makes you jump."

Jesse laughed in a low voice, but he didn't find it funny. He was ready to sit down and try to piece together some information. His stomach felt queasy and his head ached. He needed time to be alone with his own thoughts. But then again, that scared him. He didn't want to re-live the tornado, or what Hallia had told them.

Once they passed through the park, it felt strange walking on a street, as if the pavement would erupt from below because they were the ones walking on it. But it was either that or cut through yards, and that seemed wrong and more conspicuous. The neatly cut lawns, the piles of leaves in bags, and the swept driveways felt surreal. Nothing really bad had happened here. Why? Jesse knew the answer. The aliens were looking for them, the Youth Triumvirate that happened to be at a Molleena high school drum line practice. He wished he had his phone to call Sofia. At least she had been at home. He made himself believe she was okay.

They wound their way through the subdivisions. The moon and yellow glow from the streetlamps lit their way. Soon they approached Route 6, not a highway, but a two-lane street with cornfields and wild grasses on both sides of it. It led to a spur for 355, which was the fastest way to Chicago.

"Let's stop soon," Hayden said.

"You're right. Should we camp under that bridge up ahead?"

"Sure," Hayden answered. Kate nodded in agreement.

They picked their way through bushes and down a slope to a spot below the bridge. The ditch was covered in dead leaves and patches of grass that came to Jesse's hip. They hunkered down on a bed of brush and rocks and rubbed their hands together for warmth.

Kate unzipped her pack and pulled out the orb. "Okay, I'm desperate to be warm. We need to figure this thing out."

"All right," Jesse said. "Can I have a look?"

He took the cold ball in his hands. It felt like an oversized marble.

"I don't know – should I try to concentrate and use my mind like you did, Hayden? To get it to work."

Hayden scooted over and squatted next to Jesse like he'd seen his little brother Dorian do when he played with trains.

"Yeah, try to imagine it heating up," Kate added.

Jesse shut his eyes and tried to think of hot things: visiting his cousins in Alabama, the beach at Lake Michigan in Chicago in summer, marching in the hot Labor Day parade in his drum line uniform, but no thoughts made the orb heat up. In his hands, it gleamed like a pearl from cold ocean depths.

"Let me try," Hayden said. Jesse handed it over and watched. Hayden closed his eyes. Nothing happened at first, but then letters appeared on one side.

It read:

K. Emotion + Hands = Orb Power

E. & P.

"Whoa," Hayden said. He let the orb slide from his fingers. It made a thud on the ground and rested in a nest of leaves.

"Did you two see that?" he asked.

"Yeah," Jesse and Kate said in unison.

The teens leaned over, and Jesse read the message aloud. "A little more information would be nice."

"Maybe it's like Twitter? These alien dudes can only send messages from Terria in one-hundred and forty characters or less." They all chuckled but then grew serious.

"I think it's addressed to me," Kate said.

"Oh yeah," Jesse said. He picked it up and handed it over. Their fingers brushed against each other. A pulse of heat ran through Jesse's body.

Once it was in Kate's hands, it changed from white to pink.

"That's it, good," Hayden said. "Whatever you're doing, keep doing it. It's changing colors. The message said your emotions make this happen. What are you thinking, no *feeling*, right now?"

"I'm not sure," she said. But her face reddened, and it wasn't just from the pink glow of the orb.

"Try to feel it again," Hayden prompted.

The air around them felt electrical while Kate closed her eyes and held the orb for several minutes. Soon her hair, which had grown limp from sweat, started to flare upwards like a flame.

"Cool," Jesse said. "Must be like static electricity."

The orb changed again from pink to orange. Kate opened her eyes and looked at Jesse. "Dig a spot for it."

Both boys tore at the fallen leaves and deadened grass until they could paw through the damp earth. Once they had made a wide circle that was a few inches deep, Kate put the glowing orb in their cursory fire pit. In a short amount of time, it had warmed their make-shift campsite.

All three sighed with relief and comfort. They positioned themselves around the orb's circle, curling on their sides and resting heads to feet. Jesse had the maps under his sweatshirt and against his skin. He'd thought he might pull them out and study them before morning, but sleep came as soon as his eyes shut.

He was bombarded by dreams. First he relived the horrors of the day almost as if his dreams were movies. Most of the details were exact: practice, the storm, giant aliens in the sky, the tornado, and then Hallia explaining everything that stripped away all human belief systems. Jesse tossed back and forth, and the dreams became stranger, more disconnected. He saw great balls of fire shooting from the sky and hitting the earth like meteors. Then he saw Hallia again as she grew to gigantic proportions, but then she metamorphosed into the Belite alien who brought the Bull of Heaven. The next thing in the dream was Kate and Jesse climbing up a crack in the earth, one like the bull had made for real. She looked over her shoulder and kept saying something he didn't understand. Finally, Jesse made out the words, "Help Hayden," she said over and over again. But Jesse didn't know how. Then he and Kate were lying down in the woods. She was curled next to him in some leaves. She shivered beneath the brush, so Jesse cast the length of his body over hers. Then he realized she was naked beneath him.

Jesse shot awake and studied Kate. Her mass of hair fanned around her head, and her hands were tucked beneath her chin. The orange light from the orb cast spiky shadows on her body. How many different ways could he sell out? First he lived a middle-class life in the suburbs, and second, he definitely had a thing for a white girl.

The shadows on her arm were wavering in strange patterns, so Jesse was forced to look away from the sleeping Kate and back at the orb. More letters formed on the side. They were cloudy at first, but then the message became clear:

Be ready. Another storm's coming.
E. & P.

CHAPTER SEVEN
STORM

In the beginning, there was only water
and the water animals that lived in it.
Then a woman fell from a torn place in the sky.
She was a divine woman, full of power. Two loons flying over the
water saw her falling. They flew under her, close
together, making a pillow for her to sit on.
The loons held her up and cried for help. They could be heard for a
long way as they called for other animals to come.

— Diving Woman, the Creator,
Huron story

He roars like the thundering clouds; He blazes with his own radiance,
illuminating the space between heaven and earth. Inspirer of glories,
depository of riches rouser of thoughts guardian of the divine elixir of
love source of strength a blazing king. Manifester of all, germ of the
world, sight of all creation, he fills earth and heaven with light,
he claves the cloud when he advances.

— Rig Veda, 10:1-2

Instantly, Jesse looked to the sky. It was serene with a faint glow of sunrise on a hazy morning. Maybe there was time. Questions ran through Jesse's mind: Who were E. and P., and why were they helping them? His pulse raced; he put a hand to his chest as if to steady the rhythm. They had to get moving.

Jesse shook the other two awake to look at the orb.

"Beautiful. What's next? Locusts?" Hayden said. "When these aliens get down to it, they don't waste any time."

"What do we do?" Kate sounded worried. She kept flicking her eyes to the sky. "If it's another tornado battle maybe we should just stay here in the ditch?"

"It won't be a normal tornado," Jesse said. He couldn't look right at her because he felt too embarrassed from his dream.

"I say we move," Hayden said. He had already slung his pack over his shoulder. The other two nodded.

"How do I turn this thing off?" Kate asked. "I don't want to put it in my bag and start a fire.

"Look, it's already cooling," Jesse said. "Maybe because you want it to."

"Oh yeah. Right. This is too weird," she said as she zipped it into her pack.

They moved quickly through the gloom. The sun tried to show itself in full brightness, but bulbous gray clouds muscled in front of it. Jesse felt lightheaded and agitated. How much time did they have before enormous aliens broke through the crowd of clouds? He quickened his pace across the field, and his companions must have felt his urgency because they did the same.

Now they were in between a residential area and the new construction of strip malls and superstores. What had once been farmland was now another stamp of suburbia: Target, Kohl's, Home Depot. The world woke up as usual with people hopping into cars and hurrying to work. Street lights went from green to yellow to red, and the cars obeyed.

Why weren't there school buses? Was it because of the devastation at the central campus of their high school? No, he realized, it was Saturday. Normally his mom would either be heading to her job as an ICU nurse at St. John's, or she'd be off of work and making homemade cinnamon rolls or pancakes. For the first time since what Jesse had started to think of as the alien invasion, he cried. He was silent as tears ran down his cheeks. He wiped his face quickly, but not before he caught Kate's eye. Instinctively she grabbed his hand and squeezed it. When she let go, Jesse felt his palm burn a little, or was that his imagination?

They were getting closer to Lincoln High's east campus. The school, a creamy brick building that sprawled across a lawn with small undulating hills, looked dark. "Let's cross through the school grounds and head toward 355," Jesse said with fake confidence. "Who knows when the battle will start? We may as well keep going toward Chicago."

"Who do you guys think E. and P. are?" Hayden asked as he ate an alien bar. Jesse had munched two quickly and he'd felt an instant energy boost. Even though he didn't completely trust Hallia, what choice did they have but to eat the Terrian food?

"I have no idea," he answered.

Kate shrugged but then said, "It seems like whoever they are, they're trying to help us."

"You could say the same for Hallia, or even the Belite who let me win with the bull. The question is why?"

No one had a response. Finally, Jesse said, "Maybe both sides want the power source so they're encouraging us?"

"You're probably right about that, so I feel like either side could turn on us at any minute, depending on who's in power on Terria," Kate said.

"We must have something they need, something Hallia didn't tell us about," Hayden guessed.

"Yeah, cause why else keep us alive?" Jesse asked.

"Hallia said the Belites would try to track us and kill us with beasts and things."

"But from what we saw, that Belite dude helped me, in a way."

"Maybe he was actually a Shaari?" Kate said.

"No, remember, the silver hair and skin for Shaaris and the gold for Belites," Jesse said.

"But would they use disguises to get us confused?" Kate asked.

"Good question," Jesse said. Everyone fell into silence.

"Let's look at it this way," Jesse said, kicking at leaves as they crossed over the track field, "both sides want us to succeed and that's a good thing." He longed for an ordinary worry, like trying to best his time in the two-hundred-meter race, or how to come up with a killer thesis for his history term paper. Not these worries about his family in a perpetual sleep or the fate of humanity on his shoulders. And aliens posing as gods – he had no idea what to do with that one. He felt unequipped, a snare with no holster, or a holster hanging with no snare. Always something off or missing. This was the way he had felt when his family first moved to the predominantly white New Franklin, like the old Sesame Street song, "One of these things is not like the other. One of these things just doesn't belong."

And yet, over time he had made some friends, and he had an awesome girlfriend. He excelled in school, sports, and band. If he was honest with himself, he had to admit that sometimes he liked standing out because of his color. He felt above the crowd, special. And then there were other times, where small things happened that stabbed him with the realization that the white world only accepted him because he was acting white. But then again what did this mean really? Everyone was so mixed now anyway.

Those small things stuck though, like his first-grade field trip to the nature preserve. He'd loved the hike and the talk on birds of prey. At the end of the trip the leader, an older white woman who worked at the preserve, had given each child a stamp on his or her hand. It had been a print of a deer hoof. She'd said to a girl with milky white skin, "Yours looks beautiful because of your nice fair skin." Why did he have to be the next to get a black stamp that didn't even show up on his hand? No one even noticed her comment, but he had, and he'd stuffed his hand in his pocket with shame. Was his stamp not beautiful?

Jesse hadn't noticed, but Kate and Hayden were looking at him. They must have thought he had more to say, but he didn't. What was he going to tell them anyway? *I was just thinking about being black again.*

"Once we get to 355, it's not like we can walk on the highway. What do we do?" Kate asked.

"We'll look at the maps I got. I think those topographical ones are the ones to follow."

All three were walking single file along Route 45 when the sky began to darken. To their left was a large field, a copse of trees, and beyond that more woods that most likely butted up against another new subdivision. To the right of Route 45 was a strip mall with a bagel shop, hair salon, and a food mart.

Hayden tapped Jesse on the back and pointed to the black clouds. "Doesn't look good."

"Let's get off the road and find cover," Jesse said.

"Where? The bagel shop up over there?" Hayden asked.

"No," said Kate, "let's head across the field and find cover in that cluster of trees. I don't think it's a good idea to be near buildings."

"Why?"

"Because they collapse. Remember the gym? We would have been crushed if Hallia didn't protect us," she answered.

"Yeah, but a tornado will get us anywhere," Hayden countered.

They stood immobile in the ditch on the side of the road. A light rain started. The sun had completely disappeared behind clouds.

"Do you think this will be a regular storm, not an alien fight?" Kate asked.

"Doubt it," Jesse said, "I say we do what Kate said."

Hayden nodded, and they sprinted into a clearing of wild grasses and clumps of dead leaves. How had he never noticed so much nature butting up against buildings and highways? Why this thought came into Jesse's mind he didn't know, but then there was no more time for random fleeting thoughts.

Darkness came. Then bright light. A shower of it, spilling above them like thousands of fireflies.

"Ahhhh," Kate screamed, looking up and pointing. "They're coming again!"

The sky peeled open like a knife running along the skin of an orange. Masses of Terrians filled the sky. Hayden pulled at Jesse and Kate, and all three hit the ground, momentarily hidden in the tall grass. Jesse made himself look up for a moment. In awe he saw the gigantic beings throwing punches at each other or shooting fire from their enormous hands. The fire smashed into invisible shields thrown up with a whoosh of their liquid-like arms. Clusters of giants materialized out of nowhere. Some rode in on chariots that were the size of airplanes pulled by massive horse creatures and bulls much like the one Hayden had fought.

"Let's move," Jesse said, popping up. The three crouched and sprinted. Drifts of fire sparks rained down to Earth slowly.

"Wave it off," Hayden shouted.

Wave what off? The fire? If more than fire sparks came down, there was no waving it off, Jesse thought.

They ran. Darkness – purple and green sky filled his vision. Fire, more rain, or was it? Gooey blobs fell from the sky. No time to look up, Jesse thought. He pulled at Kate's hand. She whimpered and yanked on Hayden who nearly fell.

Embers floated and went out mid-air like bubbles.

"Uuuugh," Hayden yelled. "Got goo on my back." He stripped off his pack as they ran.

"Damn, there's ice coming down now!" Jesse yelled over his shoulder. "Move to the trees."

Salty sweat poured down Jesse's face. "Run, run, don't look up. Don't look up!" he shouted over his shoulder. Kate's face was white as the hail coming down now.

Crash. Ping, ping.

Behind them icy balls were denting and destroying cars and buildings. He heard the smash of ice on metal, the crash of cars out of control, and outdoor signs busting apart from the barrage.

Once they reached the cover of trees, Jesse shouted, "Don't stop. We need to get away from them!"

"Do you think they're looking for us again?" Kate yelled back. Her voice was a shriek in the howling wind.

"No time to consider," Hayden said, sliding up next to Jesse and yanking on Kate. "We need to find some effing cover."

Ping, ping. Slam.

The hail ricocheted through the naked branches like metal balls in a pinball machine. Each sound made the teens crouch or squat and then race off when the sound lessened. A piece of hail the size of Jesse's fist flew sideways through the tree line and nearly cracked Kate on the shoulder.

"Watch out," he said and shoved Kate forward.

Boom. Thunder clapped. The wind went from a howl to a wild, churning roar. Monstrous gurgles sounded overhead.

Then the tree plucking started. Why throw trees when they had fire and ice at their fingertips? A Belite charged the earth in liquid light, stretched his giant hands as if they were elastic, and snatched up a maple tree.

"Back the fuck up," Hayden shouted and back-pedaled, grabbing Kate's and Jesse's jackets.

Jesse almost pissed himself. He tripped and skidded on his backside. The uprooted tree loomed above him, the roots dangling like tentacles. The Belite threw the entire tree as one would a javelin.

Pop! It pierced one Shaari who was driving a chariot. The tree blasted through the Shaari, leaving a gaping hole that re-formed sluggishly. The tree had done the most damage! Why?

"Come on, Jesse." It was Kate pulling on him this time. Her hair whipped around her face, and her eyes were wide with fear. "They're yanking up the tree line. We have to move!"

They ran with the sound of trees exploding behind them. Jesse almost collapsed into Hayden he was running so fast. Hayden caught him and all three did a crouch-run back into the clearing outside the harvested trees.

Rocks, dirt, twigs – all were spinning and flying at them with alarming velocity.

"AHHHHH," Kate yelled and buckled.

"What?" Jesse screamed and pulled her up.

"Ice spikes."

"You okay?" he shouted.

"Yeah." She answered, or he thought she said that.

Purple light. Green shadows. No, no, no. Jesse did not want to die under this. They had to live. They had to find shelter.

WHOOOOSHH. A sound like rushing water reverberated.

All three hit the ground with their hands on their heads.

Silver and gold forms snaked above them. The sky flashed purple and green, then blue and orange.

"Let's go into a store or something," Jesse shouted.

"Didn't Hallia say to stay away from human interaction?" Hayden yelled, breathless.

"Do we have a choice? We need to get away from here," Jesse said.

No one had time to answer. Jesse caught a glimpse of a ray of fire that channeled into a beam that was cutting a chunk of earth out of the side of a small mound in the field. "Look at that," he said.

"It's coming from Hallia," Kate said. "She's there. In the sky."

Jesse saw her. Once again it looked like she was saving them. She had made a near perfect shelter out of the hill. A rough mound of dirt and grass had a hollow center. After she finished, she came down to earth looming above them as tall as the pines.

"Get in," she said. "I'll close this, and it'll look like a hill on the outside."

They filed in and squeezed together. Hallia was about to seal it up with the same type of force field that she had used in the gym, but before she completed it, Jesse said, "Wait, what if something happens to you? How do we get out?"

"Use the orb. Concentrate, Kate," Hallia said. Her voice was thunderous. Her skin rippled silver streaks across her enormous face. She turned, her hair swirling like waves of water, and flew back into battle with two trees she had pulled from the ground as if they were carrots in a cartoon garden.

Kate was shaking with fear next to Hayden. Jesse was jammed on the other side of him, uncomfortably squeezing his girth as close to the dirt side as humanly possible. Though their shelter supposedly looked like a hill on the outside, the teens now had a window view of the continuing battle. They all shook from the release of adrenaline.

Some Belites were working now, making an ice ball the size of a hot air balloon. The Shaaris were on it though. A team of ten threw fire with the force of ten fire hoses, breaking the great mass of ice and making a churning whirlwind of fire and water in the sky.

"Hope that doesn't make it down," Hayden said. "It's just hanging there, waiting to fall." Jesse shivered.

The three huddled closer to each other and covered their ears to the sound of rushing water and cracking fire above them. Jesse wondered how the average human population, the ones not like the three of them, interpreted this tumult from the sky?

Others rallied around an injured Shaari; one in particular pulled her compatriot aside, loaded her on another chariot, and drove away from the battle. Jesse watched their path intently, even as explosions erupted around them. He wondered if they could kill each other. Well, of course they could, right? Or what would be the stakes in the battle. These were not gods. They were another species that had wars just like humans did.

For awhile he lost sight of the chariot with the injured Shaari, but then he saw them circling the outskirts of the battle. One female alien was bent over the other. Because of their size Jesse could just make out that the non-injured one shoved something in the other's mouth, and then into her own. All of the sudden they lost their present semi-gelatinous form and became all liquid. Then they smeared across the sky in a burst of light and silver goo and were gone.

"How long do you think this will go on?" Kate asked. Her teeth were chattering. Jesse worried that she might be going into shock. "What if I have to get us out with the orb?"

"You'll do it," Hayden said and patted her leg. "Man, it's strangely quiet under here. All the explosions sound so muffled."

"Yeah," Jesse said. He wiped up the sweat from his face with his sleeve. "I'm glad we're not being stabbed to death by flying trees, but it's tight in here."

"Look at that." Kate pointed to a rift in the fighting. Both sides were moving back, almost as if they were forming lines like Jesse had studied the British did during the Revolutionary War. Both Belites and Shaaris were flying in the open air and driving their chariots to form battle lines. But why? They hadn't done this before. Jesse craned his neck to try to see some more.

Then the sky opened up like it had been slashed, and a blur of red spilled out. Jesse instinctively drew up a hand to protect his face, but none of the hail that still pounded the earth broke through, and thankfully none of this new red substance reached the ground. It pooled into one massive arch between the lines of Belites and Shaaris, but then it began to congeal into a horrific trio. A red dragon with seven heads spouted rings of fire that flew out in whips and snatched Belites and Shaaris alike. Two giant humanoid aliens rode on the back of the dragon. They had lobster-colored skin and flaming crimson hair. Their long silver and gold coats shined with bright light. One was a woman with full breasts, red eyes, and a skin-tight gold body suit. She steered the dragon's heads while a man with muscular arms and legs stood on the back of the beast, thundering so loudly it was impossible not to make out his words. They were as clear as a booming bass drum, "We've made it! Now watch the earth burn!"

CHAPTER EIGHT
BURN

The dragon stood on the shore of the sea. And I saw a beast coming out of the sea. It had ten horns and seven heads, with ten crowns on its horns, and on each head a blasphemous name. The beast I saw resembled a leopard, but had feet like those of a bear and a mouth like that of a lion. The dragon gave the beast his power and his throne and great authority. One of the heads of the beast seemed to have had a fatal wound, but the fatal wound had been healed. The whole world was filled with wonder and followed the beast. People worshiped the dragon because he had given authority to the beast, and they also worshiped the beast and asked, "Who is like the beast? Who can wage war against it?"

— Bible, Revelation, 13:1-4

"What the heck is that?" Hayden asked. He had shifted to see better in their small shelter. This meant that his left elbow jabbed Jesse in the chest.

"This can't be real," Kate said through chattering teeth.

"It's real all right," Jesse added. "We all see the same thing, right? Two more Terrians, one cut dude and a hot chick."

"Yeah, that's right," Hayden answered. "And don't forget the fire-breathing dragon we all thought was from fairytales."

"Or from the Bible." Jesse twisted to get away from Hayden's elbow.

"What do you mean the Bible?" Kate asked.

"That seven-headed beast looks just like the one John describes in the Book of Revelation."

"Really?"

"Yeah, y'all don't read the Bible?"

Hayden laughed this off and looked up at the sky.

Kate said, "No, not really, remember I'm Catholic."

"Okay, whatever, look up there." Hayden pointed. "It looks like the Belites and Sharris are working together to fight this thing. What the heck is going on?"

Jesse struggled to make sense of what happened next – the battle lines charged at the dragon. The dragon's ferocious maw spat out rings of rings of fire that encircled the aliens and cast them out of sight. Were they dead? The dragon's scales glistened in the rain. Purple and black streaks of light emanated from its gyrating tail. The red-haired woman steered the beast and secured a force field to try to protect herself and the dragon from the Belite-Shaari attack while the man threw more ice balls, some of which hit the Belites and Shaaris, sending them whirling at alarming speeds. Other giant hail balls crashed to the earth in deafening thuds.

Various Shaaris or Belites broke out of the battle lines to attack the dragon heads in smaller groups. They pulled out daggers that were similar to Hayden's and slashed at the dragon heads, but they soon regenerated.

"Is it like the Greek Hydra?" Hayden asked. "You know Hercules kills it, but at first he isn't winning because when he cuts a head it grows back."

"No, this is different. The Hydra head multiplies when it grows back. Look at that." Jesse tried to point, but the force field hissed when he touched it. He continued, "That thing grows only one head again for each neck, so the total number is always seven." Jesse wanted to add that the number seven was archetypal, that many ancient cultures had stories with that symbolic number. It meant that if something was done seven times, it was complete.

"Always seven," Jesse murmured.

Hayden snorted. "Yeah, our lucky number, right?"

"Not lucky, it means completion. At least it did in all the stories we studied – seven times, seven objects, always seven to be complete," Jesse said.

The Belites and Shaaris kept slicing at the dragon heads, but the heads kept coming back. Many of the fighters were burned with the unnatural fire that froze them in time and place, formed a ring around them, and hurled them into nothingness. But then Jesse noticed a new band of Belites and Shaaris who had joined together outside of the fray. They were all on chariots with the fiercest bulls or horses to pull them. They had long sticks with what looked like lassos of light that drooped from the ends like wilted flowers.

"Charge," a Shaari yelled so loud that Jesse actually made out the word. The red-haired aliens looked worried for the first time, but the man grimaced and slapped the dragon's necks, aiming three of the dragon heads at Earth. The dragons obeyed, and their flames scorched the trees across the clearing. The fire popped and moved rapidly toward the strip mall. Some Shaaris had focused their attention to directing some rain to the blaze, but most alien power went to taking down the writhing strength of the dragon.

Their charge overpowered the red-haired aliens. The woman was thrown off the dragon's back and was instantly manacled with airy-looking shackles of light beams. The man held onto the dragon's neck and kicked and slashed at any approaching fighter. But his efforts didn't last when a bull charged and threw him from the dragon. It took three Belites to hold him down, but they finally managed to get light shackles on him as well.

The unexpected Terrian alliance managed to weave the lassos into an intricate net, snaring the dragon and dousing the flames. The creature squirmed and spat, then slumped awkwardly. The net appeared to have a drugging effect, because the dragon fell into a trance-like slumber.

Jesse shuddered and rubbed his eyes hard before looking again.

Belites and Shaaris must have decided to call a truce because they gathered up their wounded and possibly dead into chariots. The red-haired aliens still writhed and yelled, but a Shaari came up to them and injected something into their arms. Suddenly they, and their guards, became red, gold, and silver smears of light. They were gone.

Systematically the remaining Belites and Shaaris left too, but they did what Jesse had witnessed earlier in the battle: They ate something before they transformed and shot out of Earth's atmosphere. Meanwhile, sirens blared from the nearby street. Fire trucks lined the area and hosed down the burning trees. Piles of dead leaves had caught fire, sending gray and black streams of smoke into the sky. The hail had stopped as soon as the battle had, but the clearing in front of the teens looked like a golf range with baseballs covering the green.

No one said anything. Jesse was breathing hard, and he heard both Kate and Hayden panting.

"I can't believe we just saw that," Hayden said. "Do you think battles like this one are happening all over Earth?"

"We have to find out," Jesse said. "I know we have to live off the grid and all, but we need to know what's happening! How many humans have died in all this?"

"We agree, man, chill a little. It's too tight in here for that kind of emotion." Hayden said and gave a nervous grin. Jesse took in a slow breath and let it out.

Kate sat in silence. Her eyes darted from fire patch to fire patch. Her hands grabbed onto her bent knees so hard they looked almost transparent.

"It'll be all right. They have control of that one," Hayden said. "It'll be put out soon."

"It's not only that. I don't see any more Shaaris. Do you two?"

"No," both boys answered.

"So that means no Hallia, and no Hallia means that I'm supposed to use the orb to get us out of here."

"You got this, Kate," Hayden said. "Just do what you did last night, you know, when you lit the orb."

"But this is different, isn't it?" Kate asked.

"Let's see," Hayden urged.

Jesse felt sweaty in the tight space. All three grew silent as Kate closed her eyes and concentrated. The rain had ceased as soon as the Terrians had left, but their fires still popped on the horizon. Jesse's eyes followed one firefighter as he yanked one of the largest hoses from the back of the truck and then hooked it up. The burst of water crashed into the flames, but like the dragon heads, it seemed to become more vital when attacked. Jesse wondered how to counter such a force.

Their safe haven from the battle was heating up. Kate's concentration had managed to light the orb just as she had done the night before. It glowed a dreamsicle orange, and all three teens, who had already been perspiring in the dank ground, began to pour sweat.

"Good, Kate, you lit it all right," Hayden said. He swiped the dripping sweat from his face. "But I think you're right. This is different. You need to blow the hatch, baby, not heat us up in it."

Kate smiled nervously. "I know. I think I can turn it off."

Within a minute the orb cooled, and they all sighed with relief.

"Awright, you can do this," Jesse said with as much hopeful inflection that he could manage. "E. and P. said that emotion and your hands will bring orb strength, so it's not just lighting it that you can do. You can draw power or produce some kind of strength from it. Try to visualize yourself getting strength from it and pushing the force field away like it's a door. I use visualization in track, with my relay handoffs. I hit the mark perfectly, ninety-nine percent of the time."

Jesse leaned forward. Kate looked like a wet kitten someone had tried to drown. He gave her a reassuring smile, and she nodded back and then closed her eyes.

Nothing happened. Hayden and Jesse looked at each other eagerly at first. Then Hayden was about to give her more instructions, but Jesse put a finger to his lips. Anxious minutes passed with Kate's eyes locked shut, her hair stuck to her cheeks and neck, and her hands glued to the inert orb.

Jesse stared outside again. Another fire truck and some paramedics arrived. The paramedics jumped from their van and started working on a firefighter who had been crushed by a fallen branch. Jesse tried to see if the firefighter was all right, but he couldn't tell. Within minutes the injured man was lifted into the van. The sirens blared, and the truck spun out of sight.

Kate had made no progress. Hayden tapped his fingers as if his knees were snare drums. Kate opened her eyes and gazed at his knees; she slid the orb onto her lap.

"I can't do this," she said. "It's not working."

Jesse hoped Hayden had something to say, but he was contorting his body to reach behind his back to get his water bottle from his pack. Jesse leaned back an inch and grabbed it for him.

"Thanks, man." Hayden took a long gulp. "You two want some?"

Kate shook her head, her splotchy face anguished.

"Sure." Jesse drank and tried to think of something else to say. He thought for sure the visualization thing would work, but it didn't. He wanted to throw the water bottle at the force field, or shove at it in a fit, but he knew that wouldn't do a thing.

"There may be something you two can do," Kate said. "I think I know what I need." Her voice was low. Both boys stared at her, and her pale face grew red as the fire outside.

"You mean to get us out of this tomb?"

"Yeah, but please, both of you have to agree that you won't make me explain anything."

Both boys nodded in agreement.

"Then what are we waiting for?" Hayden asked. "Let's do it."

"I think I need to be next to Jesse."

"Why?" Hayden's voice turned sharp, accusatory.

"You both agreed I wouldn't have to explain." Her voice grew stronger.

Hayden quickly shifted to a light-hearted tone. "Okay. How we gonna do the switch? No offense, dude, but I'd rather have Kate slide across my crotch than you. You got a nice butt and all, but you know." Hayden smiled like he did when Jesse saw him trying to charm the girls in the line.

"All right," Kate said. "Here I go." She slipped out of her pack, clutched the orb to her stomach, and slid across Hayden's lap. Hayden held her there momentarily, shifted his weight to the right, and set her down in the middle like he was passing a football.

As soon as she was next to him, Jesse felt her heat. He assumed it was from all of her efforts with the orb.

"Okay, now what?" Hayden asked.

"I try again," Kate responded with more confidence.

Jesse felt her lean a little closer into this shoulder. He sat as stiff as a statue after that, afraid of her body next to his own and the power she seemed to have gained by her proximity to him. Kate closed her eyes again. Jesse glanced to Hayden, but now there were no looks back and forth to check her progress. Hayden stared off in the other direction, apparently ignoring Kate.

She pressed closer, and despite the heat and sweat from running and being crammed in such a small space, Jesse shivered. He felt the dew of sweat on his closely-shaved head start to drip into his eyes. He blinked it away. Nothing changed with the orb, but he felt something, orb power or Kate power. He wasn't sure which. He closed his mind to this and searched the scene outside for the hurt firefighter. But no, he had already been taken away. What else could he think about? He had no idea. He tried to make his mind go completely blank, but then Kate's thighs stretched a little and her left leg moved closer to his right. He tried as hard as he could to think about the particular shade of blue her jeans were and nothing more, but then she let one hand go of the orb and touched his arm. A jolt struck his body, surging to his crotch and down his legs. Her eyes shot open and she turned her head as a robot might to look at him square in the face. Her lips were wet and her eyes blazed with light he realized was reflected from the orb. It was glowing not orange but a purple hue. Kate took her other hand and jabbed at the force field, which snapped away with a pop and a hiss. They were free.

CHAPTER NINE

GALES

The space of the universe was in the shape of a hen's egg.
Within the egg was a great mass called no thing. Inside no thing
was something not yet born.
It was not yet developed, and it was called Phan Ku.
In no time, Phan Ku burst from the egg. He was the first being.
He was the Great Creator.
Phan Ku was the size of a giant.
Phan Ku separated sky from earth. The light, pure sky was yang,
and the heavy, dark weight of earth was yin. The vast Phan Ku
himself filled the space between
earth and sky, yin and yang.

— Phan Ku the Creator, ancient Chinese story

The Master said, He who will not worry about what is far off will
soon find something worse than worry close at hand.

— The Analects, Confucius

After Kate had freed them from their earthen shelter, the three
teens sprinted away from the emergency vehicles and toward the
uprooted trees. It didn't take long for the smog from the fires to
burn Jesse's lungs. He glanced sideways at Kate who coughed, yet
still looked triumphant from her accomplishment with the orb.

Neither boy had acknowledged the fact that she had managed to get power from it. On Jesse's side of things he didn't know what to say. He had so many questions about how she did it and what he had to do with it, but both boys had promised not to ask why she'd needed to be next him. Because of this, neither had said a thing, not even a thank you.

"Let's follow Maple Road. It connects to 355," Jesse said. Hayden nodded in agreement. Kate gave a thumbs up.

Once out of sight of the emergency workers, their run became a trot, and then without discussing it, they walked. The clouds had disappeared, and a bright sun illuminated the cornfields that sprawled on both sides of the road. The gloom and gray had changed to a brilliant blue in the sky.

Jesse watched a flock of crows dance above the harvested corn stalks. They swooped and cawed, seemingly looking for food, but the intensity of their synchronized flight patterns, which made black swirls in the air, was jarring; it was as if something made them behave like wind-up toys with mechanical wings that never caught wind for flight.

"What's up with those birds?" Hayden asked.

"God knows, well, no, He doesn't. If we can believe what we've been told, there is no God, only aliens," Jesse said. He bit down hard; he was angry and still stunned by the recent events. "Maybe the crows are picking up on the alien activity. Who knows? Y'all know anything about birds?"

"No," both Kate and Hayden said in unison.

Once they got to the spur and toll booth for 355 they sat down in a ditch to discuss their next move.

"We can't just walk on the highway. We'll get stopped or hit," Kate said. She had dirt smeared across her cheek and Jesse had an urge to wipe it off.

"What about those maps, Jesse?"

"Yeah. I'll get 'em out." Jesse reached under his shirt and pulled them out. "Let's have a look at the topographical one." He unfolded it so everyone could see. "See here, it shows a hiking path through the tree line that runs right next to 355. I don't think it's a real hiking path, but it'll probably be clear enough that we can move through it, stay out of sight, and follow the highway. Sound okay?"

"Sure thing," Hayden said and stood up. He stretched like a cat and jumped up and down. "Let's hit it."

"I also want to know what's going on in the rest of the world," Jesse said. He flung his pack over his shoulder, and the three followed the ditch to maneuver around the toll area. "This is crazy stuff. We can't be the only ones seeing it, can we?"

"After we go a ways, I say we stop and one of us goes into a gas station or something and tries to get some news. I'm up for it," Hayden said.

"Yeah, screw this. We can't do everything Hallia told us. We're human after all, not Terrian." Jesse flexed his hands in anger. Why now? In some ways he wished that the god deception was still intact, and then life would go on as usual. But then his mind countered that because he wanted the truth, not some force-fed, made-up religion from an alien species.

As if reading his mind, Kate said, "Religion isn't faith. So the Terrians think they've played gods, they're wrong. There is a God out there – for all of us." Her face was splotchy and glistening with a fine sheen of sweat.

"That'd be nice," Jesse said and looked her in the eyes, "but I do think the truth is they been playing us since humans wanted to find something beyond this world."

Kate's eyes flashed hurt for a second, but she recovered. It was enough to make Jesse regret his bluntness.

"Okay, enough," Hayden said, "how about we sing songs or play car games instead of talking about all this stuff. Pretend it's a weird road trip."

They all laughed, and Jesse was especially grateful to see Kate smile.

They hiked through the tree line that ran next to 355 for some time. Like Jesse had suspected, it wasn't a real hiking path, but the Terrians were right to highlight it because there was just enough space for the three to walk single file on the damp ground that was plagued with tree roots and buried rocks. No one spoke, but Hayden continued to hum a song Jesse didn't recognize, probably some alternative music. Jesse had a drum beat in his head, some Black Eyed Peas tune the line had performed last year for the spring competition.

Cars raced along the highway next to them, and things seemed pretty normal, so Jesse assumed that the battle, at least the one they had witnessed, was contained to their area. Soon the wind started to pick up; it made an eerie whistling through the trees. They were lucky that they weren't in the open because it wasn't long before the wind blew in earnest. The chain-link fence that ran along the highway banged in the air, and despite the tree cover the teens slowed their pace in order to brace themselves against the wind. Jesse glanced to the highway where cars slowed as well because the gales pushed on the metal with force.

"Man," Hayden said, "I hope this isn't a prelude to another battle."

"What?" Kate asked. Jesse had heard him because he led the group through the trees with Hayden directly behind him and Kate in the rear. Hayden turned to repeat what he had said to Kate, but the wind had become so strong at that point that Jesse couldn't hear him.

The whistling of the wind turned into a howl. It took all of Jesse's strength to walk against it. He started to pull himself forward through the woods by holding onto trees and stepping. He looked back. Hayden held Kate by the arm. They were hunched like an old couple. Hayden braced himself and steadied Kate who looked like she may take flight at any moment.

"She's gonna blow away, Jesse," Hayden yelled, and Jesse just made out the words.

"I know. Let's find a place to stop." But there was nowhere to stop for a good half mile, which in normal circumstances wouldn't have been a long way. In this case the walk was interminable. The wind started to send garbage and leaves in the air; they tossed about in swirls while entire trees were stripped of their remaining leaves after a particularly big gust.

Finally, there was a break in the tree line. Jesse scanned the horizon: A hill rolled into a valley with an industrial complex. Large cement cylinders sat on the outskirts of the crop of buildings. Again, Jesse had to remind himself that it was Saturday, and he thought this was lucky because no workers drove the now vacant trucks or lift equipment.

"Let's make a break for one of those cylinders," he yelled.

Hayden nodded and tugged on Jesse's sleeve. Jesse understood. He linked himself to Kate's other arm, and they dashed down the hill. It felt like they hit a wall of water because a gust threw them into the air and down onto their backsides.

"I know this sounds crazy," Hayden yelled, "but I think we'd better log roll."

Jesse rolled feeling like a hamster spinning a wheel because when he glanced up he saw that little progress had been made. He wasn't even halfway down the hill. Hayden had gone the farthest, but Kate hadn't realized that she wasn't rolling down the hill, but across it. She seemed paused in space while the wind whipped her hair and hood furiously. He crawled back to her and gave her a tap. Her face had been shoved into the grass; she looked up, her eyes wild.

"You need to straighten out," Jesse said. He saw Hayden rolling rapidly out of the corner of his eye. A laugh drifted off into the vacuum.

"I can't move," she said.

"Yeah you can." Jesse pulled on her backpack. The sky was darkening, and he was getting scared himself. He wasn't sure if this meant yet another battle, or if it was residual effects of a battle taking place somewhere else.

In one quick toss, Jesse flung Kate down the hill. She log rolled a good distance. He rolled after her and was amazed when he landed an inch from her body. He crawled to where his face was next to hers, which was again in the dirt.

"You all right?"

She looked up and smiled brilliantly. He grinned back.

"Let's go again," he said with the fleeting excitement that comes from remembering being a small kid.

He gave her another toss and she cleared the hill. Hayden pulled her up and into the cement cylinder. Jesse soon joined them.

"We have to stop meeting like this," Hayden said after Jesse had crammed in next to him. "I'm going to charge for one of those buildings and try to break in a window. We can't stay in this block of cement for the night."

Jesse looked at the sky. Was it night? He had lost track of all time, and without his cell phone he couldn't check. He watched

Hayden disappear behind a building. His entire body felt numb from fatigue and strain. He closed his eyes for a moment and quite possibly fell asleep. He woke to Hayden yanking on his sweatshirt.

"I can get us into one of the warehouses. Follow me."

They hunkered down and pressed together to fight the wind. When they reached the window that Hayden must have pried open with his dagger, they sent Kate in first to squeeze through the small opening and then let them in through the side door. Once inside they all walked clumsily. The wind rattled the windows and outdoor signs. Some pallets that had not been secured well banged on an outside wall every now and then from surges of wind.

"Too bad Chicago isn't all downhill from here, maybe we could just log roll the whole way," Hayden said. Jesse laughed remembering their awkward roll down the ravine to the bike path. Was that only one day ago?

Jesse examined the empty warehouse: There were more pallets stacked along the cement wall, small forklifts, a conveyor, and some loose gravel and decorative stone in large bins. The pallets outside knocked periodically on the outer wall; each new round of clanging made Kate jump.

"Jesse, let's go outside and move those," Hayden said.

"All right."

He and Hayden stepped outside; a cool gale flung the metal door open. They struggled against the force, staying close to the side of the building. Once they found the pallets they worked together, floundering with each whip of air. They pulled the flats as far from the building as they could manage without being launched into the early evening sky with the slatted wood acting as a kite.

When Jesse and Hayden returned inside the warehouse, Kate had already lit the orb, which gave off a soft light. It warmed the room, creating the sense of a hearth within a stone home from hundreds of years ago. Kate hunched her body toward the orb and used her fingers to comb through her matted hair.

"Wow, it feels great in here," Jesse said.

Kate looked up and gave a satisfied smile.

"Yeah, you're getting the hang of that thing. I say we dig into some more food and camp here for the night." Hayden sat down on the cement floor. "Too bad Hallia didn't pack sleeping bags or toothbrushes. My mouth is rotten. I'm totally buying brushes, toothpaste, and hygiene stuff tomorrow."

"You got money?" Jesse asked.

"A little cash. I'll spot you two."

"Thanks," Jesse said. He had never thought that brushing his teeth would be so appealing, but it was.

"And a roll of toilet paper too," Kate said.

"Sure." Hayden smiled. "Jesse and I have it easier, but I've been holding back a giant crap, waiting till we hit a gas station. It's that or squat in the woods and wipe with dried leaves. Who knows what I'd catch?"

"Dude – come on." Jesse gestured to Kate. "Lady present."

They all laughed and sat around the orb. Each rifled through their packs and tossed their packages of alien food into a pile to sort and trade like it was Halloween. They ate in silence, all mesmerized by the glow of the orb and the whistle of the wind. After eating just two packs of food, another granola-like bar, and a sealed strip of something that looked and tasted a lot like beef jerky, Jesse spoke, "Maybe this stuff is like elf food, ya know, like in the *Lord of the Rings*."

"Dunno, man, never read the books."

"I love the movies," Kate said between bites.

"Yeah the movies are great, but the books are better."

Kate gave a small smile, and Hayden tore into his own beef

jerky-like food. He spoke while chewing, showing red strips in his mouth, and Jesse saw Kate look the other direction. "All I know is that I'm glad this stuff fills us up, but I'm dying for some real meat, not these petrified strips of God knows what alien crap."

They chewed in silence. Jesse wanted to make another attempt at conversation, but he was afraid it would fail again. He wished that it were just he and Kate who were chatting around a real campfire. Then Hayden wouldn't be there to interrupt or even make her laugh. He shifted his mind to the maps. He unpacked each one, unfolded them, and spread them out on the floor. This was the first time he had a chance to really see them in detail. When he came to the tied package with the maps of Union Station and other possible locations for the power source, a thin book dropped from between two pages that had been sealed together. The binding, cover, and pages were old and yellowed. The script must have been Terrian.

"Whoa, what's that?"

"I'm not sure, but it looks old and important and alien," Jesse said. He gently turned the pages. There was a page or two of alien text and then some space, or the text blurred because of age.

"Won't do us much good if we can't read it. I'm hitting the sack." Hayden fluffed his backpack like it was a pillow and was asleep within minutes. Kate looked over Jesse's shoulder at the Terrian book. She smelled like outside air and autumn leaves.

"What do you think it says?"

"I wish I knew, but I can't stop trying to read it," Jesse said. After a few long minutes of silence with Kate straining to stay awake, as if her watching him attempt to read the script helped his progress, Jesse looked at her. "Go to sleep, Kate, you're exhausted."

She nodded and curled into a crescent moon shape. Soon Jesse heard her quiet breathing. He continued to pore over the script again and again until his eyes hurt. But he forced them open and searched for meaning or patterns. His eyes closed momentarily in sleep, but he snapped them open. Then he felt compelled to try again. For hours Jesse continued, and he found that even when he got the urge to give up and close down for the night, his eyes opened, and he tried again. And then, one time he closed his eyes and he saw the text in his mind's eye. He kept his eyes closed and the script unscrambled and became words he could read and understand. His eyes shot open; his heart raced, and then he looked at the cover of the Terrian book. It read: *The Ancient Terrian Fragment of Human Divinities*. He wiped the sweat from his hands on his pants and turned to the first page. He read. *In the beginning...*

CHAPTER TEN
INFORMATION

In the beginning we, the Ancients, saw the universe as a color spectrum, pinks, oranges, blues, the black of nothingness and the light of stars. One seer had a vision of a unity tether stretching from our planet, Terria, to Earth, the planet of possibility, of nascent wonder, where humans' minds were so pliant, so full of amazement, that we could not help but to link ourselves to such a species. Humanity, the sprawling, expanding species, started to question, to ponder, to hope for a being that created them, that offered a paradise, and an after-world after their deaths. The way of the Ancients is a peaceful path, where we can bring humanity the gods, the answers, the pure light of paradise that lives not across the universe, but within their own minds.

— The Ancient Terrian Fragment of Human Divinities, Jesse Woods, translator

Jesse shot awake; for a moment he had no memory of where he was. Then he saw Hayden sprawled on top of his backpack in deep sleep. He looked over and both Kate and her backpack were gone. He jumped up. The orb still glowed and warmed the room, but when his eyes scanned the warehouse there was no sign of her.

"Kate!" Jesse's voice cracked.

"I'm here." Her feint answer came from one corner of the warehouse.

He ran toward it. "Are you okay?"

"Yeah, I'm changing clothes."

He stopped in his tracks and looked toward two large gravel bins, behind which Kate was undressing. His face got instantly hot. "Oh, okay, I was worried," he stammered. His body stood stock-still and his eyes locked onto the gray barrels.

"I'm fine. I'll be out in a minute."

She emerged in a new outfit: blue jeans, a gray turtleneck, and a fleece jacket. She looked shocked when she saw that he was so close to where she'd changed, and apparently frozen in place.

"I feel better now that I changed. You all right?"

"Yeah, and no. I have a ton of stuff to tell y'all."

Hayden was still asleep, but Jesse jostled him awake. He sat up and wiped his eyes like a toddler might. He slumped over and looked at Jesse through half-open lids. "Whas up?"

"I actually read most of that Terrian book last night." Jesse felt anxious to convey what he had learned.

"How? It's written in ancient alien or something. So you managed to crack the Rosetta Stone of alien script?"

"It seems so, just like you glowed and killed a supernatural bull the other night, and Kate can light this orb and keep us warm." Jesse glanced at her and she reddened. He felt himself grow hot too. He took a step away from her and concentrated. "I have so much to tell you both."

"All right, all right. Just let me find the equivalent of some coffee or something to get me to wake up. Five minutes, I'll be ready. We can get moving too, and then talk. Sound good?"

Jesse nodded, but felt like the five minutes would be an

eternity. He killed the time by going behind the gravel barrels to change clothes. He ate a quick alien bar and went back to their camp. Hayden had hardly moved, but Kate was packing up her old clothes and the orb. Jesse followed suit and rearranged his stuff, clutching the alien text and standing over Hayden.

"Okay, okay, I'm moving you two. Man," Hayden said. He stood and pulled his pack over his shoulders. "We hit a gas station and I'm buying a greasy sausage biscuit and some coffee."

The three walked out into sunshine on a crisp autumn morning, but the destruction from the gales the previous day was apparent: Upturned trees lay with massive roots jutting out, the pallets they had moved had blown farther from the buildings, and debris stirred on the ground from vestigial winds of the day before. They picked their way through blown leaves, candy wrappers, empty pop bottles, and even roof shingles. Jesse motioned for them to enter the woods that butted up against a wire fence, which was as tall as cell phone towers; on the other side of the fence early morning drivers raced along Route 355.

Once in the woods, Jesse turned to his companions; though he had hardly slept, his mind felt electric. "Can we talk now?"

"I really want to know what you read." Kate slid up beside him on the path, and Hayden stepped in closer behind the two. There was not enough room for all three to walk side by side.

"I'm dying to tell you." Jesse looked right at Kate and realized he had spoken mainly to her. Hayden must have sensed the slight because he pressed in closer to them and slapped Jesse on the back in a friendly manner.

"Go ahead, tell us what you read. We can analyze how you read the stuff later," Hayden said.

"What I read is a fragment written by ancient Terrians. They weren't called Shaaris or Belites thousands of years ago, only Terrians. Their scholars-slash-peacekeepers were called the

Ancients. Like Hallia said, Terrians first discovered our planet when modern humans were developing."

"Did she say that? I hardly remember, but I was also pissed as all get out," Hayden said. Hayden nearly tripped Jesse as he leaned in to hear.

"Yeah, she said something like that, I think. What about you Kate?"

"I remember that too and she said they saw snippets of the future and that humans started to wonder about an afterlife."

"Yeah. In the fragment they noted how the Neanderthals buried items with their dead, you know, because they thought people needed them in an afterlife. They took an interest in our progress because our species are so similar."

"So this fragment is their archeological notes on early humans?"

"Yes and no," Jesse answered. His mind was racing. "From what I understand, they sent scientists to blend into the different modern human groups and make observations. Kind of an anthropology project or something. When modern humans migrated out of Africa, they still remained scientific observers, but then it started to change over time. Civilizations cropped up, and some Terrians thought they could help humans by providing them with what they wanted: supreme beings."

"What arrogant asses!" Hayden huffed. "Not to mention they could score a little human sex, right?"

"Hallia said they had to make laws or something to stop Terrians from propagating with humans," Kate said.

This wasn't going how Jesse had intended. He really wanted them to understand how the Ancients really wanted to make both species better.

"Yeah, for sure, there must have been breeding, and it was

arrogant of them to think of themselves as supreme beings and all. But if you read their stuff, it's beautiful language, you would see that these Ancients were trying to do good things for both species. They had these seers that foresaw a link between our species. They saw a need for our species to be united to save us both."

"Save us from what? Looks like the Terrians don't mind killing humans. Think of our friends!" Hayden snuffed the air and spat on the ground.

"I know, I know. But just listen," Jesse said. He took a deep breath. His insides felt hot and tight. He didn't know how to communicate what he had read. How had he read it anyway? What if he misunderstood something? No, he felt he was right.

"Look," he started, "Terrians saw themselves as millennia ahead of us, so they formed this Consortium that discussed the future of Terrian involvement in human development. It gets a little confused here because I think this must be a copy of a primary document, so there are chunks out of the text, but the gist is that they voted and decided to become our gods. This would ensure our link to each other over time. They also wanted to help us become more like them – in their image, sound familiar?"

"But how many different gods were they? It's not like there was only Jesus and God back then. Weren't there all these groups with a load of their own gods?" Hayden had forced himself alongside Jesse. He looked mad. The three of them squeezed as best they could on the uneven ground, but soon Kate slid behind them. Jesse felt her presence; she seemed sad and tense.

"You're right, Hayden. They sent emissaries to blend into budding civilizations, and these became the prophets, seers, philosophers, shamans, and healers of our earliest civilizations. The emissaries guided human beliefs and ideologies. You throw in a few 'visions' where humans thought they heard or even saw their gods, which were Terrians that fit the image, and poof, you have a religion. The emissaries responded to whatever the human population wanted and provided it in their gods, so different gods for different civilizations. It really was an altruistic endeavor, but this was only a fragment. I'm dying to read more."

"You kind of sound like these Ancients have charmed you a little." Hayden's voice sounded bitter.

"Naw, man, I'm just freaked a little by being able to read the thing. What's up with that, and with all the weird stuff we've been doing? What if we're part alien?"

"No way. Even Alien-Bitch said as much." Hayden stopped and kicked the ground. Kate tripped on a tree root, did an odd jog, and fell into Jesse. He caught her and helped her to her feet. They stood in a triangle and stared at each other. Jesse felt energy pulse through his entire body. Was this what it felt like to use more of his brain? He wanted to pursue the idea that they were all part alien, but Hayden looked pissed, and Kate dejected, so he kept his thoughts to himself.

"What about the power source?" Kate asked, obviously wanting to break the awkward silence.

"Oh yeah, that's a weird one. The stuff on the power source is pretty garbled. But I think the Ancients planted them as they said, 'To keep the sacred in their motives to help humanity'. If I understand it right, it's something that should help solidify our union, so we can help each other now, in the present. They put different power sources in various places around the planet, but the crazy thing is that only one of them is the real deal. If I understand it right, there is a small sect of Keepers who hold this knowledge and have passed down where to move these power sources, cause it doesn't take a rocket scientist to figure out that Union Station wasn't there when the ancient Native American tribes were here, and that was probably about when the first of the power sources were planted."

"But what is it?" she asked.

"That I don't know."

"I still don't get why the Shaaris wouldn't go to their own Keepers to get them?"

"I'm not sure about that either," Jesse said. His mind clicked with options. "Maybe they tried and it didn't work, so they decided to get help."

"From us? That doesn't make any sense." Kate readjusted her back pack and sighed heavily. "I wish Hallia would have explained more."

"I know she saved our butts two times now, but we can't trust her. Something is up. There's more to this, and I think they're all a bunch of users: Shaari, Belite, or Hot Red-headed Chick and Muscle Man." Hayden punched the air.

They went over and over what they had observed thus far: gold hair and skin for Belites, silver for Shaaris, and the red for whatever the dragon group was. Each time they thought they reached some purpose of why them and not the Keepers, they had no solid argument. There simply wasn't enough information, and it wasn't like they had any means to acquire it. They even pondered that the fragment could be a false one, to set them on a wrong track. To this Kate broke in with, "No, they need us for some reason, so why give us wrong information to get the power source? As far as we can see both Shaaris and Belites want us to succeed at something they can't do themselves."

It was the most she had said about anything, and as usual, it was the most lucid. Jesse chewed the side of his cheek and thought more on it. "The Ancients must have rigged the power source somehow, you know, so that the future Terrians would need human help to get it. This would serve as a safeguard, in case the Terrians went over the top with their god role."

"All right, I'll give you that, but it's a little whacked. I mean come on, how much more over the top can you get than becoming another planet's gods?" Hayden gave a harsh laugh. "These dudes are too full of themselves, ancient or modern; they screwed with our minds."

"Yeah, but these Ancients really wanted humanity to achieve the best of ourselves. Maybe they went about it the wrong way." Jesse felt torn; if he really thought about his feelings, he realized he felt an affinity for the Ancients. They saw life as one interconnected web, and they really wanted to weave their future with humanity for the betterment of both species. They didn't want to dominate or deceive. At least not in the beginning, at least not all of them.

Jesse kept his mouth shut. He couldn't capture the beauty in the Ancients' motives without using their language. Maybe they were being used, but Jesse couldn't help but think that the Ancients were very different from the different groups of Terrians they had already encountered. Wouldn't it make sense that Terrians got more corrupt as time went on; hadn't this happened to humanity?

They moved in silence as sunlight filtered through the canopy of trees, sporadically warming their faces while they walked. To Jesse the patterns of light on the path looked like Legos scattered on the floor of his brother's bedroom. He brushed the thought away because it made him miss his little brother Dorian that much more; if he thought too long about the three-year-old's doughy arms and hands intently building something with Legos, he would surely cry again, especially because of the lack of sleep and new feelings. What were his new feelings? He glanced at Kate who studied her feet as she hiked. He wanted to take her hand.

Because of this urge he felt three levels of betrayal: She was white; he was dating Sofia who he hoped was safe; and oddly, he didn't know what kinds of problems would develop between him and Hayden if he went with Kate. Went with Kate? He almost smacked himself in the head to stop such thoughts. He had to focus!

The tree line opened up to a clearing with tall prairie grass surrounding an exit from 355. The road split in two directions. North of the exit a lone gas station stood with several semi-trucks parked and a few travelers stopping for gas or coffee.

"You guys want me to go?" Hayden asked.

"Sure but be careful. Try not to have much contact," Jesse warned. "We'll wait for you in this ditch."

Hayden nearly ran to the gas station, and Jesse couldn't help but laugh. He and Kate walked down the ditch and sat on their backpacks in the late morning sun. She bit her thumbnail and Jesse scratched the side of his head and ran his hand along his jaw, feeling for some growth of a beard that wasn't there.

"Jesse," she said. He jolted a little at the sound of his name.

"Yeah."

"Do you think that this is all the end of the world? You know, the Apocalypse."

Kate hunched over, bit her thumbnail harder, and then started twisting a strand of hair. Once again, he wanted to take her hands in his. He moved to do so but pulled his hands back; he was thankful that she kept staring at the ground, as if the answer would sprout from dirt. Was it the Apocalypse? It very well could be, or at least one disastrous alien war was about to hit Earth, and how could humans fight it?

"No," he lied, just a little. "It's gonna be all right, Kate." His voice was firm, assuring. She looked him in the eyes and gave a half smile.

"Even if it's not true, it helps me to hear you say so."

Right then Hayden showed up and worked his way down the slope.

"We're set amigos!"

He passed out toothpaste and brushes for each of them, sausage biscuits, coffee, water, and a roll of toilet paper. He handed it to Kate, and she smiled as she tucked it into her pack.

They crouched down and ate in the ditch. The meat and buttery biscuit melted in Jesse's mouth. He would have slammed the coffee, but it scalded his tongue on the first drink.

"Find out any news?" he asked between bites.

"Yeah, saw some of the news and I bought a paper. Dude, there's weird stuff happening all over the world, hurricane in Chili, earthquakes in Asia, and odd storms in Europe. Whatever is going on with the Terrians, they are full-blown bringing their business here. And check this out, we're not alone." Hayden spoke through mouthfuls of sausage and opened up the newspaper. The headline read: *Illinois Resident Reports Alien Sightings*. "If you read the thing, this was a reputable professor, not some crack pot reporting UFOs. He had the balls to say something, but then later he was found dead in his home from an apparent suicide. Guess who's behind that one? I'll bet anything it was God, you know, Hallia and the Shaaris."

CHAPTER ELEVEN

BRIDGE

Do you hear the beating of your own heart, dear child? Does it sound like thunder, a pounding life force, the sky's own pulse pulling us closer?

— The Ancient Terrian Fragment of Human Divinities,
Jesse Woods, translator

The snapping turtle came to help. The loons put the woman on the turtle's back. Then the turtle called all the other animals to aid in saving the divine woman's life.
The animals decided the woman needed earth to live on.
Turtle said, "Dive down in the water and bring up some earth."
So they did. A beaver went down.
A muskrat went down. Others stayed down too long, and they died.

— Divine Woman, the Creator, Huron story

"Let's get moving," Jesse said. He was unnerved after hearing about the dead professor and Hayden's assessment that the Shaaris were behind it. He wanted to get clear of the open space surrounding the gas station and resume their hike in the woods. After a frantic, yet thorough, brushing of teeth and spitting in the grass, all three stuffed their toiletries in their packs and walked the length of the ditch until they got back to the tree line that ran along the highway. Jesse kept looking over his shoulder as they walked. For some reason he had chills all over his body. He drained his now lukewarm cup of coffee, hoping this would help, but he couldn't shake the chills or the feeling that someone or something was following them.

"Can you slow it down, man?" Hayden shouted. "My insides are bubbling."

Jesse turned and saw Kate trailing him a little, but Hayden had started to lag behind a good twenty feet. He stopped and watched Hayden slowly reach the group with a pained expression. Maybe the food hadn't agreed with him. His normally ruddy complexion looked ashen. Kate must have noticed as well because she looked at Hayden intently and handed him her water bottle as soon as he had caught up. Jesse wanted to warn her against this, just in case Hayden was becoming ill, but it was too late. Hayden chugged half the bottle.

"You all right?"

"Yeah. Just tired. You two woke me too soon." Hayden glanced away and ran his fingers through his spiky blondish hair. "I think we're around Downers Point, or some other faceless suburb. Right?"

"Sounds right." Jesse decided he'd pull out one of the maps to allow Hayden to rest. He unfolded it and ran his finger along a blue line. "We'll cross the Des Plaines River soon. There's a huge bridge. It must have some space on the shoulder to walk along."

No one said anything. Hayden held in a deep breath and exhaled slowly. Once he straightened up and gained some color back into his face, Jesse pressed on in silence. He felt better since they were covered by the nearly bare trees, but soon he started to worry that the bridge would leave them open, high up, and very exposed. But how else could they cross? Wait all day to try to sneak onto a barge? The barges would most likely run downstream and not simply ferry across the wide river. No, he thought, they had to risk the bridge and cross it as quickly as possible.

The tree line broke when it looked to be about midday. Brown grass covered slopes that had clusters of native grasses; one patch in particular looked like slender stick men topped with bushy Russian hats. They waded through the waist high plants, each not able to resist touching the soft tops with the palms of their hands. The bridge was in sight and Jesse got that prickly feeling again. He saw that even his hands showed goose pimples. He rubbed his hands together in an effort to warm himself, but the prickles persisted. When they reached the bridge he felt like someone was sticking needles into his skin. He remembered how his mother had gone to an acupuncturist for back pain. She'd marveled in how the pressure points brought relief to her lower back. But this wasn't anything like relief; he was scared.

The slopes had led them below the level of the bridge, but above the river valley. Hayden looked like he felt better because he motioned to the group to follow him up the hill that brought them to the causeway. Hayden paused along the chain fence at the start of the bridge.

Jesse didn't want to make anyone nervous, and they had no choice but to cross the bridge, but he felt like he had to bring up his feelings. He had never liked heights, but this was something different. "I don't feel good about this."

"Why?" Hayden asked. "You were the one who led us this way." His voice had a hint of accusation in it, but he curbed it with a smile. "You afraid of heights?"

"A little, but this is different. I feel like someone is watching us."

"I'm scared," Kate added, "but I pretty much feel like that all the time now. You know, like we're always being watched."

Jesse was grateful she'd spoken up; otherwise it could have easily become a back and forth with Hayden.

"So, you feel all right about crossing?"

"Yeah, man, let's go," Hayden said.

"I don't think we have a choice," Kate said. She gave him a half smile and a piercing look with those blue eyes that heated his chills instantly. "Come on." Kate waved them on, running toward the walkway on the side of the highway bridge.

They had a wide expanse of cement along the shoulder of the bridge, but they fell into single file without discussing it. Jesse followed Kate and focused on her backside. It felt a little cheap, but watching the swing of her hips calmed his nerves. He heard Hayden's determined steps behind him. The wind picked up and knocked the fence, and each metallic thump solidified Jesse's plan to avoid looking down. Out of the corner of his eye he caught the form of a barge sloshing through the murky water.

Jesse was good at judging distances, probably because of his running experience. He figured the bridge spanned at least two miles. The wind started to blow harder and fear crept through him. What if another battle started? What if the bridge collapsed? He wasn't usually such a worrier, but since his surreal night of reading and the odd feelings since the gas station, he couldn't help but imagine cement explosions that would send them plummeting into the frigid river below. Maybe Kate sensed something too because with about one fourth of the way to go she turned abruptly. Her brow furrowed into severe lines and her eyes danced with alarm. She wasn't looking at Jesse, but at Hayden. Jesse no longer heard Hayden behind him, so he turned too.

Hayden buckled at the knees and fell. They ran to his side and pulled him up to a sitting position. Each held onto one of his shoulders, and Jesse thought that if either one let go, Hayden would topple over, possibly onto the bridge with its speeding cars. Hayden's head lolled in a terrifying circle and his fingers twitched.

"Hayden!" Kate yelled, but her voice was lost in the rush of cars and the now screaming wind. "Hayden, can you hear me?"

He didn't answer; his head slumped onto his chest, and Jesse checked for a pulse. His heart rate was way up. Jesse peeled back his eyelids and then Hayden's eyes shot open by their own volition. He sat up straight, his back as rigid as a plank of wood. He blinked twice, almost like he was an old antenna receiving a transmission, and on the third blink, his eyes were red and glowing.

He spoke in a cold and monotonous voice: "We have found you, Hayden. Be our emissary, and we will rule both worlds. We have found you, come to us, open your mind. We'll show you all the power your body and mind can unleash. We have found you, Hayden. Be our emissary, and we will rule both worlds. We have found you, come to us, open your mind. We'll show you all the power your body and mind can unleash." He repeated the same message, in that icy voice. Kate stared and shook with fear, and though Jesse was scared too, he wanted it to stop. So he braced himself, and right when Hayden opened his mouth to speak it for the fourth time, Jesse pulled back and punched him square in the jaw.

Hayden flew backwards, and Kate fell into the fence, shocked and grateful that Hayden's eyes no longer glowed red.

"What the hell did you do that for?" Hayden's voice was venomous, but it was his own.

"Your eyes were glowing red and you kept repeating some alien message."

"What?"

"Look, can you walk? The winds are picking up and we're too exposed on this bridge."

"Ah, yeah, I can walk." Hayden stood. His legs wobbled, but he regained his balance and walked ahead. Once across the bridge, Jesse led them down a hill with thick growths of bushes and trees. He slashed at branches that crossed in front of his face and held them back for Kate and Hayden to pass through. They were now farther from the highway, but Jesse had a plan. He wanted to reach a train yard that he had seen on one of the maps. From what he could tell, it was for industrial transport only, so he hoped to find a box car to ride in. He assumed this was possible from movies he had seen; at least he hoped it was. They needed to get to Chicago and fast. Hayden was easy enough to take, but seeing him possessed was unnerving.

The woods opened into a valley with freight cars sitting on rust-colored tracks. One long train had carloads of wood, steel, and other materials. Jesse quickly scanned each car to see if there were any ones that had sliding doors. He couldn't tell from the distance. He saw some men on a platform, so he pulled Kate and Hayden behind a cluster of bushes.

"You wanna hop a train? Don't you think we need to discuss this?" Hayden said.

Jesse bit down hard and muttered. "Okay. You want to hop a train? I saw this line heads north on the map. We could get off on the outskirts of the city."

"Can we get on?" Kate asked.

Jesse looked again at the immobile train. "I think if we're gonna do this we have to act fast. This one will move soon."

"All right," Hayden said. "But what about the 'no transportation' thing Hallia talked about?"

"No one will see us. I think we need to risk it," Jesse countered.

Hayden bit down and shook his head. "I dunno. What do you think, Kate?"

"I think we should go. If no one sees us, then it's the same as walking through the woods."

"All right," Hayden said. "Let's make for the end of the train. There better be an empty one."

They dashed down the hill, crouching. Jesse's heart beat furiously. When they reached the train cars, he sprinted along the side frantically looking at each one. The slatted ones with visible contents were stocked full of materials, but two at the end had doors, and a chance of being vacant box cars. Hayden was already on it. He yanked at one door, trying to slide it open. Jesse pulled too. It let out a sharp sound of squeaky hinges. Jesse scanned to see if anyone heard, but no one was in sight. Hayden hopped on and grabbed Kate's hands to hoist her up. Once on, the boys slid the door shut and all three huddled in silence and darkness in the corner of the train car.

"What if we don't move again today?" Kate whispered.

"I think we will," Jesse said. He could hear her breathing. She put her head on her knees and exhaled a shaky sigh.

"Do we need to whisper? I'm dying to talk to you guys about what happened to me on the bridge."

"I think we need to keep quiet until we move." Jesse decided to trust his instincts on this one. Didn't his prickly chills predict the scene on the bridge? He didn't want to take a chance. He knew that they had to get going and fast, but now he was more cautious. Somehow, he knew that time was running out. Time for what? Like Kate had asked, was it the end of the world? Possibly. Everything was already changed with this new knowledge. But he had to save his family, and he had to find out if Sofia was okay. He had to get to the power source, to find out more about the Ancients because he knew that they were different from the Terrians now. They intended peace and unity. They predicted a need for Terrians and humans to work together. But why?

After what felt like an hour huddled in silence, the train lurched. Kate stirred and Hayden sighed with relief. Jesse welcomed the metallic grinding of the wheels on the tracks, the constant vibration and rocking motion, and the clanging of material in one of the cars ahead of them. When the whistle let out an even series of sounds, something like a church organ, he relaxed and opened his backpack to get some water and food.

"Okay you two. Fill me in," Hayden said. He stretched his legs and rubbed his hands together for warmth. "You think we could have some orb heat now that we're moving?"

Kate pulled out the orb, closed her eyes, and lit it instantly. Jesse was impressed with her skill. He pushed back the question of if he had anything to do with her improving power, like it seemed when she blew open their earthen shelter.

Jesse repeated what Hayden had said while possessed on the bridge.

"It was almost like you were a radio transmitting the same message. The question is who sent it, and why you?" Jesse rocked sideways and caught himself with his hand.

"I don't remember a damn thing about it. Well I remember the punch. Still hurts by the way."

"Sorry about that. I didn't know what else to do."

"Do you think it was the red-haired aliens?" Kate asked in a low voice. "I mean, your eyes glowed red. I dunno, just guessing." She looked away.

Jesse felt her uncertainty.

"It's as good a guess as any," he said. "How many alien groups are there? It's driving me crazy."

"I know it's nowhere near bedtime, but that possession thing knocked me out. I feel like I'm going to pass out." Hayden gave a wry laugh. "I have to shut my eyes for a while." He pulled his pack to a far corner and flopped on it. "I don't think I can take another round of guesses about this stuff. We're just gonna have to wing it – at least for now."

CHAPTER TWELVE

CORRUPTED

Olorun was the Owner of the Sky and the Highest Being. He lived in the sky with other spirits. In the beginning, the earth was all watery, just a marshy place, a waste.

Sometimes, Olorun and the other gods came down to play about in the marsh-waste. There were long spiders' webs hanging from the sky. They draped across sweeping spaces like graceful silk bridges.

Yet there was no solid land anywhere. No ground on which to stand. There could be no human beings under the sky until there was a hard place for them to plant their feet.

— Owner of the Sky: Olorun the Creator, Yoruba story

Full darkness engulfed the rocking train car, but inside Kate's orb glowed, sending off a soft light and warming their small cabin. When Hayden first fell asleep, both Jesse and Kate watched him nervously, afraid there could be another alien transmission complete with flashing red eyes and robotic voice. After watching him for what felt like an hour of silence, they finally relaxed when Hayden slept peacefully and started to snore.

Jesse looked around the train car, his mind racing through different topics. With Hayden asleep he really wanted to talk to Kate. Now that he had the opportunity, he couldn't think of anything to say. All he wanted to talk about was her history with Hayden. He also *didn't* want to talk about Hayden. He wanted to know why she needed to sit next to him in the earthen shelter in order to gain power from the orb. He felt rather ridiculous about this.

In the last twenty-four hours especially, they had many things to figure out: who were E and P? How did he read the Ancients' text? What was the power source? Which group of aliens spoke through Hayden and why? But none of those things felt as relevant as Kate herself. He longed to know what she was thinking.

"It's hard to believe that Nazis crammed about a hundred people into one cattle car. I'm surprised anyone even survived the trip to concentration camps." Jesse cringed internally at his involuntary choice of topic: Nazi Germany, lighten up! He knew how to charm 'em, he thought.

Kate stirred and turned toward him from across the orb. "That's horrible. And all those Jews who died and said the – what was it, Kaddish, I think, their prayer for the dead. What did the Terrians do for them? I hate them, Jesse, I really do." Kate turned her cheek onto her bent knees. A wet circle formed on her jeans where tears fell.

He scooted over to sit right next to her and put his hand on her shoulder. She blinked and looked at him through her tears. "I know," he said, "it's enough to make me want to kill them all, but then I read that Ancients' fragment and I..."

She sat up and wiped her tears on her sleeve. "Jesse." Her voice was a mere breath. He squeezed her shoulder and she took his hand in hers. They held hands like small children do, palm to palm. The softness of her palm shocked him; his felt rough, even calloused, in comparison, like he worked outdoors. He dared not make the slightest shift that would make her let go. Eventually he had to move his weight from squatting to sitting, but she kept her hand in his.

"So, you think the Ancients didn't really want to be gods for humans?" she asked.

"Naw, they did decide on that, but the motivations were to guide us to something, I'm not sure how to say it, but something more. I believe they really wanted to do this slowly. Their technology and abilities with mind and body, well, if we got that while we were just figuring out how to irrigate crops, they thought it was too much. I don't know where this is going, but I have to find out."

"You think fate brought our species together?" Kate asked.

"Not sure I believe in fate. I don't have the answers, but I think the key to this is finding a way to get to a relationship that is like what the Ancients wanted. I haven't worked it all out, but whatever has happened on Terria, it's not good, and it's not at all how it used to be. Kind of like here."

Kate slid a fraction of an inch closer to Jesse. "I know I keep saying this, but I do believe there is some kind of God out there for all of us."

Jesse didn't want to hurt her, but his words came before he had a chance to edit them. "I haven't thought much about God since my dad died. Haven't prayed. I go to church for my mom, but not because I believe the stuff."

"How did he die?"

"He was shot. We still lived in Chicago, my mom, my dad, and me. He tried to stay away from his family's business, but my uncle, his brother, was thick in gang activity and selling smack.

My dad tried again and again to get him out of trouble, but it never stuck." Jesse swallowed hard; he had never told anyone in New Franklin the whole story, not even Sofia. He worried that they would think that he and his family were lowlife. "Anyway, I was six and my mom was taking me to my granny's house because she had to get to nursing school. She dropped me off, and I was playing army men for what felt like ten minutes, and she was back, and at first I was so happy to see her, but then we all packed up and called a cab, which was something we never did, and went to County hospital. My dad died almost right away from gunshot wounds. He'd been over at Uncle K.T.'s place, fixing the damn plumbing, when some hoods came wanting their money. There was a fight and my dad got hurt."

Jesse couldn't stop the tears then. They were surprisingly hot down his cheeks. He let go of Kate's hand to put his face in his hands for a moment. He only looked up once he knew that seeing her wouldn't bring on some very un-cool sobs.

Her expression was like one he had seen on his mother's face the last time he really looked at her. They were in the kitchen the night before all of this happened, before everything changed. Damn aliens and fire from the sky. He wanted to go back, but then Kate wouldn't be rocking with him on a train car. What was it about Kate that made him think of his mom? Obviously, Kate looked nothing like his mother, but she gave off the same quiet gentleness, the same feeling that made Jesse feel connected, not alone. He would have broken down again, but she smiled and held his face in her smooth hand.

"Your mom is lucky to have you." She held his cheek and he burned from his face to his feet. "So you live with your mom and stepdad in New Franklin. You're the only child from her first marriage."

"Yeah," his voice sounded gravelly. "Kate."

"Yes." She dropped her hand, and he missed it instantly, but he found he could think clearer with it off of his face.

"There are things I want to ask you, but I don't want to make you upset or cross a line."

"Go ahead, ask me."

Hayden stretched and made a sound like he was about to wake. Kate shot up and pretended to be digging through her bag. Jesse felt enraged; he wanted to punch Hayden again, but this time because of his crappy timing. Hayden turned to them and rested his head on his bent arms.

"I hope I haven't gone all *Exorcist* on you two while I slept."

"No," Kate said and smiled. "You were sleeping like a baby."

"Is it dark outside?"

"Yeah, must be early evening, at least I think so." Jesse tried to keep the frustration out of his voice. Kate glanced up quickly at him and down again, as if she caught his hint of bitterness and understood why.

Hayden sat up and rummaged for food and water. Jesse longed to be alone with Kate. He craved her voice speaking only to him, her eyes looking only at him, and her body next to him. He couldn't help himself; as Hayden crunched an alien bar and chugged water, Jesse watched Kate out of the corner of his eye. She curled herself into a ball with her face shimmering from the glow of the orb. Jesse imagined running his hand along her back and down her jeans, where he could feel her taut body beneath the denim.

Maybe Hayden saw something in the way Jesse looked at her because he scooted within the orb's glow and plopped his things down with a thud. The only sound for a few minutes was the grinding of metal from the wheels on the tracks. They all jumped a little when the train let out a series of long whistles.

"So, wanna talk and try to figure some stuff out?" Hayden asked, eyeing each one cautiously.

"Sure." Jesse got his own water and drank. He needed a moment to collect himself.

"Have either one of you seen images of your families since the gym?" Hayden asked and the others shook their heads no.

"Me either," Hayden paused. "And what about Sofia, Jesse? She wasn't at practice, so let's assume she's all right."

"I hope so," Jesse answered. Why was he bringing this up? Did he hear some of his conversation with Kate? Did he sense something?

"I wondered if you had a vision of her asleep, you know, how we saw our families?"

"No, but I hope she's all right."

"You're the only one of us who's dating anyone."

"Yeah, so?"

"I just wondered if you saw her. That's all." Hayden put his hands up in mock surrender. "I didn't mean to pry. You two have been an item for awhile, just wondered if you were all right."

Jesse felt badly then because Hayden's voice was genuinely concerned.

Kate jumped in, "I'm sure she's fine. You'll see her soon, Jesse." She forced a reassuring smile at him, and he felt guilty and sick. He did care for Sofia and definitely didn't want her blown away by a tornado or fire, but if he was honest with himself, when Kate was around, he only thought and felt for Kate. But Sofia was his girl; she had been for some time.

"Yeah, she's fine I'll bet, and ready to hit the bass drum as soon as..." Hayden trailed off. Who knew when or if things would return to normal? "And I wondered if you guys had any ideas about what the heck happened to me on the bridge. Do you think they're trying to possess me?"

"Who's the *they*? Shaaris, Belites, or what I'm gonna start calling the Red Aliens, you know, the ones with the Biblical dragon," Jesse said.

"All right, so which one?" Hayden asked.

"I'd say it was the Red Aliens," Kate said while staring at the orb.

"What makes you say that with such confidence?" Hayden smiled at her, but Jesse could tell that the whole scene on the bridge had jarred him.

"It makes the most sense to me." Kate tapped her fingers on her knees as she spoke. "We know that both the Shaaris and the Belites will stop fighting each other to get control of the Red Aliens. And did you notice that they tried to protect Earth from the dragon attack? So it seems to me that the Red Aliens are real trouble for any Terrian, something they need to control. But from what we saw, I don't think the Red Aliens will stop. They're trying to make the earth burn, as they said."

"Okay, now I'm totally freaked if *those* are the ones taking over my mind."

"Hmm, not take over, but use you," Jesse said. "I keep going back to how it felt like an old SOS transmission that repeats the same thing. I'm not saying this isn't something to worry about, but it seems that they're being squashed, including getting to Earth, by whatever means. Anyway, if it happens again I can deck you. It worked the last time." Jesse tried to lighten Hayden's mood and provide an argument to calm their nerves. In essence, though, they were totally screwed if any alien was taking over Hayden's mind. Totally.

"Not the best plan for my jaw, but at least it's something."

They rocked with the train, all lost in their own thoughts. Jesse decided he had to take his mind and eyes off of Kate, so he stared at the maps of Chicago. He thought the most logical place to start to look for the power source would be Union Station. He cross-referenced the Chicago map with the one with the train lines and saw that most industrial lines went into LaSalle Street Station or Union Station, which were within walking distance of each other.

When he had led the group to the train he'd made his best guess because he'd felt in his entire body that they had to be as far from that bridge as possible. He had heard distant train whistles and the lurch of wheels on tracks trying to tote heavy freight. For as long as he could remember, when he read something, it was as if his mind had taken a picture. He'd pictured the map with train lines and had gone in the general vicinity, and here they were. But were they safe? Hallia had told them to stay off of transportation, but he'd started to think this was because of contact with humans, and quite possibly, Terrians. No, except for the gas station and then the bridge, they were not seen. Then it hit him.

"Hey guys," he said. "Maybe it was the gas station. Did you talk to anyone there, Hayden?"

"Just the guy at the counter. I asked him about the storms in Europe. They were talking about it on the T.V. behind him."

"That could be how they got to you."

"How do ya mean?"

"What if the Red Aliens found you because of a sighting in the gas station?"

"Do you think the gas station guy was an alien?" Kate asked.

"No, but somehow they use technology to cue into what's happening here. I don't think it's all brain power, no matter what

Hallia said." Jesse felt he was on to something, but he had no way to prove anything. "She warned us about using cell phones and things to track us."

"But I threw mine in the woods on the bike path."

"Yeah and after that, the Bull of Heaven came down," Kate said.

"Maybe it's the security camera, the TV, or something," Jesse mused. "Think about it. Right after that, we headed for the bridge and it happened."

"You might be right," Hayden said, but he didn't seem convinced.

"That might explain why you, Hayden," Kate said, and this did hit home. Relief passed across his face and he slumped down again and stared at the ceiling.

"Okay, say you're right," Hayden said, "This means we can't buy anything else. We're stuck with alien food and one roll of toilet paper. Sorry, Kate."

They laughed and fell silent; it seemed that the enormity of their task hit them all. The once familiar places like gas stations and restaurants became taboo. Jesse wondered how they would move around the city itself without being detected. Hayden must have had the same thought.

"We need to wear our hoods and nip some hats or glasses before Union Station. I don't want this to happen again."

Jesse lay back on his hands and tried to relax. He longed for sleep, but his mind danced from thought to thought, image to image. He kept reliving the events of the last two days, tornados, death, storms, and alien battles. He pictured his mother and the rest of his family asleep, hoping their slumber would bring about his own. Hayden seemed just as agitated because he took out his dagger and clutched it, ready for anything. Once this started, Jesse surely couldn't sleep. What if the Red Aliens possessed him and he had the dagger, then what? He chanced a glimpse at Kate who appeared to be sleeping, but then he positioned his gaze back to the ceiling where he could watch Hayden through the corner of his eye.

Time clicked on with the rocking of the train car and the occasional hiss of whistles. Hayden's eyes were growing heavy, and when they finally closed, Jesse relaxed and allowed his own to shut.

He woke to heat on his face and an odd sensation all over his body. Had he been dreaming about Kate again? He couldn't remember.

Kate crouched over him, and he felt like pulling her into his arms for a kiss.

"Jesse, wake up," she said and moved to shake Hayden awake.

He and Hayden sprang up.

"Look," she said pointing to a swirling curl of color on the orb.

Jesse knew another message was coming, probably from E and P. He kept staring at it until the cloudy wisps formed into letters. Jesse's heart pounded in his chest. They message read:

You've been corrupted. Now you will attract Belite-Gelf battle fire. Hide. – E & P

CHAPTER THIRTEEN
JUMP

*In the beginning God created the heaven and the earth.
And the earth was without form, and void; and darkness was
upon the face of the deep. And the Spirit of God moved upon
the face of the waters.
And God said, Let there be light: and there was light.
And God saw the light, that it was good: and God divided the
light from the darkness.
And God called the light Day, and the darkness he called Night.
And the evening and the morning were the first day.
And God said, Let there be a firmament in the midst of the
waters, and let it divide the waters from the waters.
And God made the firmament, and divided the waters which
were under the firmament from the waters which were above the
firmament: and it was so.
And God called the firmament Heaven.*

– Bible, Genesis, 1:1-8

"Corrupted. That's me, I know it is," Hayden said. He paced back and forth, stumbling once or twice when the train lurched.

"You don't know that, and we don't know what that means exactly," Jesse said in an even tone.

"It means I should leave you two alone, Belite-Gelf battle fire, what the hell! How many groups of aliens are there?"

"It's hard to say," Jesse said and began to pack his things. He had that urge again, to keep moving. "Let's get ready to go. And we aren't splitting up. We're in this together." Jesse said this with as much gumption as he could muster. He did what his mother advised when he had a sensation to be selfish. She always said, "Then do the opposite." Jesse just did the opposite of how he felt. He'd had a rush of excitement with the idea of losing Hayden and being alone with Kate, especially after the events on the train car, her hand on his cheek. He buried those thoughts and made himself want to stay together as a threesome, even though he longed to be alone with Kate.

"Yeah," Kate added. She took Jesse's cue and began to pack. "We need to stay together. And any one of us could be 'corrupted.' We've been doing our best here, but we really have no idea what we're up against."

Hayden seemed moderately assuaged. He stopped pacing and started packing. "Wait a minute," he said and paused from shoving things into his bag, "how are we supposed to *go* as you said? We're on a moving train, aren't we *going* right now?"

"Look, I got this weird feeling right before, you, ya know, seemed possessed, and now I have a feeling we need to move on."

"You want us to jump?" Hayden glanced to Kate and gave Jesse a look like *she'll never make it* when Kate was turned away.

"We'll be all right," Jesse said with fake confidence.

"It's crazy, man. At least here we're 'hiding' in a sense, just like E and P said."

Kate was finished packing; she stood looking from one to the other. "Maybe the train will stop soon. How fast do you think we're moving?"

"I'd say forty or fifty miles per hour. That's fast if we jump and land in the dark, in the woods, just because Jesse gets an itch."

Jesse glared at Hayden, his temper up. "Look, dude, I was right before, actually twice. If you remember, my punch brought you back." He took a step toward Hayden and balled his fists. Hayden did the same, and Kate pressed herself between both of them. Her scent made Jesse relax a little.

Boom! A train car in front of them exploded and the three dove to the floor. Metal crunched as the train attempted to stop, but they kept hurling into the night. Then another series of pops told them that more fire rained from the sky, hitting the train and making it jerk like a body lacerated with machinegun fire.

"Okay, your idea sounds about right," Hayden yelled and coughed. Smoke billowed in from the cracks in the car. They all stayed low and slid on their bellies to the door.

Jesse was the first to reach it; he tried to breathe any fraction of fresh air, but the air was clouded and acrid. Once Hayden and Kate reached the handle, both boys signaled to each other to heave it open. They couldn't see anything but smoke after the door slid like a curtain to reveal a night of pitch and fire.

"I can't see a thing," Kate said between coughs and sobs.

"I say we hold hands and jump, that way we land together," Hayden shouted.

Jesse craned his neck out the door and toward the front of the train, which was a blaze of orange light. The wind whipped their bodies so hard it was a struggle to hold on. An emergency alarm echoed repeatedly and punctuated their fear with a hauntingly consistent blaring beep.

"All right, on three," Jesse clutched Kate's hand and she squeezed back. Hayden took her other hand.

"One, two, three!" They jumped into the ominous blur of gray and black, their bodies instantly obscured while the train raced and screeched, a line of light like the after burn of a rocket launch.

Hayden must have spun off to the left and lost Kate because Jesse didn't let go of her hand until he had to in mid-air. Jesse's body hit the ground hard, but he felt a bit like a cat as he curled into a ball, rolled, and landed on all fours, his eyes instantly scanning for his companions. Fire balls still streamed from the sky, but as soon as they jumped the fire shifted to the trees where they had landed from the train, which now raced in its own direction, trying to screech to a stop with emergency breaks.

"Get down!" Jesse yelled into the smoke-filled air. He had no idea if the others heard him, but he put his stomach to the ground and crawled in the direction he thought they'd be. He couldn't see anything, except for when orange balls of light blazed from the sky and struck the earth. The trees and brambles crackled as fire danced to life. Small woodland animals panicked and ran. Jesse panicked too; his heart raced and sweat poured down his face. He had to stop and breathe into his shirt to keep from suffocating under the blanket of smog. This was it, he thought; he was going to die from smoke inhalation. In the distance a seed of sound came: Maybe a siren, or the train alarm, dotted the generalized terror of fire breaking branches, roaring and popping, and then the smog and soot seemed to press on him like giant stones. He'll be pressed to death, no, his mind was going. He crawled and held his breath; he saw only his hands clawing the dirt, clutching tree roots or brambles in order to get to Kate, who must be close, but where?

Something, maybe flecks of ash, pinged his face. The smoke pressed him down lower, lower, and he focused on his hands in the dirt, clawing one at a time. *Do this. Do this*, he kept saying in his mind. He hoped his lungs would hold out. But they burned and burned and his head felt so light. Here, he came to moss. The green was cool to his cheek. His eyes slid in and out of focus; one moment he saw his hands clawing his way through brush and smoke to find Kate, and the next moment everything went black. He popped his head up again. *Do this. Do this. Find Kate.* But he was so tired, and his lungs had a campfire in them. He set his head on his arms to rest, for a minute. Orange and purple inky splotches ran across his closed lids, and then they smeared to blue. Kate.

Jesse shot up, but it wasn't by his own volition. He was suddenly returned to the fiery reality when someone grabbed his backpack and yanked him to his feet.

"Come on, it's stopped. We gotta find Kate." Hayden pulled harder on his sleeve and dragged Jesse through the fog by hoisting his arm around his shoulder to carry Jesse's weight. He opened his eye a crack to be sure it was Hayden. It was, Hayden singed and blackened with torn clothes that were covered in ash and mud, but he was alive, more than alive, he seemed energized to have Jesse there to save. They did an awkward three-legged race type of walk through the gloom.

Though fire no longer rained from the sky, many trees were ablaze. The smoke had cleared somewhat, enough to see each footfall and a little way in each direction. The two boys stumbled through the haze, stopping momentarily by a maple tree when Jesse started a coughing fit.

"Here," Hayden said, and he handed a cloth, maybe a torn t-shirt, to Jesse. "Put it on your face and breathe into it. It's the only way we'll make it through here." Jesse did as he was told. When he stood up, Hayden shoved a water bottle into his hand. They both crouched instinctively when a nearby tree toppled over with fiery branches igniting bushes and dead leaves.

"We have to find Kate," Jesse shouted through the sound of cracking tree limbs. "Did you see where she landed?" He realized that he had no idea where he had crawled to search for her.

"Over there, I think." Hayden pointed about twenty feet ahead of where they were. The woods sloped downward. Jesse thought that if she had landed in that direction, she probably moved downhill to escape blazes from the sky. "You ready to move?"

"Yeah."

Hayden went to hold him up again, but Jesse shirked him off. They kept their cloths to their faces and headed toward the slope. Small patches of fire snapped at their feet; some clusters of bushes smoked and then erupted with new surges of mini explosions. Once again, Jesse mused that this fire was unearthly, alien, just like its source somewhere in the atmosphere. Luckily the smoke, which moments ago was a threat to his life, started coalescing in one great cloud and drifting like a slow lifting hot air balloon above the tree line. Soon the teens could see more in the distance, and then Jesse spotted Kate's blue jeans and her tan pack in a heap. Hayden saw her too because he yelped, "There," and sprinted to her. Usually Jesse would have been the faster one, but he trailed Hayden by two feet, his lungs burning as if coals smoldered in his chest.

When Jesse reached Kate, Hayden already cradled her in his arms while he nursed water to her lips. She gulped it and instantly choked. He brushed her hair from her face with such tenderness that Jesse burned with anger.

"Thanks for the water," she said and glanced up to Jesse from a bed of leaves that looked like tar. "You two all right?"

Jesse nodded, speechless, but Hayden said, "Just a little grilled, but I'll survive. I can't believe we jumped a train. This is crazy!"

Kate gave a weak smile and adjusted herself; Jesse saw she was hurt by the way she moved with deliberation, afraid to harm the injured part of her body.

"What'd you hurt?" He stooped beside her.

"I did something to my foot. I can't put any weight on it."

"Then I'll carry you for awhile," Hayden held her and sprang up. Kate lounged awkwardly in his arms and winced when she tried to move her foot. "I think we better move. Look at that cloud."

They all gazed at the mass of smoke that hovered above them. Jesse shook his head. "No, I know it sounds weird, but I think that's helping shield us or something. The fire streams stopped coming from the sky, and then all the smoke coalesced into that." He pointed and took a step closer to Hayden and Kate.

"I still think we need to move. Remember your prickly feeling on the train, well it turns out you were right. It's a good thing we jumped. Now I think we keep with that idea and walk. If Kate can't walk, she weighs the same as my beagle, I'll carry her." Hayden cracked a smile.

Jesse ignored him for a moment and studied Kate. It was hard to tell if her face was paler than usual with it covered in soot and dirt. He leaned in to feel her pulse, which was shallow, and heard her teeth chattering uncontrollably. "I think you're in a bit of a shock," he said to her alone and she nodded with fearful eyes.

"Hayden, put her down. We can't go yet."

"You think you're a doctor or something? What can you do that I can't?"

"I think I can help her. I want to take a look at her foot."

"No, I say we move out of this fire forest, then maybe you can have a look, though I'm not sure what you think you'll accomplish."

Jesse's blood pulsed in his temple; his hands flexed in and out. This was it. First, the conflict on the train and now this, which Jesse felt was not at all about what was best for Kate. All of it made

Jesse want to charge the cocky bastard and kick his ass. Hayden didn't back down, and he must have felt the same way because he stepped toward Jesse; they were so close he could feel Hayden's body heat and hear his breathing.

Kate wriggled in Hayden's arms, and despite her chattering teeth, she spoke, "Give me to Jesse." Her voice cracked with strain and she stared at the ground.

"What?" Hayden's voice was venomous.

Kate's face was pained, not only from her foot, but by choosing Jesse. Jesse wanted to save them both from the situation, which was strange because moments ago he wanted to beat Hayden. Hayden's lip twitched with anger, but his eyes were vulnerable and hurt; this made him think about fights between Dorian and Keisha, Jesse's younger siblings. They seldom meant to hurt each other, but once the fighting and anger took over, they didn't know how to let it go.

"Look," Jesse said in a conciliatory tone, "I don't want to fight, but for some reason I feel like I may have power to heal her. I know it sounds crazy, but all of us have some kind of alien powers here, and mine might be fixing this, at least this is the sense I get." Jesse held Hayden's gaze, which softened.

"You're right," Hayden relented. With a sigh that lessened his hold on Kate, Hayden passed her to Jesse. He looked more than dejected, almost defeated. Jesse felt ambivalent: He wanted to snatch her away with territorial gusto, but he also sympathized with Hayden who seemed to feel his place in the group as tenuous since the whole "You have been corrupted" message.

Hayden snapped his head back and said: "I suppose a glowing blue sword won't help this situation." Hayden laughed and made eye contact with Jesse. Jesse smiled and gave a small chuckle, knowing Hayden was trying to make further amends.

Careful not to disturb Kate's foot, Jesse assessed Kate's face for a pain barometer. She smiled weakly through her clicking teeth.

Still coughing a bit, Jesse concentrated on putting Kate down gently in the leaves. The cloud Hayden had viewed as sinister felt like a guardian floating above them. Jesse unlaced her shoe with shaky hands. He had never broken a bone, but by the look on Kate's face now it must have hurt something fierce.

"I'm going to work your shoe off now," he said.

"No, please, it's so painful..."

"I need to see if it's broken. Take a deep breath." Jesse tried to use a calm voice, but he felt just as scared as she looked.

"Hold my hand, Kate," Hayden offered, and she grabbed it. "At least I can be of some help."

"All right, here I go." Jesse loosened her shoe as much as possible and slipped it off. Kate screamed in pain. Tears flowed, and she pulled so hard on Hayden he fell from a squatting position to his knees. When Jesse got the sock off, and they could see where the bones were misshapen beneath her skin, Kate passed out.

"Kate, wake up," Hayden said. He started blowing in her face, which Jesse found odd.

"No, let her stay out. It may make this easier."

"Okay, but hurry up." Hayden cradled her head and sang a song Jesse couldn't place. He thought, or more accurately, he *felt* that if he put his hands on her foot and imagined kissing her, this heat and energy would do something to help her. At least he hoped so. He tried it.

He pictured Kate in front of him on the train again. Instead of being interrupted by Hayden she held his cheek in her hand, and he leaned in to kiss her lips. She tasted like strawberries, which Jesse didn't understand. That was it: "Strawberry Fields Forever," the ancient song by the Beatles. That was what Hayden was humming, but it seemed that Hayden had vanished to a faraway place where his voice only existed as a murmur.

In Jesse's imagination he kept kissing Kate. At first, he kissed her softly and then they both responded to the other's touch, so they leaned in, pressing their bodies together and tasting each other. Jesse burned for more of her in that moment and always, and then his hands lit like dual torches. They made a pale amber glow, and he knew to place them on her foot. Her skin was cold and clammy, especially to the heat of his hands.

"Dude!" Hayden almost dropped Kate's head from the shock, but he regained his grip on her, and half laughed, half cried, "Do it, man."

Jesse held on tightly, and Kate's eyes shot open. She cried choking sobs, but Jesse did not let go. He shut his eyes and saw the bones, *Intermediate Cuneiform, Medial Cuneiform, and Lateral Cuneiform. Tarsals, Metatarsals.* These bones moved the phalanges, or the toe bones. How did he know this? He remembered studying bones in Biology, but now he understood what moved what; he knew how bone, muscle, tendon, and fascia worked. In his mind's eye he saw the broken bones fuse and strengthen, slowly, but steadily. He kept his hands in place and his mind focused on the process of healing. In minutes, Kate's foot was not deformed any longer, and already the swelling was diminishing. When she realized that the bones in her foot had re-formed, she quieted to an awe-struck contentment. She looked so hard at Jesse he had to turn away.

"Whoa, can you move your foot?" Hayden asked. He must have felt awkward being between the two of them because he slid his hand out of Kate's and stood. He stretched his legs in and out to accentuate his stiffness.

"I think so."

"Take it slowly," Jesse said, but he was anxious to see how well she could walk. They moved to either side of Kate to support her as she attempted to stand. She hopped on her good foot at first, but then committed to a definitive step on the one that had been broken just minutes before. Jesse could tell she didn't put her full weight on it at first, but after a few seconds and some deep breaths, she sank into the wet bed of leaves. Slowly she removed her arms from their shoulders and let them hang at her sides.

"It feels funny, but fine," she said. She laughed nervously and shifted back and forth from foot to foot. "This is incredible. You fixed my foot. It was broken – did you two see the bones? That made me sick, but you did it. It feels great!"

They all laughed, shaking their heads in amazement.

"Okay, Healer-Man, now I feel better about jumping trains and doing other extreme sports types of moves because you have this skill in your pocket."

They walked slowly through the hazy darkness, talking again and again of their extraordinary feats, relishing in their survival.

"Thanks for finding me and saving me by the way," Jesse said to Hayden.

"No problem."

Finally, they moved in silence. Kate had lit the orb effortlessly to help them see where to step. Jesse walked a couple of feet behind her and relived the moment when he thought about kissing her and then his hands lit and healed her bones. Now he knew how she had blown open the hatch.

CHAPTER FOURTEEN

E S P

*In the beginning, there came Nothing, alone. It was something
called Chaos, or the Void.
But it was nothing all the same.
Next appeared Earth, so the gods would have some place to
stand. And then came Tartarus, the underworld.*

— The Coming of All Things, ancient Greek story

*Awed by her splendor
Stars near the lovely moon
cover their own bright faces
when she is roundest and lights earth with her silver.*

*– Awed by Her Splendor, Sappho,
Mary Barnard, translator*

Was it possible to love two people at the same time? Jesse thought
he loved Sofia; she had been his girlfriend, the only person he was
really close to in New Franklin, for three years. But now there was
Kate. Jesse caught a glimpse of her concentrated stare into the
orange orb. He longed to kiss her for real.

After healing Kate's foot, the three had walked on in silence through woods that lined the railroad tracks; both boys followed Kate who held the lit orb in front of her like a color guard member carrying a flag. Now they were in a small clearing in the woods, sitting around the orb and talking through what had transpired.

"Oh, I forgot to tell you two with everything going on," Kate said, motioning to her foot, "I think I know who E and P are."

"This is huge. How'd you skip over this one?" Hayden said.

Kate twisted a stick between her fingers and started to drum her thigh lightly with it. "I know it sounds strange but I'm having this weird merging of what goes on in my mind and what's happening with the three of us." She beat out a nervous rhythm like her leg was a snare. "It makes it hard to remember what's what."

"Me too," Jesse interjected; relieved someone had put words to the phenomenon.

"Probably par for the course with alien stuff, and I'll give you an Amen to that sister, seeing as I spoke like a Red Alien and all." Hayden crunched an alien bar, but Jesse still heard his stomach rumble.

"Tell us about E and P," Jesse urged.

"It was right after we jumped. I'm sure I broke my foot when I hit ground; it hurt so bad. I had to crawl, away from fire patches, and I felt a burning sensation on my back. I freaked out thinking that my backpack was on fire, so I rolled and squirmed out of it. It wasn't on fire. It's just that the orb was lit up. Once I got to a relatively safe place, I took it out, and when I touched it that's when I saw them, E and P."

"Who are they? What'd they look like?" Hayden's eyes flickered.

"It was a flash for about twenty seconds or something. They look just like two guys we could go to school with, about seventeen or eighteen, maybe a little older. But they're Terrians all right. You know how they all have a glow to their skin. E and P have that."

"Did they have the hair color thing to signify their alien group, maybe silver for Shaaris?" Jesse asked.

"No, they both had brown hair, and they were around an orb just like this one. I think there were other people, well you know, aliens around. I could hear stuff in the background. They were huddled together and, well, holding hands and kissing."

"Two dudes?" Jesse felt strange. Hayden let out a wry laugh.

"Yes," Kate answered.

"Whoa, that's nasty," Jesse said. He couldn't refrain from making a comment; homosexuality always creeped him out.

"They're helping us, Jesse. I'm grateful for them," Kate said quickly.

Jesse was ashamed of himself. He wanted to gloss over E and P and move on to another topic, but Hayden spoke through his chuckles.

"This gets better and better, gay aliens, Red Alien possession, Dr. Jesse Woods Medicine Man – I'm ready for a cable channel to snatch this one up. Forget about the power source, let's pitch this idea to someone." He laughed harder, and Kate joined in, but Jesse wanted to move on to something else.

"I really get the sense they want to connect to us, that they're worried about how we're doing," Kate said. "I haven't gotten that feeling from Hallia, even though she's obviously saved us two times. She needs us to do something for her. Don't you feel that's the reason she's making sure we stay alive?"

As Kate carried the conversation, Jesse wondered if either of them noticed his discomfort, how the idea of gays, even gay aliens, made him so uncomfortable. He felt itchy, like he had to scratch something as hard to reach as the back of his eyeballs. He knew he had to get over it and focus, so he did.

"Yeah," he said, "I think you're right about Hallia. I just wonder who they are. We have the Shaaris, Belites, and we're thinking that the Red Aliens are Belite-Gelfs, right? I figure it that way."

"You might be right," Hayden said. "Didn't Hallia say Belites would try to kill us? She didn't say what Belites. That's just the kind of double talk that makes up a world's religions. Anyway, if the Red Aliens are the Belite-Gelfs, they seem totally rogue."

"That makes the most sense," Jesse added. He didn't remind Hayden that they all had agreed previously that the Red Aliens had been the ones to possess him.

"Then who do E and P belong to?" Kate asked.

"Except to each other." Hayden sniggered. Jesse gave a quick laugh, more out of obligation than thinking it was funny; he wanted to forget about E and P.

"Please," Kate said, "don't make fun of them. I can sense how they feel about each other. Not all the time, but in those few seconds when I saw them in the orb. They love each other, and they're..." She searched for words.

Hayden blew up his cheeks to suppress a laugh. Jesse stared off as if the tree line offered something of great interest.

"Scared," she finished. The hazy sky hung beyond the still lingering black cloud. Sporadic moonlight cast odd shadows through the treetop. A chill ran through Jesse.

"Well, let's hope we're hidden enough to camp tonight." Hayden broke the quiet. "Let's get some rest. You have a new plan for tomorrow, Jesse?"

"Get clean," he said and scraped at his dirt-caked hands.

"I'll say. I feel like a volcano dumped twenty pounds of ash on my head."

"My hair is so gross." Kate struggled to get her fingers through a knot.

Jesse pulled out one of the maps and studied it under their light. "There might be a creek or something about a half mile from where I think we are right now. The only thing I have to go on is the railroad tracks."

"I'll check it out first light." Hayden adjusted himself on his backpack, looking up at the obscured stars. Before long Jesse heard his heavy breathing. He listened for Kate who slept so soundly he feared she was dead, or maybe awake?

"Kate?" he ventured, but she didn't respond. Jesse kept his head up, gazing at her and hoping she would wake, but she didn't. He put his own head down and soon fell asleep.

The morning came slowly; the black cloud above them had dissipated, but it left a cover of gray that snuffed out any sunshine. Kate slept huddled near the orb, but Hayden must have gone to search for the creek. He'd taken the map, but Jesse didn't need it. He wrote a note to Kate with a crude sketch of where he thought the creek would be; he also gave her the option to wait until one of them returned to lead her back. He stood over her wondering if he should wake her up, but he didn't, figuring that she needed the rest after the ordeal with her foot.

He grabbed his toothbrush and the other clothes he had and headed for the stream. The idea of fresh water on his skin was a big motivator to move quickly through the cool morning. Even though the water would be freezing, Jesse didn't care. He trotted the last quarter mile or so.

He came upon Hayden, naked and singing, in ankle deep water. He squatted in the weak trickle like a chimp; his back was to Jesse, but once in awhile he raised his hips to submerge his face; his junk made a dangling shadow on his thighs, and this made Jesse stop dead in his tracks. Chill, he thought. He showered with dudes all the time in the locker room. But the E and P kiss hung in the air.

"Hey, amigo!" Hayden pivoted in the squat position and spooned water down his back. "The water's like ice, but it's getting the grime off. If you come in, please know my dick isn't usually this small, it's the temp."

Jesse was more than uncomfortable; he felt like running. "Dude, keep it in the water. I don't want to see your stuff. This E and P situation has me weirded out as it is."

"Why? What's your hang up with gays?" Hayden continued to scrub at his arms with his fingernails.

"I dunno. I've always thought it was..." What? A sin? Jesse bit back his multi-layered thoughts. He had gotten that idea from church. Hayden must have had a similar thought.

"Look, if you're into these Ancients, you must know the Greeks, Romans, even some Native American tribes all accepted gays. Seems to me that the *mono*theistic ones wanted to get rid of the *homo*." He laughed at his own cleverness; Jesse stayed in his spot on the bank.

"I just don't get it. Two dudes?" Jesse felt a little stupid; he usually had better reasoning and arguments for his beliefs.

"Love's love, bro," Hayden scratched his scalp. "And sex is sex. It's hard to say what's gonna turn someone on."

"Okay. But two dudes! It grosses me out. Now we have a magic orb view of two alien dudes making out," Jesse said. He couldn't help but hate his voice. He sounded younger and whiney.

"You may want to open your mind. Kate really has a connection with E and P."

Jesse sat down. Hayden was smart. He knew how to get to the crux of anything. Was he trying to be a friend?

"Doesn't it gross you out, the sex part of it? And I don't have any clue about talking about love." Jesse threw his hands in the air, and Hayden nodded.

"Amen to that, love is a mystery to me. You know, I'm a bit of a player. In the nicest of senses, I love falling in love with a girl." Hayden looked downstream and sighed. Who was he thinking about? Jesse hoped it wasn't Kate.

"You know, if I really think about it," Hayden said thoughtfully, "if someone's gonna blow me, and they're attractive, I'm not sure I'd say no, even if the someone's a dude. Now *doing it doing it*, that's a different story. Then I'm all girl."

Jesse had never had such a candid conversation with another guy. He felt strained and on guard, and a small part of him worried that Hayden was hitting on him. Or maybe this was what it was like to talk to a close friend? Jesse was overcome with emotion: Had he not closed himself to friendships in New Franklin for over ten years? Why? Because most of the people were white? That may have been part of it, but this went deeper, down to the murder of his father.

He was lost in this reverie when Hayden snapped his fingers. "Come back to Earth, doc. Look I don't want to freak you out, or make you think I'm gonna get you in the backside, but I'm getting out now. My clothes are over there. Avert your eyes or take a gander. I know I'm a sight to behold." Hayden leapt from the water. Jesse couldn't help but laugh when he let out a series of swear words and screams from the cold air hitting his full body. He scrambled into his dry clothes.

"I'll head back and check on Kate while you get washed up. It's cold, but I feel better."

"Awright," Jesse said and stood, "ah, thanks, Hayden."

"For what?" Hayden shook his head to dry his hair into spikes.

"Talking."

"Oh, yeah, sure. Look, we've had some bumps, but I'm your friend, Jesse. You act like you don't need 'em, but you do."

With that Hayden jogged away.

CHAPTER FIFTEEN
TIRED

The Lord is my shepherd; I shall not want. He maketh me to lie down in green pastures: he leadth me beside the still waters. He restoreth my soul: he leadeth me in the paths of righteousness for his name's sake. Yea, though I walk through the valley of the shadow of death, I will fear no evil: for thou art with me; thy rod and thy staff they comfort me. Thou preparest a table before me in the presence of mine enemies: thou anointest my head with oil; my cup runneth over. Surely goodness and mercy shall follow me all the days of my life: and I will dwell in the house of the Lord forever.

— Bible, Psalm 23

Each time, Turtle looked inside their mouths when they came up, but there was no earth to be found. Toad went under the water. He stayed too long, and he nearly died. But when Turtle looked inside Toad's mouth, he found a little earth. The woman took it and put it all around on Turtle's shell. That was the start of the earth. Dry land grew until it formed a country, then another country, and all the earth. To this day, Turtle holds up the earth.

— *Divine Woman, the Creator, Huron story*

Jesse was clean and dressed when Hayden and Kate arrived at the stream.

"My turn, but you two need to get lost," Kate said. She had a flirtatious tone Jesse hadn't heard before. Maybe she felt the pure exhilaration that came from simply surviving this far. Jesse felt it too; he was grateful for the icy chill of the morning touching his body. Hayden, despite the possession thing on the bridge, had taken on an even more jovial mood. He picked up Kate, saying, "I'll dunk you, you dirty Irish lass!"

"No!" Kate squirmed and laughed.

"Yer dead, man, if you do that. Remember she controls our heat," Jesse said with a smile.

"Right, down you go." Hayden put her down and sighed. He looked like a smitten boy, but spoke to Jesse before his face got too red. "Wanna get lost for awhile and try to figure where to go from here?"

"Yeah."

Kate smiled after them while standing on the bank, obviously watching to be sure that both boys were out of sight. Hayden and Jesse walked over the slope but stayed within earshot in case something went wrong.

"I'd love to have stayed, and I know you feel the same," Hayden said. He slumped on a broken tree branch and dug at the dirt with a stick. Then he slammed at a nearby trunk like it was a cymbal. "Don't worry, you don't have to comment. She doesn't have a boyfriend only because most dudes are scared to death to be with a girl like her. Kate's world class."

Jesse had already pulled out the maps. He sat and watched Hayden scratch idly at the ground and then bang the tree trunk. Should he ask Hayden about what happened between the two of them? He didn't want any tension, but it was a chance.

"Didn't you two date?" He flipped open the map he thought they needed.

"We went on one date. That's it."

"What happened?"

"Well, I'm not going to tell tales on the activities of the night, but let me just say it was intense in its own way. Look, you're getting that heated-pissed face—"

"No, I'm not," Jesse said.

"Are too." Hayden laughed. "It was intense, but she dumped me the next day. Not sure why, it still gets me. I'd be with her now if she'd have me, but then again, like I said in the creek, I *am* good at falling in love." Hayden smiled; it was a smile Jesse was sure charmed many girls.

"Did she give you a reason for not wanting to date anymore?" Jesse craved information. They probably slept together. Jesse hated the thought. He wanted her, and he didn't want anyone else to have her, even if it was in the past. He pushed this yearning down; he had Sofia. He had to stop thinking like this.

"Not really, something like she felt we were better off as friends because of our different experiences and world views, something lame. I didn't talk to her for about a week, but staying mad at Kate is like being mad at a puppy. Plus, we were lab partners in Physics."

"Oh."

Hayden looked up. "You know, I mentioned Sofia before not to bust you out or anything. I just wonder if the Belite-Gelfs will go after her. I've thought about not saying anything, but I think you should be prepared."

Jesse had thought this, but he'd buried the reality of Sofia being in danger because of him. His body went tense with fear and something else, guilt.

Hayden pressed on, "Sorry, man. I can tell you're upset."

"Well, yeah, of course I am. Sofia's my girl. It's not that

I haven't thought about her. I have." Jesse stood up and paced. "What's wrong with me, Hayden?" He paused. If they were friends, why not talk to him like one? He thought they had crossed over into new territory since the stream. This made Jesse smile a little. It took two gay aliens to get him to say something beyond bullshit to another guy. "I feel like a complete idiot. I think I'm into Kate, but then there's Sofia, and all this." He gestured to the woods surrounding them. "This could very well be the end of the world, and I'm thinking about getting with a girl."

Hayden laughed out aloud. "Dude, it's always the right time to think about getting with a girl." Hayden slapped the side of his shoulder. "She digs you too, man."

Jesse's face got hot. Kate was walking toward them from over the top of the hill. Her soaked hair stuck to her face, which had a freshly scrubbed sheen. She smiled widely, and Jesse saw that she had the orb in her hands; it glowed with heat, and something else. He couldn't make it out until she was nearly next to them. A soft whoosh of air blew from it. Kate started to circulate the sphere around her head, attempting to dry her mass of red hair.

"Cool," Hayden said. He looked from Jesse to Kate and must have realized Jesse's discomfort because he started babbling nervously, asking how she got the orb to blow air. He even pulled out his dagger to compare their skills.

Jesse regained his composure after he was sure she hadn't heard any of their conversation. Again, he winced internally at this middle school mentality. He focused and started to walk ahead.

"We better move," he said and pointed in the direction of the train tracks. "I think our route should follow the tracks as best as we can."

The other two trailed Jesse with Kate taking up the rear; she continued to swarm her hair with the air from the orb. After a few minutes, Jesse glanced back and saw she had grown even more adept at it because she palmed the orb with one hand and scrunched her hair with the other to speed up the drying. What else could the orb emit?

The sun attempted to break through the haze of the morning. How much of it was leftover smoke from last night Jesse didn't know. He tried to follow the general path of the tracks, but this made him wary because of the possibility of human contact. Surely there were still people cleaning up from wherever the train had finally stopped. But the woods were eerily quiet. It seemed that even woodland creatures stayed hidden. Did they fear another bombardment of fire from the sky? Twigs snapped beneath his feet, and the air smelled like burning leaves that had been doused with water. Some leaves still clung to blackened branches, but the normally vibrant trees of October in the Midwest looked dingy and weathered, almost like they were hanging on, afraid that this year's death would be the last one.

They walked in silence through the dreary morning. Each occasionally took some water or alien food from their bags. Jesse tried some Terrian Energy Mix. He marveled at his ease with reading the label. This small success didn't make it taste any better. The chips and nut-like chunks were rock hard and gritty. But it filled him up.

Kate lagged at times having lost the invigoration from turning the orb into a hairdryer. When they approached the area where the train must have halted, they peered over a hill while on their bellies and watched workers with hazmat suits and masks clear debris. After looking on for several nervous minutes, the three slid backwards on their stomachs and crept away. After watching the workers, people with everyday lives to return to, Jesse ached to call or text someone, especially Sofia. He longed for their familiar day-to-day. The inability to reach her or anyone outside their triangle of teens gnawed at him; he worked hard during the long morning hours to control his feelings of powerlessness, making sure that they didn't turn to rabid fear. Their lighthearted mood at the stream seemed like it was weeks ago. Their desire for human food wasn't helping; though the alien supplements filled the void, thoughts of human contact and hot food, steaming heaps of pancakes, spaghetti, loaves of bread, a greasy burger, even his mom's broccoli and cheese casserole, not his favorite, made his mouth water. He forced himself to focus on getting to Chicago.

At midday Jesse looked back: Hayden seemed almost dazed, and Kate, although not limping, plodded wearily at the rear. They were approaching a suburb. The trees thinned into a residential area. Through a break in the tree line, Jesse glimpsed neat brick homes much smaller than the ones in New Franklin. He pictured outdoor toys and bikes angled in the yards and trash bins at the ends of driveways, ready for the next day's pick-up. After the woods stopped, the tracks went on to a small station with one platform and a vast parking lot for commuters. The generic placard reminded Jesse of New Franklin's train station.

"We need a plan to get through the town," he said. They had become so removed from normal daily activities that they stood at the edge of the woods as if they were on the cusp of another world. Kate shivered and twirled her hair with her fingers, a nervous habit Jesse had noticed.

"Put up our hoods, hug the tracks, and move fast," Hayden said. He yanked his hood up fiercely.

"Awright, let's go."

They started with a brisk walk, maneuvering to the station platform, working through a light number of people waiting for an afternoon train. They all kept their heads down, Hayden especially.

Jesse turned away from the two women and one little girl on the station's bench.

"When's the train coming, Mommy?" the girl asked.

Her voice was so innocent and beautiful to Jesse that hot tears pooled in his eyes. He pressed his fingers to his lids and marched on, trying to forget about Keisha, his little sister. Her voice had the same soft cadence, the same gentle inquiry in her best moments.

With the tracks to their left, they wove mostly through parking lots: the train station lot, a McDonald's, and a bank, and then a long length of space kept them moving behind strip mall after strip mall. Jesse glanced back at Hayden, who seemed nervous and thoughtful, and Kate wiped tears from her eyes. He suspected they were wrestling their own sadness and trepidation. Jumping from a moving train almost seemed easier than creeping as ghosts through the territory of their former lives.

Then they came to neighborhoods along the base of a hill. Jesse saw that they could climb the hill and walk on a thin strip of land next to the track. Without speaking he started up the slope and his friends followed. Even though he was in top shape, his thighs burned. He wasn't used to so much walking without decent rest. Kate practically crawled up; panting, she collapsed at the top and sat. Jesse and Hayden plopped on the damp grass next to her. Luckily, they had filled their water bottles at the stream, because their thirst was acute. Each chugged water and hunched on the ground with nothing to say. After long minutes and when all seemed a little revived, Jesse stood and led the bedraggled group in a single file.

Their feet thudded on the dead grass and leaves. No trains were in sight, but here and there they came upon wooden slats or large spool-like objects that must have been discarded from freight trains. Would anyone ever pick the stuff up or use it again? No one, save train workers and vagrants, probably noticed the things, and now Jesse gazed at the objects as long as he could until they passed them. How many abandoned objects were thrown from trains without a thought of how lonely they would appear to three desperate teens walking along the tracks? Jesse thought that feelings of guilt for Sofia or his repressed desire for Kate would be better than this dismal hollow in his chest. Or anger. It wasn't hard to revive the anger he felt at the Terrians. Energized, he put one foot in front of the other. Despite his feelings of fatigue and despair, he continued to lead the group along rung after rung of track.

Rap songs, ones he listened to every day after practice, punctuated his steps; he thought they would spur him on, but instead a memory surfaced of one of the last times his mom had come home from work. He'd been blasting Lil Wayne, and she had burst into the room and turned down the volume on his computer.

"That's awful stuff, Jesse," she'd said, her eyes tired. "I don't want Kiki or Dorian hearing all that cussing."

"Awright, awright," he'd answered. Later when he had finally emerged from his room, he'd found his mom and stepdad Michael drinking wine and listening to Billie Holiday.

"Now *this* is music!" His mom had stood and grabbed Michael for a dance. Jesse had looked away, always embarrassed by their relationship. Later, when the two had played "Strange Fruit," they'd held hands while Jesse's mom cried.

Michael had wiped her tears but looked directly at Jesse with a defiant and angry face, saying, "Lynched black people. That's the 'strange fruit.'"

This was the hard part about Michael: Jesse couldn't hate him. His six-year-old self had tried to hate him when Michael had started to show up with his mom after work. They'd cook meals together and after a time, Michael had started to play Legos and army men with Jesse. It had snuck up on him; he liked Michael a lot. He had yearned for his visits, and now Jesse still had the taste of bile in his mouth because each time he cracked up with Michael or sought him out, he felt he was betraying his father. In his worst moments, in the solitary wanderings of his mind, like now, when he had countless hours with his own thoughts, he hated his dad for being stupid enough to go fix his brother's sink and get killed. He hated himself for thinking that though he loved and adored his biological father, his stepfather was a better man.

Why? Why did Jesse think this? He loved his dad. At the heart of it, Jesse viewed Michael as having a strength his father had lacked. Michael broke away from the hood. He left the streets at a young age to live with his grandmother in Milwaukee; he went to small charter schools and then put himself through college; he studied radiology and now traveled throughout the Midwest scanning patients on high-tech equipment that could catch cancer earlier than usual. But all of this didn't make him a better man than Jesse's dad: Michael was there. He didn't take off all night and run with his brother once in awhile, worrying his mom to death. He did what he said he would do, and he loved Jesse's mom like the sun rose and set by her movements. Jesse missed Michael so much he thought he would crack. In the same instant of this surge of longing, the sun made a rare appearance through the haze and then ducked back behind the pall of thin clouds. He realized how much he depended on Michael's stable force when things were crazy, how he often slapped Jesse's back and said something like, "You doing all right, kiddo, more together than I ever was." This was a high compliment from someone with the unflappable strength of a military general.

Jesse couldn't take it; he had to stop these thoughts that only made him feel more isolated and desperate. He turned to the group.

"I think we might as well head back to the tree line along the track. We'll be in the thick of the woods for awhile as far as I can make out." His voice cracked because it had been so long since he had spoken.

"Sure," Hayden said. He and Kate followed Jesse to the woods. Jesse held back and then walked beside both of them when they caught up.

"How's the foot, Kate?" Jesse asked.

"Fine. I still can't believe you fixed it." She smiled brightly at him and wiped hair from her face. Good, he thought: All he had to do was spend some time right next to her and he'd be fantasizing about going up her shirt or combing through her hair. This way he wouldn't feel weak and scared. Remembering his own father's failings always seemed to bring out those feelings, and now, with all the alien shit, the emotions were that much worse.

"Maybe we should talk about something to help the time pass?" Hayden was tired too; he had dark circles under his eyes, and though he tried to add vigor to his voice, it had a gravelly quality to it.

"What should we talk about?" Jesse asked. He was anxious to get his mind on other things.

"Drum line," Hayden offered.

"I can't," Kate stammered. "It makes me too sad to think about everyone being–"

"Oh, yeah," Hayden finished for her and shuffled along in silence.

"How about we try to come up with a plan once we get to Union Station?" Jesse had no desire to do this because his mind was a blank. It was easy enough to go virtually unseen when they followed train tracks through suburbs and woods, but Chicago? How could they avoid human contact there? What constituted as contact anyway? One question only led to more.

No one gave a response to his suggestion probably because they didn't have any ideas either. After another fifteen minutes of no conversation, Kate spoke.

"We could make more guesses about why E and P want to help us?"

"Okay, anyone have any ideas?" Jesse thought it best that he kept quiet on the subject.

"Like I said, I know they're scared. We also know they communicate with us through their own orb. Anything else?"

"They have information we need, and they give it to us right before something bad happens," Hayden said. His eyes got an excited glint. "Maybe they're spies?"

"Who they spy for?" Jesse asked.

"Dunno. Just throwing ideas out. We're swimming here. We can't even make logical guesses on that one. Why is that?"

"We don't know who they are," Jesse said.

"Right. See, we can't make guesses because I think we have a new group of Terrians on our hands."

"Maybe."

"I wonder what they want from us," Kate said.

Jesse couldn't stand her sad expression. He had to think of something to say, and fast.

"Who knows, but I think you're right to think like that. As far as I can see, they all have an agenda, we just don't know what—" Jesse stopped midsentence because ahead of them a pool of gray liquid hovered above a group of evergreen trees.

It reminded Jesse of a giant animal bladder, one pumped

with formaldehyde and ready for dissection in his Advanced Biology class. It swayed in the light wind and slowly turned for a few minutes. Hayden had his dagger ready.

Soon the liquid bubble dripped to the ground and made a humanoid form of average human height. Hallia stood before them. She had no brilliant glow any longer. In fact, she looked beaten and gray.

The teens approached her; Kate had stepped in front of the boys and turned slightly over her shoulder. She glanced hard from Hayden to Jesse, and it almost seemed that her blue eyes emitted a twinkling light. Suddenly Kate's voice echoed in Jesse's mind. She repeated the same sentence three times: *Don't tell her about E and P. Don't tell her about E and P. Don't tell her about E and P.*

CHAPTER SIXTEEN
HALLIA

In the Name of God, the Merciful, the Compassionate
Praise belongs to God, the Lord of all Being,
the All-merciful, the All-compassionate,
the master of the Day of Doom.
Thee only we serve: to Thee alone we pray for succor.
Guide us in the straight path,
the path of those whom Thou hast blessed,
not of those against whom Thou art wrathful,
nor of those who are astray.

– The Koran, "The Opening"

Hallia's once shimmering silver hair made ashen gray strings around her sallow face. She had blue and purple bruises on her arms, neck, and cheeks. A deep gash was crudely stitched with what looked like Silly String. Her hands shook a little, but she stuffed them in her outfit. Her tight-fitting dress was gone; she wore a gray and silver body suit, something like a janitorial outfit here on Earth. A small satchel hung at her hip from a long strap that crossed her chest like a beauty pageant sash. She glanced over her shoulder like a fugitive, and then she turned to the three anxious teens with a false smile.

"I am so very proud of all three of you for all you've accomplished."

"Save it," Hayden said. He held his dagger in front of him and walked toward her until the blade touched her neck.

"Mr. Monroe," Hallia started, her eyes tired.

"What's with the Mr. and Miss crap? Just call us by our names. We're running this little meeting. We want answers."

"Very well, Hayden." She punctuated his name like an elementary school teacher might do when a child squirmed in his chair. "You don't need the dagger with me. I'll not fight you."

Jesse got a chill with that one: Was she flirting with Hayden? Hayden may have felt it too because he put his dagger hand to his side and gave her an *I dare you to keep it up* look. The kid had guts; that was certain.

"I came as soon as I could. There has been much," she paused and searched for the right word, "*activity* on my planet, and I'm afraid some is spilling to Earth."

Hayden still stood inches from her face. "We need a breakdown of the Terrian groups. We're tired of trying to figure who's who and what they want."

"What do you think you've figured out?"

Jesse stepped in, remembering Kate's words in his head. *Don't tell her about E and P.* He wanted to be careful. "When you hid us in the earthen shelter, we watched that sky battle. Who were the two red-headed aliens with the dragon?"

"Belites. I told you they were your demons; they even bring the nightmares from your Bible, things like that dragon. Let's just say that the Belites are known for their skills with what you call genetic engineering. As a result, they have created beasts that roam our planet like jungle animals do here, but ours are things from your fairy tales and myths."

"Or religions," Hayden said; his tone was like acid on skin. Hallia gave him a thin-lipped smile.

"We think the red-haired ones are different from the golden-haired Belites," Jesse pressed. "You all rallied to take them down during the battle. They can't be plain old Belites."

"You're right, they're not." Hallia motioned to a bed of pine needles. "Shall we sit and discuss things?" She sat and crossed her legs. She grabbed a handful of needles and rolled them on her palm absentmindedly. The teens joined her. They all sat in a circle like they were at summer camp.

"Go on," Jesse said. Kate was right next to Hallia; she leaned closer to Jesse when Hallia shifted her weight.

"They are a renegade group of Belites that are considered criminals on my planet. They formed soon after what would be the start of your twentieth century. They want dual world dominance, and they don't care what lives are destroyed in the process."

"Why do you call them Belites then?" Hayden asked. He was twirling his dagger like it was a magic wand.

"They started as part of the Belites, but then a couple of rogue leaders began a hateful underground movement. They are now known as Belite-Gelfs."

Jesse dared not look at Kate for fear he would give something away. Hayden, too, was silent, but broke in: "So when you said Belites would try to kill us and use beasts and stuff against us, you meant these maniacs?"

"Yes."

"Some clarification would have been helpful," Hayden said, holding her gaze.

"If you recall, Hayden," her voice was thick, "our conversation was interrupted by battle fire. I had to save you. And save you I did. Twice."

No one said anything to that. Kate picked at something on her jeans. Jesse didn't know how much time they had; he had so many questions.

"I don't get something. I read that Ancients' text you left in my bag," he started and Hallia's eyebrows shot up.

"You were able to decipher it?" she asked.

"Yeah, more on those questions later, but I need to know, why don't you just track down the Keepers on your planet and have them get the power source? Why us?"

Hallia stared at Jesse, and then a small smile crept over her face. "I'm pleased to hear that your skills are manifesting in such an advanced manner; I want to know more about what the three of you can do."

"First, answer the Keepers question."

"We did try that," Hallia said, looking at the pine needles in her hand. "We were unable to acquire the necessary information, so we focused on Earth sources. As I said in the gymnasium, you three are one of the Youth Triumvirates searching for possible power sources. The Ancients were thorough. Not only did they have Keepers, they had six possible main locales for the power source, each with their own Youth Triumvirate. We, the Shaaris, have a legion that only works on scouting for possible youths; they usually are clustered in one area, like you three. I'm your Guardian, but I also guard my planet's knowledge. And we have little time; this is a pleasant respite from my time in battle the last three days, but I came to give you what you'll need once you make it to Union Station."

"So we are supposed to start there?" Jesse asked.

"Yes, you all have proven that you are worthy of that information."

Hayden stood, pissed as all get out, "Proven – what the hell is that supposed to mean?"

Hallia leapt up and placed her slender hand on his shoulder. "Hayden, you have been somewhat tested up until now."

"Yeah, we've noticed."

"Good. Let's just say that not all the Youth Triumvirates are fairing as well as the three of you, so this leads us to believe that you may be the ones to find the real power source."

"And what about the other kids?" Kate asked.

Hallia gave Kate an icy stare. "They are fine, Kate. I just meant that they're not manifesting quite the Terrian powers that you three are, so we sense you are the ones that have the right combination of gifts from the Ancients. You can use these skills to acquire the real power source."

"So, to clarify, we weren't part Terrian, right?" Hayden shrugged her hand away, but placed his own palm where hers had been on his shoulder. Hallia glanced at it and then back at Jesse and Kate.

"Correct, you're not offspring. Some of your ancestors were given gifts by the Ancients and they have been genetically passed to you. As I mentioned, your skills were triggered by events – meeting me, the trauma of the tornado – and with mind expansion, emotion, among other things, they are enhanced. This is partly why you see the battles for what they are, but average humans see horrible natural disasters. It's all part of what the Ancients set up thousands of years ago, to ensure our god status; they wanted to provide hope in life beyond this world, but in a controlled manner. They wanted *you* to carry out their goals."

"Do you ever think that Shaaris have changed what the Ancients wanted?" Jesse asked.

"No, but yes, how's that for the dialectic that most Earthly religions possess. Times and planetary goals change. We Shaaris have adapted to our roles."

"By killing, right? Did you kill that professor in Shanberg who saw the aliens too, and spoke out? The one the police said was a suicide." Hayden fumed and paced in front of the group.

"I know nothing of that, but again, my role is to be Guardian to all of you."

Jesse was angry, but also very curious; his mind raced as he tried to pinpoint what to ask next. Hayden beat him to it.

"How do they find us, the Belite-Gelfs?" Hayden asked.

"I think you know the answer to that question already," Hallia said. She gave a sympathetic smile. "Part of what you just experienced – the fire from the sky – is the result of the Belite-Gelfs homing in on you, Hayden, but you're not alone in this: Others with what we call *The Glow* can be tracked and marked, so to speak. It's their way of attacking Earth. Once you were spotted on a satellite camera, then the Belite-Gelfs were able to link with your mind. It's their mechanism to infiltrate Earth. There was a battle on the atmospheric border raging; you were marked, as others have been, and once the Belite-Gelf dragoons showed up they were able to penetrate our protective borders. You, and a few others they have connected to, draw their fire to Earth. Their biggest goal is destruction."

"Why?" Kate asked. She was the last to stand. Hallia wouldn't keep her gaze; she pointed to the sky. "There was a great battle above you, between Belites and Shaaris, and the Gelfs are the least in numbers. They want more followers; they want to dominate both planets by hateful means. All of us, Shaaris, Belites, or humans, have a common enemy with the Belite-Gelfs."

"You didn't really answer my question," Kate pushed, and Jesse wanted to give her a thumbs up. "How did they get that way?"

"Another long story," Hallia said. "Do you want to know what you face in Chicago? The Shaaris have secured the border, but I can't say how long it will last."

The three glanced at each other and nodded in agreement.

"Good. Now you know the importance of moving undetected through this landscape. Our planets are even more linked now. When we are in battles, and the Belite resources are increasing, their power stronger, then more trouble happens on Earth. Do you understand your need to fulfill this task? Each planet's peace depends on the three of you finding the power source. Our research has shown that Union Station is the first locale, but after that, the trail runs cold. On the ceiling of the Great Hall, there are decorative engravings of flowers. One of those has the power source, or at least the first clue in retrieving the power source."

"Do you mean that we may have more to do after Union Station?" Kate asked.

Hallia's eyes, which had blazed with energy moments before, softened at Kate's question. "Kate, your journey is just beginning. Even I cannot foresee what all you will have to do."

"How exactly are we supposed to get to the ceiling of the Great Hall? It's fifty or more feet high," Jesse said.

Hallia turned to Hayden. "You have *The Glow*, take this." She handed him a capsule that looked like one of those "Grow Your Own Dinosaur" toys. Jesse had left three colored capsules in water overnight when he was eight, and in the morning, they had grown five times their original size by absorbing all the water.

"What is it?"

"Because of *The Glow*, your body chemistry will respond to our Liquid Light. This is what we use to metamorphose to travel here. This is a small dose. You won't be able to enhance. We're not sure humans will ever be capable of this, but you will be able to fly to the height of the ceiling."

"Wicked! By enhance, do you mean, get to be giant-sized, right?"

"Yes," she answered.

"How long does it last?" Hayden asked.

"We aren't certain. You should have enough time to retrieve what you need."

"*Should* does not give me confidence."

"You have to understand that we are in new terrain as well. We're doing our best to preserve the old order, but we don't really know how our technology will react to your body chemistry. We don't experiment on humans.

"Liquid Light allows us to travel unaided by a ship, faster than the speed of light.. It changes our bodies to base liquid material that does not need oxygen to survive, but once we are in an atmosphere with oxygen, like each of our planets, then we can re-form to humanoid shape. Terrians can alter their size, but we doubt that humans will have the same capability."

"Should I test it out now?" Hayden's eyes sparkled with energy.

"No, we aren't sure what multiple doses in your system will do."

"So I'm your guinea pig."

"Sorry?" Hallia wrinkled her brow.

"Another test."

"In a sense, yes, but it has to be one of you who gets the power source. The Ancients devised it for one Youth Triumvirate, and one alone. We aren't even sure how you accomplish this, but we know we are not able to do it. Believe me, we've tried."

Hayden took the capsule and put it in his pocket. "Do you even know what the power source is?"

Hallia began to pace on the bed of pine needles. Cones crunched under the weight of her boots. "No. Most think it's a weapon, some think it's secret knowledge, and others believe it is a key to eternal life. We need it to remain your gods. If the Belites get it, especially the Gelfs, who knows what they will do to our planets."

"What if we don't want you to be our *gods* anymore?" Hayden asked

Hallia considered his words. Her eyes bore into his with fire like the kind that had rained from the sky the day before. "You may not want that, Hayden, but consider what is best for humanity. What would happen to the masses of believers if you took away their god? Imagine the chaos, the wars, the end of reality as it has been. Do you really want to bring that kind of hopelessness to your planet?"

Hayden walked away for a minute or two, swearing under his breath. "I want to kill you!" he shouted. "You have no right to do this!" He stormed in circles. Hallia watched him with alert, but not malicious, eyes. She unzipped her satchel and tossed more packs of alien food into a pile on the ground.

"I wish that things were different. I wish it never came to this. I don't want war on my planet or on yours." Hallia rubbed at her eyes and squatted with her elbows on her knees.

After several long minutes of silence, Kate spoke up, "How are our families?"

"They are still under Shaari protection, as you saw them three days ago."

"What about my girlfriend, Sofia Calhoun?"

"As I said before, everyone from your drum line is dead," Hallia said.

"But she wasn't at school the day of the tornado."

Hallia arched her eyebrows and sighed. "Then I do not know. This is an oversight. We will find her and provide protection, Jesse. Like I said, things have been getting worse on Terria."

"Do you think she's in danger?" It felt like someone had punched him in the gut.

Hallia stood and motioned to the sky, which still had a dull gray hue. "She could be a target. If the Belites want to manipulate you, then they will go after her."

"And what if you want to manipulate us?" he asked. His heart pounded in his chest. Hayden had rejoined the group and looked at Hallia with defiance.

"There is no need. I can see that the three of you understand why you need to find the power source."

"What will you do with it?" Kate asked; her hands were shaking.

"It depends on what it is." Hallia started to move off from their circle. Her eyes darted to the trees above. "Whatever it is, we will secure its power to help everything on Earth and on Terria to go back to how it was before."

Jesse, Hayden, and Kate watched as Hallia stepped off to stand in a gap in the trees. "Be careful. Shaaris will provide border support at the cusp of your atmosphere, but it is a hard fight. You must do this quickly. I don't know if I'll see you again." She took out two capsules from her bag and put them in her mouth. She gazed on all three individually, lingering over Hayden before her body pooled into a gray liquid mass. The liquid ball floated for a few seconds above the tree line and then darted into the sky and out of sight.

CHAPTER SEVENTEEN
NAMES

> An endless road. Letting oneself be pushed by the mob; letting oneself be dragged along by a blind destiny. When the SS became tired, they were changed. But no one changed us. Our limbs numb with cold despite the running, our throats parched, famished, breathless, on we went.
>
> We were masters of nature, masters of the world. We had forgotten everything – death, fatigue, our natural needs. Stronger than cold or hunger, stronger than the shots and the desire to die, condemned and wandering, mere numbers, we were the only men on earth.
>
> At last, the morning star appeared in the gray sky. A trail of indeterminate light showed on the horizon. We were exhausted. We were without strength, without illusions.
>
> — *Night*, Elie Wiesel

"This gets better and better," Hayden said. He let out a huff and swished his dagger in the air.

"Yeah, it's a lot to take in." Jesse's stomach churned with anxiety. What if the Belites, or worse, the Belite-Gelfs, got Sofia?

Kate had already started moving. "I'm nervous. I think we better get going. By the way Hallia looked, I'll bet the Shaaris are taking a beating, and I really don't trust them. I know she's holding stuff back."

"No kidding. She kept glancing down when she got to certain bits, the telltale sign of a liar," Hayden said.

After walking quickly for a few minutes, Jesse asked, "What was up with how she looked at you?"

"Yeah, I felt that." Hayden smirked.

"It's disgusting," Kate said. "She could be your mother."

"She's hot though."

"Hayden! She's also an *alien*," Kate said while shaking her head.

"I know. I can't help it that I can even attract a forty-something alien chick." He smiled. "What can I say, I got *The Glow*."

Jesse laughed at the same time Kate made an annoyed grunt.

They walked on until late afternoon. Sometimes the only sound they heard was the crunch of autumn leaves under their feet; other times they spoke in a rush about what they had learned from Hallia. They went over and over the new information. What exactly did all the Terrian factions want, especially with them? What was the power source? What kinds of genetically nightmarish beasts awaited them on their journey? And the question at the forefront of their minds was how would Hayden be able to float along the ceiling of the Great Hall in Union Station without being seen?

To that question Kate said, "I think the orb is the answer. I'm working on what I can do with it."

"Yeah, I thought that if you can blow dry your hair, then what else can the orb do?" Jesse said.

Kate was along his right side and she smelled like pine needles. He inhaled and let out a long breath. But this was it, no more thinking about her, he vowed. After the confirmation that Sofia could be in danger, Jesse was determined to focus on her, and that meant not thinking about Kate. She was a friend, and that was all.

When they had to maneuver through residential areas, they kept silent. Jesse usually led with his head down, and Kate brought up the rear. Without saying anything about Hayden being marked by Belite-Gelfs, the other two automatically cushioned him between them, as if they were ready for anything to rain from the sky and home in on Hayden. Jesse tried to imagine a massive line of Shaaris keeping a protective border at Earth's atmosphere. Were they gelatinous-liquid giants at that point, or a normal humanoid size? What kinds of weapons did they have? Jesse couldn't believe that this was real and not something he had made up from his childhood games, when he used to have intricate battle scenarios with army men or superheroes. If the three of them, this make-shift Triumvirate, were the superheroes, then Jesse was worried to the point of frenzy. They were average kids from the suburbs. And yet, they had gifts from the Ancients, gifts that even Hallia was impressed by.

When Jesse heard the hiss and grind of school buses in one neighborhood that had an arch of vibrantly golden, brown, and orange leaves above the street, he longed to be a child jumping off the bus and dashing home for a snack and cartoons. But he and his friends avoided the buses, the children, and the homes as best as they could; they were pariahs in a sense. What if more battle fire broke through the alien front line and zeroed in on Hayden? It would destroy the neat homes and pristine lawns. Kids and families would be blown apart. Giant aliens could snatch up the brilliant trees and leave craters the size of tractor tires. No, Jesse thought, they could not be noticed, and they had to get to Chicago as soon as possible.

The sun set behind the shield of gray clouds, and once true darkness was upon them, Kate lit the orb. She was still at the back of the group, so it cast a single beacon that flickered in front of Jesse because Hayden's head obscured the beam as he walked on the uneven ground. They could no longer move right next to the tracks because of a rusted metal fence. They picked their way through the woods, careful to avoid a shallow stream much like the one they had bathed in that morning. Was that really the same day? Jesse was numb with disbelief. Soon the woods broke up and the teens had to wander through one industrial parking lot to another: Several were lots for semi-truck trailers; some housed construction materials; and many were parking lots filled with commuters' cars. Kate became adept at turning the orb off and stuffing it under her arm like a football when they had enough light from streetlamps. That was when the October chill was the worst. Jesse realized that the orb was giving off even more heat than before, and he especially missed it in the parking lots.

When they were kicking up dust and fallen leaves in yet another lot with vacant trailers for semi-trucks, Kate let out a delighted yelp. She quickly looked around to see if anyone outside of their group could have heard her. The building and parking lot looked empty. Jesse wondered how this worked: Did companies rent the trailers instead of owning the entire truck? Kate broke him from his banal thoughts.

"Check this out you two," she said. Her hair fell around her face, making a curtain around the orb. Her eyes danced with excitement. Jesse and Hayden huddled around her. She pulled her hair back over one ear, and that's when Jesse saw what made her look like a kid on Christmas: It was another message on the orb.

Once he made out the words, the thrill ebbed. It only read, *Hi.* Then a faded and slow-forming letter followed the message: *K.*

"Did you write that?" Jesse asked.

"Yes." Her joy was infectious.

"Cool, Kate, are you sending it to E and P?" Hayden asked.

"I tried to. Let's see what happens. Can we stop for awhile?"

Hayden nodded. "Do you think these trailers are locked?" He didn't wait for a reply. He was already checking the sliding doors at the backs of the trailers. The others followed Hayden's lead until Jesse heard a "hell yeah" from a distant trailer and then the metallic clanging of a cargo door.

Hayden climbed into an empty trailer. "The lock popped open when I stuck the dagger in it and made it glow. This is so cool."

They settled in, all three cross-legged and staring at the letters Kate had formed on the orb. When nothing happened in the first fifteen minutes, they broke out the food packages and ate in silence. The longer the evening wore on, the more despondent Kate seemed.

"Maybe we should move on?" she asked.

"Naw, we might as well sleep here for the night," Jesse said. "It's isolated enough, and we need a plan for tomorrow anyway. The way I see it, we'll hit Chicago in the morning. I don't think we should walk through the night and end up at Union Station before dawn. What do you two think?" Jesse said this partly because he thought that Kate needed rest. She had dark circles under her eyes, and her slender form appeared even thinner after a few days of the alien food.

"I agree," Hayden said. He walked the length of the trailer and stuffed his hand into his pocket. "I really want to try this Liquid

Light stuff out." He held it up to the light of the orb, and then put it back into his pocket.

"Okay, rest does sound good. I just wish that E and P would write back to me."

"Maybe they're busy making gay love." Hayden laughed and started to do jumping jacks.

Kate reddened and stretched out on her back. Jesse had a vision of being on top of her but blinked it away. Sofia, Sofia, he thought. She watched the movement of light on the ceiling, obviously in deep thought.

"Kate," Jesse said; his voice cracked, so he covered it up with a cough. "You said the orb was the answer to helping Hayden when he's looking at the flower things on the Union Station ceiling. What did you mean by that?"

She turned to her side and tucked her hands under her ear. Again, Jesse pictured her next to him in bed. When she licked her lips before speaking, he had to repeat his mantra: Sofia, Sofia, in order to gain control of his thoughts.

"I kind of thought that I could make smoke, but now I wonder."

"Good idea, you just need practice." Jesse smiled at her.

"Yeah, I guess."

"I say practice outside before the sun comes up, but we might get fire trucks after us," Hayden said.

"I know. That's why I wanted to ask E and P. But I suppose my message didn't get to them."

The evening dragged on. Jesse studied the map of Union Station but saw no easy way to get into restricted areas, which were plentiful, and definitely no easy way to scour the ceiling without having the police called instantly. Even following the tracks into the station wouldn't do, because after a certain point, any pedestrians on the tracks would be arrested. Jesse plotted a rough path around the station, but anything could change once they neared their destination. His stomach got tight thinking about all the unknowns. Now that he knew about what was going on at the edge of the sky and further into their solar system, he became even more frightened.

Though Hayden would have an occasional outburst of something like, "We'll obliterate any Terrian that gets in our way," Jesse could tell that he was nervous, especially about the Liquid Light. He kept getting up and down, swinging his dagger around, drum-tapping his thighs, and bounding around the trailer. He often checked his pocket for the capsule.

On one particularly violent explosion of movement and swearing, Kate sat up.

"Hayden, you're making me more nervous about all this. Please sit down for awhile."

"Oh. Sorry."

"Wait." Kate knelt at the orb and laughed. "It's a message."

They all leaned in then and stared, waiting for the letters to be fully realized.

Hi, Kate.

"Great! Oh, now I need to concentrate and write back." She put her palms to the circle and closed her eyes. It wasn't long until E and P's message was gone, and her response was in its place.

What are your real names?

Eruk and Palk. Are you all okay?

Yes. Can you come to Earth? Kate asked.

Kate stayed in the exact position with her eyes locked shut. Hayden opened his mouth to speak, but Jesse shook his head; he knew that this was Kate's show.

No. Shaaris control Liquid Light. Eruk and Palk wrote back.

Can you get some?

Difficult. We are shunned.

Kate opened her eyes and glanced at Jesse momentarily. Before she could formulate a response, more words formed.

Ghettoized. Part of Resistance.

Ghettoized? Shunned? This could be because of their homosexuality, Jesse thought. He felt sick and ashamed of his earlier behavior and how he called them nasty. How was he different from those who kept Eruk and Palk in a ghetto? Was there a different reason for their lack of rights? No, Jesse knew it could be because of their sexuality, and what other reason would make it all right? Nothing.

Why are you helping us? Kate asked.

You give hope. For peace. Fairness.

We want that too.

Good. Do you need help now?

Yes. Can I make smoke with orb?

Yes. Do you know how?

I'm not sure. Kate wrote. Her hands were shaking.

Remember emotion. Touch helps.

And there was a smoky haze on the orb before a new message came into focus from Eruk and Palk.

With him.

Kate's eyes shot open and she dropped the orb.

"Get them back, Kate!" Hayden said. "I want to know how they knew about the whole corruption thing with the Belite-Gelfs."

Kate was flustered; she grabbed the orb and closed her eyes again, but nothing happened. The moment was gone, and who knew how long Eruk and Palk could keep this up? What kind of risks were they taking by helping them? Kate gave up and relit the orb so it warmed the trailer.

They all lay down as if to go to sleep, but Jesse suspected that his friends were lost in their own thoughts. He could feel Kate's tension to his left. Was he the "him"? Jesse kept replaying part of the message: *Touch helps. Touch helps. Touch helps.*

With him.

CHAPTER EIGHTEEN
NERVOUS

We will have emissaries on Earth. We will observe, blend in, and then bring a basket brimming with fulfillment. From cluster to cluster of human habitations, throughout time and advancements, we will not leave our posts as gods. We will provide guidance without corruption; we will listen and match the spiritual callings of each community; we will not lead with brutality or manipulation, our intentions pure. Good. We will carve pathways to a blessed future where our planets will hold each other in a compassionate union, where the way of life and light will save all of us.

— The Ancient Terrian Fragment of Human Divinities,
Jesse Woods, translator

Jesse woke with two residual images from his scattered dreams. The first made him close his eyes again, longing to return to the dream landscape because Kate was there, looking older with a shorter haircut and wearing a yellow dress. She stood on tiptoes to say something to Jesse who was burning with desire for her. The dream cut away then, to the desert scene he had dreamed before: The white-eyed man spoke to him from the back of the elephant-like creature: *You'll have to choose, you know. I've been watching you, Jesse Voshon Woods. You thought you could solve everything with a neatly ordered life, with regimentation. But you have no control over anything, except maybe what you'll do next.*

Jesse sat up, forcing himself to break from the images from his dreams. Hayden was brushing his teeth and spitting the paste in the corner of the semi-trailer. He wiped his eyes and glanced momentarily at the sleeping Kate. Guilt washed over him. Despite his vigilant effort to focus on Sofia, Kate had entered his subconscious mind. And who was the white-eyed dude? If he was a real person from one of the Terrian groups, Jesse was completely freaked out.

Jesse rubbed his eyes, shifting them to Kate again. The question of whom the message from Eruk and Palk referred to burned in his mind. He couldn't help but wonder if there was touching with Kate in his future. He suppressed these thoughts and jumped up to join Hayden in getting ready to move on.

Kate woke while he and Hayden were studying the map of Union Station. She ate quietly, and then did an awkward tooth brushing with the water from her bottle. She didn't even think to spit on the floor like he and Hayden had done. Jesse thought that she must have swallowed her toothpaste so as to be polite. Somehow this warmed her to him even more. *Touch helps*, he thought and sighed. It seemed that Hayden read his mind because he slapped Jesse's shoulder in a kindly manner, and said, "Yeah, I know," for his ears only.

Jesse led the group in their peculiar march toward the city. He marveled at how this new routine of camping out around a ball of light and warmth had become oddly comforting, as if it's what they had always done. It wasn't only the new feelings he had for Kate, the ones he worked at dampening; it was the fact that for the first time since he was five, he had let down his guard to make friends. Sofia was a friend, in a way, but he made sure he was always in control; an automatic façade went up, even with her. It armed him against criticism or judgment; it helped him navigate a world in which he always felt a little ill-at-ease, as if someone would come up to reveal that he was a fake. A fake what? He tried to investigate this idea: a fake black young adult, one on the verge of being a black man. No, he was no fake; he was real. Did he worry that he was too white? Yes and no. He bit down hard on his lip while they edged another series of industrial lots; he was tired of the same conversations he had in his head. At least he had different worries now: aliens and war. And yet his everyday worries were not completely replaced with the new terrors that came from the sky.

Every suburb or neighborhood was alive with activity. Jesse realized it was a weekday: Was it Tuesday? They were nearing the city. Trains ran along the track, and they often couldn't hug its path because of residential areas, vacant lots in the process of new construction, busy suburban streets, or more industrial buildings. Stations were packed with commuters, and thick puffs of exhaust billowed from smokestacks. Finally, the sun broke through the cloak of gray from the day before; at times Jesse had to shield his eyes when he kept looking to the sky to be sure no giant aliens were tumbling from it.

"We're close now. Let's take a break in that Super Saver lot," Hayden said.

"Do you think it's safe?" Kate asked. It was the first time she had spoken in two hours.

"Don't worry. I won't go in and buy us some doughnuts." Hayden smiled, but Jesse could tell he was concerned.

"Let's go a bit more. I think I see a park up ahead," Jesse offered and started for the splash of green between a strip mall and another neighborhood. He couldn't even guess what suburb this was, and he didn't want to take out the map and appear to be tourists. Who visited a place as nondescript as a Chicago suburb?

No children were on the swing sets or play structures at the park, which had naked trees, a sand pit with shovels and buckets, and a baseball diamond. Jesse worried truancy officers might stop them, but he hoped it was close enough to a time when some schools started. He mentally constructed a lie about being seniors on a half day program. They climbed the play structure and nestled between slides and monkey bars, hoping to go unseen. Jesse pulled out the map of the station.

Kate kept flicking her eyes between the street and Hayden. What if it was Hayden she wanted? This sent a jolt of panic through Jesse despite his new effort to focus on Sofia. The thought made him want to fight Hayden all over again. On the practical side of things, Hayden already had a job to float along the ceiling and search for the power source.

"Okay, what's the plan?" Hayden asked while rubbing his hands together. The morning chilled them because Kate had to put the orb away in populated areas.

Jesse looked at Kate who was visibly uncomfortable with the subject matter, so he decided to speak first.

"Well, we know we need a diversion so that you can float along the ceiling and find the power source. Kate thinks she can make smoke, so that will be your cover."

"That's a start, but where will you two be with the orb and the smoke?" Hayden glanced from one to the other and suppressed a smirk.

"I think this stairwell will work okay," Jesse said and pointed to a marble staircase at one end of the Great Hall.

"Looks good."

Kate said nothing; her face was red, and she kept twisting one strand of hair around her finger.

"What do you think, Kate?" Hayden asked.

She jerked as if struck and nodded.

They sat in awkward silence for several minutes. Hayden did a couple of rounds on the monkey bars until Jesse signaled for him to come back. Hayden squatted next to Kate and put his hand on her shoulder. She tensed even more.

"Kate, talk to us. You're a major player in this one. We need to know that you can do this."

She kept working the strand of hair, and Jesse wondered if she'd yank it out of her head. She still didn't speak. Jesse wanted to make her respond, but he also felt her discomfort and wanted to ease her tension.

"Kate," he said. She gave him a panicked expression, but when their eyes connected, her stare softened. He went to speak more, but no words came; they were locked in his dry throat. Her lips moved, but she said nothing as well. They held each other in this manner for several luminous seconds. Finally, Hayden coughed and jumped up to start another swing across the monkey bars. After he turned and was on his way back to them, he laughed and spoke.

"Ahem. Yeah, from what Eruk and Palk said, I think we got the smoke thing covered. Then I guess once the smoke starts, I'll eat the Liquid Light and float to the top." He stopped and panted a little from his exertion. "I have numerous concerns though."

Jesse was grateful Hayden kept talking; he could hardly stand to be near Kate and not kiss her. Sofia! Sofia! He told himself and focused on Hayden's speech.

"The fire department will be called. They'll find the source of the smoke and it'll be you two. Then what? You get hauled in and then the police find me in the air, or worse, the Shaaris have no idea how this stuff works on humans, so I fall from fifty feet up incurring near fatal injuries. Good thing I got you, doc, that's if you aren't downtown at that point. Anyway, we're pretty much screwed. Oh yeah, and what if I end up on some surveillance camera, then I'm on a satellite dish, and the Belite-Gelfs mark me. Then we are truly, truly screwed."

Jesse nodded to all of this, but his insides reeled. He was embarrassed. Of all times to be flipping out over a girl! But he couldn't help himself; when she looked at him like she just had he felt an electrical current through his entire body. It was difficult to regain composure, and he hoped that she felt the same way.

"I can move the smoke," she said finally.

Hayden gave her a quizzical look. "Whad'ya mean?"

"I can start it from the orb, but if Jesse and I hide somewhere after I start it off, then I can make it grow without showing that it's coming from the orb."

"Cool, but are you sure you can do that?"

"Yeah."

"How are you sure?" Hayden asked.

"Are you sure that you can find the power source?" she volleyed right back to him, and then to Jesse, "And you seemed sure that you could heal my foot."

"True," Jesse put in, but Hayden seemed uncertain.

"Wanna practice?"

"No, I know I can do it," she said. This shut Hayden up.

Jesse made himself scan the map instead of think about how she'd make the smoke.

"Here, maybe we could hide in this janitor closet while you make the smoke expand. We'll start here, on the stairwell with

Hayden, and then move to this restricted area, and then into the closet."

"It's probably okay. I doubt anyone will search a closet when they want to evacuate the station. I wonder if people won't see me anyway," Hayden said.

"Because not every human sees the Terrians, is that what you mean?" Jesse didn't give Hayden a chance to answer. "We can make guesses from Hallia's cryptic information, like maybe the Shaaris put up some kind of force field. We do know we can't do that stuff, at least not yet. Also, like Hallia said, we don't really know how the Liquid Light will work in your system, so we need to be sure you have cover. Plus, what if there are other people with 'gifts' from the Ancients, like that professor. They'd see you for sure."

"Good point. I just wanna get it over with."

"Me too, man, it's scary as hell," Jesse said and slapped his shoulder. Hayden punched the air and went down a slide on his stomach. Kate was already down the stairs and heading out of the park.

She turned after Jesse and Hayden caught up to her.

"Remember when I sent you two the message when Hallia came?"

"Yeah, I wanted to talk about that, but the whole Liquid Light thing made me forget about it. How'd you make that happen?"

"I concentrated on the words I wanted to say to you two, almost like I saw the words in my mind, and then I imagined sending the words to both of you. I sensed it worked, and neither of you said a thing about Eruk and Palk."

"Right, so let's use this," Jesse said with excitement. "We can practice as we walk this last stretch." The idea of sending mental messages to each other was thrilling. "Hayden, when you get the power source, concentrate on a message."

"All right, I'll say 'got it.' Sound okay?"

"Sure. Kate and I will make our way to the Canal Street exit, if it's clear, but if there's anything that separates us, let's concentrate on two cross streets and wait for each other there, like Jackson and Canal, or something."

"Good, yeah, I imagine it'll be chaotic with the fire department and stuff," Hayden said. He ran his fingers through his hair and warmed his hands nervously.

"Sound okay to you, Kate?" Jesse couldn't keep eye contact with her, but it didn't matter; she was staring at the ground or watching her feet.

"Yeah, all right," she said quietly.

They walked the next hour or so in silence. Hayden practiced his message. After twenty "got its" Jesse said they could take a break. He let his mind wander to Kate only once in awhile; the possibility of being physically close to her made him jittery. That was paired with the fact that they were going to start what appeared to be a fire in a major train station in one of the busiest cities in the United States. And what was going on above their heads, on Earth's outer atmosphere? Were Belites, specifically, the Belite-Gelfs breaking the front line, readying themselves to link their battle fire to their "corrupted" and marked humans, which included Hayden? The thought made Jesse chill. Would they see the Bull of Heaven or the dragon again? And what other beasts that roamed Terria, the ones from Earthly myths, would charge from the sky to destroy the world? He shut his mind to the unending questions and focused on following the tracks to their left.

When they came to yet another industrial area: Keelly's Construction, A & E Industries, and then a business that sold storage bins, Jesse wondered why it was that his stepdad Michael always said that America hardly made anything any longer, and that would kill the country. No, Jesse thought, aliens will, and then the world order will dissolve into chaos if they didn't retrieve the power source. There was a part of Jesse that hoped some other group of three teens was the one to find the real power source, and then they would be free of it. No, as assuredly as Kate's and Hayden's presence had become, so had this new knowledge that they were the ones. He could tell Hallia thought the same thing.

Jesse stopped in a parking lot of an abandoned warehouse that was covered in gang graffiti when the familiar Chicago skyline loomed like a talisman in front of them. What did this city hold for the three teens, this scared Triumvirate?

CHAPTER NINETEEN
SMOKE

She walks in beauty, like the night
Of cloudless climes and starry skies;
And all that's best of dark and bright
Meet in her aspect and her eyes:
Thus mellow'd to that tender light
Which heaven to gaudy day denies.

One shade the more, one ray the less,
Had half impair'd the nameless grace
Which waves in every raven tress,
Or softly lightens o'er her face;
Where thoughts serenely sweet express
How pure, how dear their dwelling-place.

And on that cheek, and o'er that brow,
So soft, so calm, yet eloquent,
The smiles that win, the tints that glow,
But tell of days in goodness spent,
A mind at peace with all below,
A heart whose love is innocent!

— She Walks in Beauty Like the Night, Lord Byron

"Come on. Let's shoot over to Canal Street," Jesse said.

They all wore hoods over their heads and slouched like any other teenager who walked down the busy street. But Jesse's heart pounded, and his hands were sweaty. Kate's face had lost all color, and Hayden kept taking deep breaths. Jesse imagined white curls in the air during a frigid December. He had always loved Chicago at Christmas time. Now he wondered if he would ever see another Christmas, or if humans would survive the fallout from the alien war, and if they did, who would celebrate a holiday that was the equivalent to an alien hoax? He rubbed his hands together and shielded his eyes from a lone ray of sun breaking through the clouds.

The ray must have worried Hayden because he turned to Jesse with alarm. Jesse shrugged it off but guided the other two more rapidly through the afternoon crowds. The squat gray building waited for them, both ominous and banal in its regularity. What would happen to the travelers if they messed this up? And if they didn't mess it up, how in the hell would they know what to do next? He pushed through the peddlers and singers and walked through the Canal Street doors with a fake confidence very much like the one he armed himself with before each track or drum line competition. Like his mother always said, "Fake it 'til you make it."

"This way," he said and led Kate and Hayden through the food court. He followed the signs to the Great Hall, careful to keep his head down. He glimpsed Hayden next to him with his chin tucked to his chest. Kate gave Jesse a small nod before they entered the expansive room of tall columns, a marble staircase, an arched ceiling with their destination flowers carved into it, and wooden benches that had probably been in the station since it was first built. There was an old time coffee and sandwich shop in the hall; the smell of roasted chicken and bread made Jesse's mouth salivate instantly. He strode past it and toward the marble staircase without speaking to either of his friends. Hayden let out a sniff, muttering, "Dang," under his breath. Jesse assumed it was in response to his own hunger. Kate adjusted her backpack like an average traveling teen.

There was one woman on the top of the stairs. She was probably in her sixties, her gray hair tied back in a loose bun. She took a series of pictures of the elongated view of the Great Hall and smiled at the three teens when she passed them on the stairs. Hayden positioned himself along the outer wall, leaning casually and pretending to text. Kate and Jesse hid behind a pillar at the top of the stairs the best that they could, crouching like five-year olds in sand, only there were no buckets and shovels between them, just the orb. Jesse realized in one panicked moment that their entire plan pivoted on this one object, and Kate's ability to control its power. Jesse glanced at Hayden who gave him a barely visible nod.

When Jesse focused again on the orb, Kate already touched it with her left hand. Then she grabbed his hand with her right. A jolt ran through him as if he were a lightning rod. He shut his eyes for a moment and then opened them to see Kate with closed lids and a look of utter pleasure on her face. He was embarrassed and completely turned on by her expression. He didn't know what to do, so he sat stock-still and clutched her hand. He thought about caressing her palm, but he didn't want to break her concentration. He squatted and tried to think about anything but Kate to keep himself from sprouting an unceremonious erection right before the smoke started and they had to sprint to the janitor's closet.

Suddenly, Kate's eyes shot open, and it seemed like she flung something at Hayden simply with one penetrating look. But nothing was there, and then it was. Hayden was completely engulfed in smoke. Jesse heard his feet clomp the floor, and nothing more. Then the cloud of smoke drifted to the top of the ceiling. They had to assume Hayden was in it because he no longer slouched along the granite wall. Jesse pulled on her hand and led her down the stairs and to the black door that said "Authorized Employees Only" on it. Soon someone noticed the white smoke floating along the roof because people screamed and scattered. Kate closed her eyes and held tightly to the orb in one hand and Jesse in the other; the smoke cloud spread like peanut butter on bread. Hopefully Hayden wasn't dying of smoke inhalation. Why hadn't they thought about that detail?

"Do you think Hayden will be okay with the smoke?" he whispered to Kate.

"It's more of a puff, not real smoke. Think of it as floating in a cloud. And, I can sense him, Jesse, he's okay. He's touching each flower with this knife, systematically. He'll find it," she said, the whole time with closed lids.

People scrambled, and alarms went off. When someone burst through the door they were stalking, they slipped in and went right to the closet. Jesse didn't think about anyone locking a closet that held brooms and mops, but it was. He cursed as he tried to yank it open.

Kate kept her eyes closed and murmured something.

"What?" he asked.

"I need to get in there. The smoke is thinning."

Jesse only had the one hand to work with because he knew that Kate needed to be connected to him. That was it. Why didn't he use this connection to bust the lock? He had healed her foot; Hayden had opened the lock on the semi-trailer, why couldn't he do this? He grasped the door handle with his free hand and concentrated on what kind of touching may await him inside that door.

The doorknob sprang to life, and they were in.

"Keep the lights off," Kate said in an unusually deep voice.

She yanked hard on his hand and led him to one corner of the closet. She pushed a large bin out of the way and practically tripped him. She opened her eyes for a moment to set the orb on the floor gingerly. Then she did something amazing; she lay back as if the tile floor were a bed and brought Jesse to cover the length of her body with his own. He was out of his mind with desire for her; her taut body moved with his on the floor as they kissed. He kissed her forehead, her cheeks, her eyelids, her lips, and down her neck. Several luxurious minutes passed in this way: He pressed against her breasts and legs. Each explored the other's body with tender touches. She made small moans that spurred him on until he couldn't help himself; he let his hands move under her jacket and shirt; her breasts were firm and erect beneath her bra. Kate let out another low moan from deep in her throat. She kissed his full lips with more vigor, so Jesse ran his hand down her smooth stomach to the button on her jeans.

He started to work his hand into her jeans, but he soon felt her body, which had been both supple and tensed with excitement moments before, grow rigid.

"What is it, Kate?" He didn't recognize his own voice; it was so hoarse.

"I..." she stammered between breaths, "I can't go all the way, Jesse."

"Okay." He pulled his hand off the button of her jeans and brought it up to beneath her curtain of red hair. Some strands stuck to the back of her neck because she had started to sweat.

"Please, kiss me still," she said.

"Kate, I get pretty worked up here, you're, you're —"

"Inexperienced. I don't know what I'm doing. No one dates me, except Hayden, and that was way too much for me."

"How?" Jesse wanted to jump her, but he also wanted an answer to this question.

"Hayden's so, so *experienced*, it freaked me out."

"Did you sleep with him?" This really mattered to Jesse. Really, really, and he hated himself for it. He tried to tell himself it was the past. But he didn't want another guy's hands on her. Ever.

"No, but we went farther than I had gone before." Kate paused and looked away. "Anyway, we both know he gets around, and I don't. Like now, I'm scared to death I'll get pregnant. I'm only seventeen. I don't want to be a teen mom like my mom was, and my dad, he'd kill you, straightaway. He's old school Irish-Catholic, and a burly, mean drunk at times, so he'd beat you and then make you marry me, I'm sure."

Jesse's eye twitched; he was nonplussed. Where was all this coming from? He could never think that far ahead, especially in a moment like this where all he wanted was to get her jeans off to touch her silky thighs. Stop, he thought, focus!

"Kate, step back a minute. Can we not talk about your father, please," Jesse said in a light tone, hoping to make her smile, but she only reddened. "You don't date because dudes are intimidated by you. Believe me, I speak from experience."

"What? Wait, hang on. I have to check on Hayden." She closed her eyes and put one hand back on the orb. She was really getting the hang of the thing. Jesse had completely forgotten about Hayden and their mission. This worried him, so he sat up and rubbed his face with his hands to bring himself back to reality. The closet smelled like pine disinfectant and laundry soap, scents that were soothing against the pulsing beat of the alarm system and the blare of distant sirens approaching the station.

"Plenty of smoke and he's still working," she said.

"I didn't know you'd be able to sense him."

"I didn't either, but I guess my connection to you is strong." Her face turned a crimson color, and she twirled her hair with her index finger. Jesse wanted to get back to her jeans, but he knew better. She closed her eyes again and reached out for his hand. He sat completely still and waited. Now what? He wondered what his role was going to be in all of this. Right now, he felt like the appendage, the vehicle for Kate to do some pretty amazing things with the orb. Hayden had *The Glow*, a dagger, and now the experience with the Liquid Light. What was he: the extra black man on the set who got killed, or the buddy to the main white dude hero? He grinned to himself and held Kate's hand; it felt as natural as his own skin to have her so close. He hoped to kiss her again.

He thought some more about his role: He could read Ancient Terrian, and he healed Kate's foot. No, he knew he had more gifts, and in time they too would manifest or augment. He just had to be open and ready.

"I think the station police are freaking because the sprinkler system isn't dousing the smoke; people are being evacuated." Kate spoke with her eyes closed.

"Should we leave too?"

"Let's stay here a bit longer," she said.

They sat holding hands for a few minutes. Jesse could feel tension building in Kate by the way she held his hand. Her palm began to sweat.

"Jesse, there's another thing," she said softly.

"What's that? You worried about the Virgin Birth, Catholic girl?" He smiled and she gave a small grin.

"No, well yes, that was always a pretty real fear, up until a few days ago, and I found out it was all alien stories." Kate laughed and shook her head as if to bring herself back to her original topic. "I, ah, I obviously have feelings for you..."

Kate's palm was making his own wet; he was dying to wipe it on his jeans, but he didn't want to let go of her.

"Yeah," was all he could manage. He couldn't believe this. Here he was with her, in a closet of all things. On appearance this location seemed to be a peculiar place for romance, but Jesse knew it would be fodder for future fantasies about Kate: her vulnerable expression and passionate lips.

"But," she paused, "you and Sofia have been together for so long I've gotten used to liking you from a distance. You know, the whole unrequited love thing, and I figured you'd be someone who would always be off limits. It always seemed like you and Sofia would get married after high school or college or some time."

"Really?" Jesse's heart pounded. Sofia! "Kate, I don't know how to respond to that one. I'm worried about Sofia, but I'm, I don't know, confused—"

Got it. Got it. Got it. The key phrase from Hayden repeated in Jesse's head, and he knew Kate heard it too.

"We need to go," she said, looking guilty. He felt it too; here was Hayden struggling with scaling along the ceiling searching for a power source surrounded by a blanket of smoke, and they were making out and talking about their feelings for each other. Damn, this was messed up.

They stood up and let go of the other's hand. He instantly missed her; her hand left a smoldering sensation on his fingertips.

"Wait. I need to be sure the smoke covers his descent," she said and closed her eyes. Then she grabbed Jesse one more time and kissed him hard as she stood on tip toes. Her backside was firm to his touch and her lips were as soft as warmed velvet, if there was such a thing. Yes, he mused as her tongue explored his mouth; this was probably how it felt inside of Kate: warm, wet, smooth, and what else, electric. He snuffed the image out of his mind and let her lead him out of the closet and into the smoky corridor.

CHAPTER TWENTY
RAIN

When the fire rains from the sky, when the clouds explode with unknowns, turn to us. When grief or loss has clamped your heart, and your soul is punctured, you cannot go on, come to us, your gods. Be us goddess or god, spirit or animal, the intricate web of stars sketching maps of light, we will catch you in hands wide open, from the heavens, from the distant, eternal universe, we come, we come to lead you to the way.

— The Ancient Terrian Fragment of Human Divinities,
Jesse Woods, translator

They found Hayden on the corner of Jackson and Canal. He held the ceramic flower in his left palm as his eyes frantically searched the city streets. Once he caught sight of Jesse and Kate, his face lit up with a smile of satisfaction. All three fell into step and crossed the street to get as much distance as possible from the crowds, police cars, and fire engines.

"I'm dying to talk," Hayden whispered to Jesse who nodded and signaled that they needed to move farther from the commotion.

"The Wacker and Jackson corner is blocked off," he said.

Jesse tried to see ahead of the mass of people. The streets were packed; ambulances and police cars lined the curbs. Hayden's skin glistened, and his eyes were huge with excitement and possibly worry. Jesse thought that he must still have the Liquid Light in his system.

Jesse pushed through the throng; each teen kept their hoods on and their heads down. Finally, the groups thinned and the three found a park bench to sit on in a small alcove of green space called Pritzger Park.

The sky had turned an ominous black, so men in business suits fled the park benches and mothers pushed their strollers with more velocity.

"There's some more of that Ancient Terrian writing on the back, Jesse. I was hoping you could translate," Hayden said. Then he added, "And do it quick, bro, the sky is getting creepy, and you and me both know what that means."

Jesse took the dense ceramic flower in his hand. It was about twelve inches in diameter, the size of a dinner plate, with a carving of another smaller flower in its center. When he flipped it over, he saw the text. He stared at the writing for several minutes; at first it was garbled gibberish, but the more he concentrated on the contours of the letters, the more the writing came into focus. It was no longer simple etchings; words formed, and once again Jesse was astonished that he could read the words and sort out the meaning.

"Do you want a near exact translation. There's a bit of a poem at the beginning," Jesse said.

Kate shook her head, and Hayden blurted, "Hell no, sum it up, bro."

"It says that there's one more piece to this thing," Jesse said; his eyes darted from Kate to Hayden and then to the sky with its massing gray clouds. "We need to get to the Field Museum, you know, around McCormick Place, and get the albite moonstone."

"What?" Hayden stood and began to pace, but then stopped himself and sat back down between Jesse and Kate. Kate's face had gone pale again; she drummed on her knees nervously.

Hayden whispered even though no one was in ear shot, "Doesn't that have dinosaur bones and shit? What's this moonstone business? Like we're in some nineteenth century Gothic novel or something!"

"It's got to be there, and we need it," Jesse said with force. "We need to end this thing, so the sooner we get the entire power source the better. Agreed?" He wanted to reach for Kate's hand, but now in the open air with people milling about and Hayden between them, their intimacy in the janitor's closet seemed even more surreal, definitely the stuff of dreams.

Kate leaned in, "What are we going to do with the power source once we get the whole thing?"

"Good question. I say we keep it and have leverage against all the alien groups."

"I'm leaning that way, but we don't even know what the hell it is," Jesse answered. His pulse was accelerating, and he was getting that prickly feeling again that they had to move.

"What about you, Kate?" Hayden asked. "You think we should keep it?"

"I have no idea, but I think we'll know what to do when we find out what it is. I guess we trust our instincts. I don't want to forget Eruk and Palk, no matter what we do."

"Exactly, that's what I mean, leverage," Hayden said, nodding his head; his skin rippled a blue glow and Jesse yanked at his hood to cover his face more.

"Dude, you're sparklin' like a glitter ball when you get heated."

"Dang." Hayden stuffed his hands in his pockets. "I say we hoof it. It's a hike to the museum, isn't it?"

"Yeah, we need to head south. I think it's about four or five miles or so," Jesse said. He knew this from his time in the city with his family. He thought of them sleeping on a large bed and envied their oblivion.

Jesse led the group out of the park and toward Michigan Avenue. Dense afternoon crowds moved along this busy shopping and business district. Hayden and Kate were at each of his elbows as much as possible, but when more people grouped at intersections or in front of certain shops, they slipped into their usual single file line with Kate at the rear and Jesse leading. Jesse wanted to jog, but he thought this would draw more attention than he wanted, so he kept a fast walking pace.

Kate had sidled up next to him and his heart raced. "I have no idea where I am, I hardly get to the city." She gave a tentative smile, and Jesse grinned back; it was the first interaction they had had since the closet and it felt good. There she was, resplendent with milky skin and red hair waving behind her, despite the days of rugged travel and anxiety. He wanted to take her under his arm and lead her the entire way, claim her, as if they were on a date.

"Don't mean to break the moment, but I see you two got cozy in the closet, interesting, interesting, I must say. So sexual attraction means power, hah! Our vixen alien Hallia said *emotion* enhances abilities, but she left out the sexual stuff." Hayden clapped, and little sparks emitted from his fingertips.

"Dude!" Jesse instinctively put his own hand over Hayden's.

"I know, that's what I was getting at. This glow thing is monstrous. I feel a power coming on, and I controlled it in order to descend back at Union Station. The Liquid Light is still in my system. We're getting this *down*."

"Chill a little, man," Jesse warned. "Remember those Belite-Gelfs, we need to be ready."

"Yer right, man. Oh no, rain. I don't like this," Hayden said.

Thick droplets of rain fell with rapidity from gray-purple clouds that rippled along the darkening sky like the bottom of track cleats. Jesse looked up and a shiver ran down his back. Some people had umbrellas they had pulled out and huddled under; they attempted to keep their city pace and move through the streets to get to their destinations.

Honk! Someone slammed on a horn and Jesse's heart pulsed like a timpani.

"Come on," Jesse said and motioned forward.

The street scene was surreal with the increasingly purple and gray sky in the background. Cars put on windshield wipers; taxis honked and maneuvered through tight intersections. Some shoppers held their wrapped packages and bags over their heads for protection from the increasing droplets.

Plop! Giant raindrops hit the cement.

Jesse chanced a glance to the sky, but he couldn't see beyond swaths of black-gray clouds that bulged with life. The rain came down harder, and he had to shield his eyes. Soon the drops became more like water balloons from the heavens. He and his friends covered their heads and dodged the sporadic bombardment.

The water balls crashed onto the cement with deafening cracks, scattering walkers to find shelter under awnings. Screams and water pounding rung through the air. The only saving grace was that normal rain fell at a regular pace, with only sporadic bouts of the rain-ball fall-out, but the indiscriminant nature of the assault made Jesse's heart race.

"Come on. We have to move," Jesse yelled.

He grabbed both of their hands and ran. They couldn't go

far before they had to stop and find cover from the occasional balls of water pummeling the ground.

"I don't want to look up, you both know why," Hayden yelled through the loud din of rain pounding on cars, tires screeching, and people screaming in shock.

"Keep moving!" Jesse shouted back; water streamed down his face, and his backpack felt three times as heavy because it was saturated. He dragged his friends along, now in a dead run whenever they could manage it through the growing storm and people running pell-mell.

Though the deluge poured from the sky, Jesse furtively glanced up again. He saw flashes of color, silver, gold, and purple streaks. In flickers of clarity he witnessed the fight. Shaaris and Belites were enhanced to astonishing proportions without any carriages or animals, just raw gelatinous-liquid forms trying to tear each other apart. He realized some of the massive rain balls were actually fallout pieces from some of the aliens' bodies. A few aliens had weapons similar to Hayden's dagger; others had long sticks Jesse remembered let out lassos of light just like the ones that secured the dragon from the previous battle. A roar erupted from the sky. Jesse held tighter to his friends for fear that the panicking throng would divide them.

Grant Park was to their left, and beyond that the Lake Michigan waters reacted to the tumult in the sky by kicking up thick swaths of lather. Many onlookers stared in amazement at the churning waters and movement of clouds, but Jesse didn't hear anyone commenting on the gigantic bodies fighting in the sky.

"We're almost there," he yelled and pulled on Kate just as part of a building broke off from being shot with several spikes of icy hail.

"Oh my gosh!" Kate screamed and ran faster than Jesse had ever seen her.

Hayden let go of Jesse's hand and grabbed for his dagger. They ran and dodged rain balls and hail; occasionally Jesse saw enormous hands dip from the sky and clutch a mass of dirt or a tree to hurl at an enemy. Gaps the size of SUV vehicles were left in the cement, pavement, or the lawns of Grant Park. When that happened the opposite side, whether Belite or Shaari, rallied and curtailed the rogue alien. So far, no red-headed Belite-Gelfs showed up. Jesse cringed to think of what they would do.

"Shit!" Hayden yelled and shoved Jesse and Kate to the ground. Ice spears whizzed over their heads, and then a rain ball, also known as alien goo, dropped directly on the back of Kate's head, drenching her hair and backpack even more.

Automatically Jesse touched the back of her neck. As soon as his hand rubbed at her spine, he could see inside of her, just like with her broken foot, and he knew that there was whip- lash damage.

"Hold on," he yelled at Hayden who was ready to dart away. He concentrated on healing the tendons and muscles. His hand grew hot and lit the same amber color; he pressed in on her neck and caressed it. Kate whimpered with pain at first, and then, Jesse knew, with pleasure.

"All right, she's okay. Let's move, we're almost to Roosevelt." Hayden yanked at Jesse's sleeve.

They ran into the growing blackness. Flashes of blue and silver streaked across the sky, and the lake frothed more ominously in the Chicago Harbor. With each footfall Jesse became more anxious, his body bathed in sweat and rainwater. Kate's hair dripped a blue sheen; her face was dotted with the alien liquid.

"Do you feel the liquid on your skin?" he asked her when they stopped for a breath on the corner of Roosevelt and South Columbus Drive.

"Yeah, it's weird. I want it off of me."

"No," Hayden said with force and grabbed her hand, "we could use it later. Take my word for it."

Jesse nodded. "Lake Shore Drive is a hot mess." He scanned the cars packed bumper to bumper with people abandoning their vehicles to run into the streets to find cover inside of buildings. Others honked their horns, to no avail, and some avoided navigating through the juggernaut of metal by walking on the car roofs. A group of teens danced on top of a vacated mini-van repeating, "The end is near."

There were a few minutes of reprieve from the battle fall-out. Were the Shaaris really protecting the humans by putting up some of their shields?

"We have to get through," Kate panted; her hands shook, so she clasped them together and rubbed them against her wet jeans.

"Come on. We'll walk on the cars like everyone else if we have to," Jesse said.

They snaked through the cars, all the time keeping an eye on the churning water in the harbor and the brewing battle overhead. The three had just cleared Lake Shore Drive and were running across the lawn of the museum campus when fires erupted.

Pop!

A massive fire ball nearly struck Hayden, but he dodged it and dove onto the grass. More balls shot from the sky, and Jesse worried instantly that the Belite-Gelfs would soon arrive. Three, then four, and five consecutive cannons of hot embers rained down; it seemed two may have hit the steps of the Field Museum.

Alarms rang instantly, and people screamed in shock. As fast as it had started, the barrage stopped and all three clasped hands, each obviously grateful that the others were there. They had overshot the museum when they crossed the highway, so they had to run around the yawning circular structure of Soldier Field Stadium to backtrack a short distance to the museum.

Jesse's heart pounded in his chest, and he ran like it was the four-hundred-yard dash. He had a flash of their running from the first alien battle, just days ago, but it felt like a lifetime had passed. He slowed, following Hayden who had his dagger in one hand; the blade glowed blue, and Jesse saw the same sparks dance off of Hayden's fingertips. When they reached the steps of the Field Museum, Jesse's heart nearly stopped from shock; nothing could have prepared him for the chaos. A mass of people must have been herded out the front and side doors when the fire balls had struck. Injured men, women, and children writhed in pain. Family members called out for each other as small fires blazed in the grass or on the trees. The great marble stairs leading to the entrance of the museum was almost split in half, the granite scarred with soot and ash. Smoke billowed up over the great height of the ceramic dinosaur on the lawn, obscuring the battle, which made Jesse anxious. His mind raced as he scanned the panicking crowd.

"What do we do?" Kate said while tears from shock and smoke streaked her cheeks.

"You two get in and get the moonstone. I need to try to heal the injured people," Jesse said.

"All right," Hayden said.

Jesse watched Hayden lead Kate to the side of the museum, yelling, "We need to find our mom!" as he pushed through the numerous clusters of people.

Jesse lunged backward when an alien's liquid hand stretched from the sky. It plucked a tree from the ground in seconds, leaving a gaping hole. Jesse saw it graze two Shaaris who were battling another Belite group with daggers, and then the tree began its dangerous descent. It whipped back and forth in harsh gales.

"Outta the way!" Jesse yelled.

He shoved and yelled at people, but it was impossible to tell where the gyrating limbs or massive trunk would land. People pressed and screamed. The sky pulsed with an unnatural energy. Jesse felt faint.

One mother held her three daughters to her breast, and then she flung them to the ground, covering their bodies with her own. Despite the mayhem, he ran toward the family; something about the woman reminded him of his own mother. His own mother would have shielded him and his siblings in the same way.

A tree crashed down ten feet from where Jesse was; he ducked reflexively and covered his head. When dust and dirt cleared, more cries filled the air. His lungs burned from the smoke of various fires. He tried to stop people and tell them to retreat into the city, but few could focus on his words.

He found the mother on top of her daughters, moaning in pain. He crouched by her side and made eye contact.

"I can help you," he shouted. "Are your kids okay?"

The girls ranged in age. They all had curly, ash blond hair just like their mother's.

"Girls, are you hurt?" she asked as they sobbed and clutched each other.

Winds whipped, and huge clouds moved across the sky; Jesse heard sirens and screams, but he tuned it out and focused on the mother's thigh.

"May I touch your leg?" He did so without an answer. "You've broken a femur," he said.

"It hurts," she responded through chattering teeth. "Are you a doctor?"

"Better. Sit still and hold your kids," he said.

"Mama!" the little one cried, but the oldest grabbed the

baby and held her saying, "Shhh now, Zoe, shhh, now, the man is gonna help Mama, okay." The blue-eyed girl stared at Jesse, her gaze said, *You better do this!*

He closed his eyes and concentrated on the damaged bones; his hands lit and warmed her leg. Just like with Kate's foot, he felt the broken bone mend itself as if his hands were flames from a welder's torch. The mother didn't move, and the girls were tough, Jesse thought, because they stopped crying and held each other despite the churning crowds, bleeding people, and desperate screams.

The woman opened her eyes and gave a thin smile. "It's fine. I think I can walk. But how?"

"Don't ask. You all have to move out of this area, please."

"But my husband's inside," she said. For the first time tears appeared in the woman's eyes.

"He'll find you, but you need to get your girls to safety."

She nodded.

"Tell me one thing before you go, what do you see in the sky?" He had to know.

"What? It's awful! It's blue, silver, and sometimes purple streaks, and then this crazy weather. The fire! Now hail and water! People keep saying it's Armageddon."

"No, it'll be fine," he said with an authority he didn't necessarily feel.

"Who are you?" she asked while covering her daughters when an onslaught of rain balls hit in a bunch.

"I'm part of a team who is going to make this stop, I promise," he yelled and pushed the family forward because hail suddenly fell and stuck in the ground two feet from where they stood.

"Go!" he shouted, and they were out of sight.

From that point on, there was no time for conversations or even to think. Jesse ran from one injured person to another. He quickly assessed the damage as best he could and put his hands on the area to mend the problem in seconds. He was growing more adept at the process. Each new effort seemed to inform the next until he knew that he actually stopped internal bleeding in one man who had been impaled by a tree branch.

But he couldn't save everyone. Though he ran through the area at his fastest speed, he was not quick enough for some who died instantly from hail balls that struck their heads, or ice spikes that wedged into a vital organ.

When he saw a father holding his son and weeping, Jesse cried, wiping snot and soot on his sleeve. He went to the man, and tried to comfort him, but more fire rained down, hitting the earth and creating an explosion of light and smoke. He lost sight of the father and ran to another group of wounded.

Then, out of nowhere, he saw an iridescent bubble just like the one Hallia had put them in a lifetime ago during the tornado at school. Hayden and Kate were inside, and he could tell by their expressions that they were scanning the crowds for him. He waved, but it must have been impossible to see him with the accumulation of smoke and the swarming crowds.

He tried to gain his own bearings and then concentrated on two words: *Solider Field*. He could see the structure a short distance away, and there appeared to be less chaos in that direction.

Soldier Field. Soldier Field. Soldier Field.

He ran toward the stadium while repeating the phrase and focusing on his friends. Soon he saw the bubble move off from the museum area and head toward the stadium. He kept running as fast as possible, his legs pumping like a stamping machine on an assembly line. Then the sheen was on top of him, engulfing and cradling his body in a peculiar sensation of slime and warmth. Hayden and Kate were there, both with tiny scratches with tributaries of blood trickling down their faces and hands.

"Are you two all right?" Jesse instantly touched Kate's face and attempted to heal the cuts.

"Don't worry about," she said softly. "We got the moonstone."

Hayden pulled out a pearly silver sphere the size of one of those super balls that bounced like crazy. He stamped out a memory of his younger brother and sister sending the rubber ball darting willy-nilly in the kitchen while his mom made supper. She had shoved them out of the kitchen as she'd stifled a laugh.

"How?" It was all he could manage to say. His body sank with fatigue and despair. People were continuing to die beneath them.

"Hall of gems," Hayden said, panting. "Precious stones are behind glass. It was a bitch to get upstairs against the flow of people, but we kept at it. In the chaos I used my handy alien dagger to slice some marble off the banister. I hurled a chunk of it at the glass once we spotted the stone. More alarms went off, and when the guards showed up I made this." Hayden signaled to the bubble around them.

"How?" Jesse felt like a parrot repeating the same phrase in the same monotone cadence.

"I just thought it into existence and moved my hands in the basic shape. After it formed around us, in seconds, the guards couldn't see us. I heard one say he saw two kids and then we disappeared into thin air."

The three sat and considered the phenomenon in silence for a few seconds until Jesse had an idea.

"Can you make a shield, to help people get clear of this area? If the Shaaris or Belites really care about humans and are trying to shield us from the battle, it's not enough."

"Yeah," Kate said. "I think they're more focused on killing each other."

"I think I can do it," Hayden said, "but I'm starting to feel a bit weak."

"You have to try, people are dying down there!" Jesse tried to stand in the bubble, but he slid helplessly along the side. Kate put a hand on his own; he grabbed it back and squeezed it to his cheeks. Tears ran down his face, and he didn't even care if he appeared weak. The others cried too then, all releasing their own tension and haunts through the salt in their tears. Kate hugged Jesse, and then he pulled Hayden into the circle. The embrace lasted less than a minute because the bubble shook from a shock wave coming from a torn apart sky. The bubble spun out of control, and the teens were thrown. Jesse attempted to focus on the cause of the disturbance, but he could only make out the enormous aliens, whether Belite and Shaari, scrambling and assembling into new battle lines.

He knew what would come next, Belite-Gelfs. The bubble stabilized just as the sky cracked in half. Hoards of red-headed aliens tumbled through. The last ghastly sight was not the dragon this time, but a new beast, one bigger and more terrifying: A Chimera choked through; its trio of terrors took in the new atmosphere. The main body was of a lion that let out a deafening roar; the goat's head stuck out of the lion's back and rammed its razor-sharp horns in the air; and the lion's tail was a snake whipping and hissing at the rear of the massive beast.

"It's the size of a small airplane," Jesse whispered.

"Yeah, we're totally screwed," Hayden said, his voice echoing the reverberations of all of their fears.

CHAPTER TWENTY-ONE
CHIMERA

*Glorified and sanctified be God's great name throughout the world
which He has created according to His will. May He establish His
kingdom in your lifetime and during your days, and within the life of
the entire House of Israel, speedily and soon; and say, Amen.*

May His great name be blessed forever and to all eternity.

*Blessed and praised, glorified and exalted, extolled and honored,
adored and lauded be the name of the Holy One, blessed be He,
beyond all the blessings and hymns, praises and consolations that are
ever spoken in the world; and say, Amen.*

*May there be abundant peace from heaven, and life, for us and for
all Israel; and say, Amen.*

*He who creates peace in His celestial heights, may He create peace
for us and for all Israel; and say, Amen.*

— Kaddish Prayer

The three shocked teens huddled while watching the ghastly
Chimera lurch in the sky. Jesse was thankful for being in the
protective bubble, but he also knew that they had to get out and
fight. Do something, he thought. No one, especially not the fleeing
humans, would be safe from that thing, and now the Belite-Gelfs,

the aliens who seemed consumed with destruction, were on the scene. Kate folded herself deeper into his chest and shook. If only things were normal, and they could be holding each other and watching a movie. But this was no movie; it was as real as the fire that suddenly streamed from the lion's mouth and scorched a group of Shaaris. They scattered; some blew up in a shower of silver goo and others writhed from burns. Some alien bodies caught fire instantly and burst into dangerous orange and blue flames. Carriages with horses appeared from out of nowhere. Some attempted to control the conflagration while others gathered wounded.

"Is that monster from the Bible?" Kate asked.

Jesse almost laughed; she really was a Catholic who never cracked the spine of her Bible. He had a flash of himself at Bible study, white shirt and wool pants, following along while the minister spoke in a booming voice about sin and the afterlife; Reverend Martin always found a passage to corroborate his points. Why was he thinking about that? He thought this may be a sign that he was losing his mind, or maybe his brain was altering, and memories, imagination, and reality were merging even more. He spoke to find a touchstone.

"Naw, it's the Chimera, from Greek mythology," he said.

"Don't suppose you remember from Ms. Gamble's class how to kill that thing, not that it will help, but you never know." Hayden touched the sides of the bubble and closed his eyes momentarily. He opened them and a ripple of blue washed over his face, almost like there was water under his skin.

Jesse concentrated. He knew that if he thought hard about the Chimera, he would be able to see the pages he had read in AP World Literature last year. He put one hand on his eyelids and focused. Within minutes he saw the pages in front of him, and he remembered reading the book while he had been stretched out on his bed relaxing on a Saturday afternoon in spring.

"Bellerophon flew up on the winged horse Pegasus, tied a piece of lead to the end of a spear, and shoved it into the lion's mouth. The heat in the beast's stomach melted the lead and choked the thing to death," Jesse recited.

"Good to know," Hayden said. "Now what?"

"We get out the power source," Jesse said. "Remember no one knows what it is. It could be a weapon—"

Jesse was unable to continue because their protective sphere popped like bubblegum, and they were falling from thirty feet in the air. Because of the strong winds, Kate blew from his grasp, and all three writhed in the ashy air, bracing for an unforgiving fall on hard ground. Ten feet down, five, the green lawn of the museum campus was coming into view despite the twists and flips Jesse's body did midair. Three feet, and then, poof! A cushion of smoke cradled him. He coughed and tried to sit up but found he couldn't. He was floating on a cloud until his backside hit the earth with a soft tap. The cloud enveloped him, making a shield for any other assault from the sky.

"Kate!" he yelled, "Hayden!" His voice barely reverberated back at him, and he worried that somehow the smoke was muting any sound. Though he had grown used to the muffled sounds of the overhead battle while in the bubble, he now worried that no one could hear him.

Jesse wiggled in a peculiar manner for what felt like several minutes, but before long, the smoke dissipated, and he saw Hayden next to him. Kate was hunched over the orb. After she saw that they were safely on the ground, she slammed it into her pack and tossed the bag over her shoulder.

"Thanks," he said to her, but the loud crashes and crackles

from fiery branches and burning buildings made it nearly impossible to hear each other. Both Belites and Shaaris were battling the onslaught of Gelfs, and a team of ten or more tried hopelessly to bring down the Chimera with the light lassos that had worked on the dragon. But there were too many red-headed aliens now; they raced through a tear in the sky and spilled into battle in a continuous stream. When one of the hideous heads of the beast belched flame, a Shaari or Belite tried to douse the infernal fan with liquid, but more and more fire struck Earth, sending all the people from their immobile cars on Lake Shore Drive, and even greater numbers mobbed and crushed one another as they attempted to flee the attack.

"We have to help them. Try a bubble again, but think of it as a tunnel, one covering Roosevelt Road. Then we'll try to send people that way," Jesse yelled at Hayden. His pulse was pounding; his eyes burned from the spreading smoke. He heard fire trucks in the distance, but they were most likely jammed between cars with no drivers.

Hayden moved his hands in an arch. His skin glowed, and his eyes squinted in concentration. Soon a protective shield, much like their bubble, curved the expanse of Roosevelt Road. Sparks and hail bounced off its top. All three started pushing people toward the street, gesturing and hollering as much as possible.

"This way!" they all yelled and shoved, but some people were in such a panic they ran in the wrong direction. Jesse saw one woman get struck with two fire balls at once; her skin burst into purple and red flames. She ran at a break-neck speed toward the lake, but the wind made the fire fan out all over her body with some smaller sparks flying off and catching in the gales like fireflies. Instead of helping her, Jesse froze in horror. A senseless chicken with its head cut off, he thought; he remained in one place. Then he thought, *she burns like a cattail torch, she burns like a piece of paper*, but those were lines from a poem. His photographic memory failed him, for he could not conjure the page with an author or title. He could not see the entire poem.

"Come on. There's nothing you can do for her," Hayden said. He pulled hard on Jesse's arm. Both boys flinched when ice and fire balls the size of watermelons started falling from the overhead battle. Smoke obscured the details of the fight, but Jesse sensed it was not good. Once in a while he caught a glimpse of iridescent scales snaking across the sky, and then more liquid drops from the aliens' bodies rained down. The ice and fire balls must have been as hard as meteors because they made melon-sized craters in the earth. Blinded by smoke and filled with fear, many people were crushed, or they fell into the holes, breaking ankles or feet. Jesse ran to heal the broken bones while Kate and Hayden channeled people through the Roosevelt arch that was held up by Hayden's mysterious strength from either the Liquid Light or *The Glow*. Jesse wasn't sure how long it would last, but he was grateful for Hayden's confidence and bellowing voice.

Jesse ran from person to person, healing broken bones in seconds so that the stunned wounded could flee the explosions. When he came to his first burn victim, he shuddered. The burnt skin smelled a lot like scorched meat in a pan. He swallowed the rising bile in his throat and steadied the squirming middle-aged man. He focused on repairing the skin, smoothing its surface, something like icing a cake. After his arms no longer seared with blisters and pain, the man stood in shock, his teeth rattling like door hinges coming loose in the wind.

"Go," Jesse said and pushed him toward the safe passage.

Then Jesse heard Hallia's voice in his head.

Find the power source and give it to me. Find the power

source and give it to me. Find the power source and give it to me.

He immediately found Kate and Hayden in the chaos, and they nodded to him. They huddled behind a blown-out piece of concrete that ran along Lake Shore Drive.

"Does she know we have it?" Hayden asked; his eyes streamed a silvery liquid because of the smoke.

"Maybe not, how would she know anyway. We've stayed away from any contact, except now in this mess. From what we've seen, she's not a mind reader, at least she can't read our minds." Jesse let out a long breath to steady his nerves. He wasn't sure about anything, especially what to do with the power source.

"What is it anyway?" Kate asked.

"Dunno, really," Hayden said. He pulled the ceramic flower out of his bag first and then the moonstone. "There isn't any writing on the stone, as far as I can see." He handed it to Jesse.

Jesse took the smooth sphere in his palm and ran the fingers of his free hand over the surface. He stared at it with hopes that Ancient Terrian writing would appear, just as Eruk and Palk's messages came through on the orb. Nothing happened. As far as he could tell, it was a precious gem the color of a pearl with inky pink swirls inside of it. Despite the disappointment, he kept glancing from the stone to the flower, back and forth, allowing himself to ignore the screams of the injured because he thought figuring out the power source would end all of the destruction. Or would it?

Kate kept flinching with each new bombardment from a battle that felt like it was getting closer to Earth with every passing moment. Hayden closed his eyes and directed his hands to the Roosevelt tunnel, and then he turned to Jesse.

"Don't mean to break your concentration or anything, bro, but this is getting more intense. You two feel it bearing down on us?" His eyes kept darting above him and then back to the safe passage.

"I'm not sure how much longer I can keep this thing up."

"Okay, whatever we do, we can't give this to Hallia." Kate had never sounded so forceful.

"Your reasoning?" Hayden asked.

"The Shaaris control everything, remember what Eruk and Palk told us, the control of Liquid Light, the ghettos. Who knows what they'll do?"

"You're right. I don't think we can hand it over to any of them. Like it or not, we're it." Jesse had been sensing this more and more. He had even told as much to the mother and her three girls. He knew they could only trust themselves.

"Okay. Agreed. But maybe it can help us if we figure the damn thing out," Hayden said. He quickly threw his hand in one direction and a mini shield blocked a barrage of icy spikes from striking the back of Kate's head. "Wow, that was pure reaction, cool!" He waved his hands and created more shields. "Do this fast, doc, I think you're the one on this. I'll try to hold the Roosevelt tunnel and block anything from you. Kate, make some of that cushy cloud stuff with the orb to protect some people. Let's get the power source worked out we can go on the *offensive*!"

CHAPTER TWENTY-TWO
POWER

In the Name of God, the Merciful, the Compassionate
Behold, We sent it down on the Night of Power;
And what shall teach thee what is the Night of Power?
The Night of Power is better than a thousand months; in it the
angels and the Spirit descend,
by the leave of their Lord, upon every command.
Peace it is, till the rising of dawn.

— The Koran, "Power"

Jesse stared at the moonstone and ceramic flower, both as ordinary as the knick-knacks that had lined his grandmother's curio cabinet. He tried to concentrate but was often distracted by numerous things: Hayden securing Roosevelt Road and making mini-shields of protection, the Chimera burning aliens into ooze, sending the remnants falling to Earth in liquid, melon-sized spheres, and Kate generating smoke out of nowhere.

Kate held the orb with one hand and directed the mist with her other hand or even with her eyes. She was getting good with the smoke. Jesse repressed a twinge of envy because her powers were obviously expanding by only using her mind and no physical contact with Jesse. He felt unnecessary and paralyzed with fear that he wouldn't be able to do anything to help.

With their protective measures, there were less people dying from explosions and ice spears, and also less injuries. All of this should have helped Jesse determine what needed to be done to give the power source, what, he thought? Power, any kind of it. But both objects lay inert in his fingers.

If Kate and Hayden could use their minds to enhance their abilities, so could Jesse. He tried to relive his moments in the janitor's closet with Kate, thinking that their emotions for each other and their touching would spark something in the two pieces. Nothing happened. He started to pace along the partial cement wall, the flower in one hand, held like how someone might clutch a discus, and the moonstone in the other, cradled like a small baseball. After several minutes of pacing Hayden gave him a *hurry it along* sign with his hand, sending tiny fire puffs in Jesse's direction.

"Hey!" he said, jumping backward.

"Sorry. We may be making this look easy, but it's no picnic, bro. How you doing on your end?" Hayden tried the same motion in the air, and soon he made a ring of fire. His eyebrow went up. He kept moving his hand in the same motion and the ring grew in diameter. He lifted it toward the sky. Jesse saw his intention: He planned to attack or even lasso the Chimera with it.

The ring moved higher and higher as it expanded, but as Hayden did this, his other protective shields were losing strength: Liquid balls, ice spears, and fire from the sky battle broke through here and there, making people fall to the ground. Some on Roosevelt hurried more, realizing that whatever had given them a respite from the onslaught was failing. People pushed each other more. Jesse heard fire trucks moving in; they must have been re-routed to find their way to the scene without using Lake Shore Drive. He tasted blood in his mouth and touched his lip gingerly, and then without thinking, he healed the cut on his cheek from where the blood originated.

The ring moved farther from them and into the sky, closer and closer to the battle where aliens shot ice and fire at one another, lassoed each other with light rings, or even had hand-to-hand combat with daggers and punches. Sometimes those fights broke into one alien clawing at the other, and then their gelatinous-liquid bodies dripped more fluid.

Almost there, Jesse thought. None seemed to notice its slow climb or possible threat. Kate kept at her smoky puffs; she could create them almost as instantly as ice picks or fire balls were about to hit ground. Then the attacking objects disappeared into the smoke until they dropped to Earth innocuously.

Jesse felt like an extra thumb. He took his eyes off of the ascending ring and focused on the power source. It was two pieces, but one power source, so logic would dictate that the two sections fit together somehow. But how?

He squatted and stared at each object in his hands. Nothing. His hands were starting to sweat from panic. He glimpsed the aliens and the Chimera reacting to the fire ring, and all forces realigned to combat it. The air smelled like burning tar and dead fish in the lake. He licked his lips and set back to "work." He would have much rather been making a fire ring that could burn some of these damn aliens than stare at the two pieces.

The Chimera whipped its snake tail and struck down a Belite; his chest ripped and gushed blue fluid. Shaaris attempted to lasso the goat's horns, but it butted its massive head to the side, throwing the aliens hundreds of feet from the battlefield. Each one of the Chimera's heads spat smoke and fire in fury, but Hayden's own ring hovered before them with an eerie determination. There was nothing in the ring to burn, ram, or whip, but the Gelfs fought off advancing Belites and Shaaris while throwing whatever weapon in their arsenal at Hayden's fire circle. More red-headed and fierce-looking Gelfs, who were controlling the lion head, aimed the lion's mouth right at where they were. Whether they were responding to Hayden as a "mark" or the source of the fire ring, they prodded the lion's jaw with a stick until it spat a stream of flame that reached Earth. The other aliens scrambled to re-direct the attack, but it was too late.

"No!" Jesse yelled and ran toward his friends. Hayden kept his shield in place and his ring in the air; Kate flinched, but held her ground as the Chimera's attack approached at rapid speed in one searing banner of flame.

The fire hit Hayden's shield and Kate's smoke and turned into a wall of ice the teetered for a few seconds and fell on Kate's legs.

Jesse was there in an instant. Hayden must have been pissed at the attack because he swore, and his shield flashed blue and Jesse could tell it was stronger; the barrage from above bounced off the surface. He turned to Kate who was unconscious under the wall of ice.

"Kate, wake up," he said and ran his hands down her face. He felt her pulsing heart and listened for her breath. Then he tried to push the ice block off of her, but it didn't budge. He scanned the area and grabbed a long tree branch. Using it as leverage he worked at the ice. For what felt like fifteen long minutes, Jesse strained against the limb, pushing until blood vessels burst on the side of his face, and his hands had cuts from the tree bark.

Kate lay inert and vulnerable. Hayden kept his shield and ring in place, but Jesse heard him taking long, loud breaths.

Finally, the block slid an inch and then another. With his full weight and bicep strength, Jesse let out a bellow of pain and pushed with a force he didn't know he had.

"Ahhhhhh!" he yelled.

The ice flipped. It tumbled end to end and then broke into pieces like shattered glass.

"Way to go, Hulk," Hayden said.

Jesse didn't respond. He put his hands on Kate and saw in his mind that her right kidney was bleeding and her legs were broken. He concentrated and lit his hands, careful to watch every part of Kate mend with his touch. Though he knew they didn't have much time, he allowed as many minutes as he needed to make sure she was all right. If he failed — no, he stopped himself from thinking in that way.

Focus, focus, amber, light, heat, stitch the tears, fuse the bones, re-route blood flow. No clots, no hemorrhage, no seizures. Jesse cradled her head in his hands and warmed her scalp. Her eyes opened slowly; she licked her lips.

"Jesse, the Chimera?"

"Yeah, it's still up there, but Hayden's keeping it back for a bit. How do you feel?" He kept scanning her body for even the slightest wound. He wanted to work on every scratch and bruise, but she steadied his hands.

"I'm okay," she said. She stood slowly and shook her whole body like a dog just out of the bath. "Go on."

Kate picked up the orb and closed her eyes. Her smoke, which Jesse now noticed had an amber-pink hue, rose.

"I'm counting these lives, Kitty-Kat," Hayden yelled her way and she smiled.

God, she was beautiful, Jesse thought.

He crouched and studied the pieces of the power source. Sweat poured down his face and his hands smelled like a campfire. He worried the pieces between his fingers. Soon he realized that his own sweat was making a gooey indentation in the smaller, central flower in the ceramic piece. He worked his fingers in the ooze until it made a smooth hole, or a repository for another object. That was it! Jesse could fashion the middle of the flower into a receptacle for the moonstone. Then the two would be one, and from there maybe they could get the thing to power up and do something. Anything.

Snap!

Hayden slapped the fire ring around the Chimera. Neither the beast nor the Gelfs liked this much, so they directed their full assault to the source, Hayden. He scrambled in fear, but had the balls to keep his hand in the air with the ring intact.

All three beasts spat fire toward Hayden, and each burst of flame turned to ice when it hit their shields. But soon the assault came as rapid as machinegun fire. Jesse couldn't tell what all was falling from the sky; the battle itself was obscured with smoke and ash, and huge globs of alien liquid splat on concrete and dirt.

But Hayden kept trying to tighten the ring around the Chimera. With every attempt to secure the monster, more Gelfs shot direct balls of fire at Hayden. He and Kate made as many shields to deflect it as possible, but it was apparent they were stretching the limits of their skills. In flashes Jesse saw some Shaaris or Belites trying to help by attacking the Gelfs with their own weapons and rake-like hands, but now the Gelfs were more than motivated, they were incensed with the possible capture of their beast.

Give me the power source, Jesse. Give me the power source, Jesse. Give me the power source, Jesse.

Hallia's voice made a haunting repetition in his brain, breaking his concentration and causing his work with the goo to slow down. Plus, now the Shaaris knew they had both pieces. He didn't have time to question how; he knew they needed help. Kate had both hands in the air, one with the orb balanced like a waitress tray. Her red hair flared out and twisted in the wind. She looked like a witch, Jesse thought, or a goddess, Demeter who could make fields grow or the Earth cover with ice. Hayden was on his back with his hands keeping the fire ring in the air; he looked like he was bench-pressing three hundred pounds.

Jesse had to risk it; he placed the moonstone into the center of the ceramic flower and waited. Nothing happened, except more terror from above. He wasn't sure if all the aliens now got some sign the power source was found and fused, or what happened, but each alien group scrambled, re-assembled, and started to charge Earth!

"No!" Kate screamed. More cloud puffs shot from her vicinity.

"Screeeeew this," Hayden shouted and jumped to his feet. He pointed to the sky with his dagger in one hand. Jesse wanted to join them, but he stayed where he was and looked at the power source. The only thing it had done was alert the aliens to its existence. Where was the weapon? The secret knowledge? Something, anything more than a decorative flower with a slimy middle to set a precious gem. Anything!

And then it happened. Lake Michigan churned and gurgled. Massive waves rolled in from miles offshore. White froth shot twenty feet into the air. The aliens paused midflight to view what was bubbling up from the depths of the lake. A whirlpool circled, but all Jesse could do was hold on to the power source with both hands. It now glowed yellow, amber, pink, and blue colors that blinked on and off with the movement of the water hundreds of yards away.

The whirlpool circled and sprayed a wall of water fifty feet in the air. When it crashed back to the surface something was there. An object as large as a football stadium and as hive-like as a parking garage ascended. Once the enormity of the thing completely hovered over the lake, Jesse realized what it was.

An alien ship lit the ash gray sky. It was calling them.

CHAPTER TWENTY-THREE

NEGOTIATIONS

Keepers are in place. This secret group will keep the mysteries of the Ancients cloaked, hidden, a mosaic unseen beneath two worlds, a web of unyielding information passed through whispers and codes. Power weaves a string between our worlds, and despite our position as divinities, we look to humans to save us in a time when all burgeoning lives are stilled, when the worlds are aching for a trio of youths to save us both. Terrians will be committed to guiding human spirituality as they need, and to ensure our altruistic endeavor through the ages, to keep the sacred in our motives to guide humanity, until the darkening days unfold, we have hidden a power source, meant only for one Youth Triumvirate, the ones even we cannot see.

— The Ancient Terrian Fragment of Human Divinities,
Jesse Woods, translator

The previous stillness as the aliens and teens stared at the ascending ship erupted into chaos. The Gelfs flew off in a wide circle and charged faster at Jesse. Instinctively he cupped the power source to his stomach and ran closer to Hayden and Kate. He glanced up and saw all the aliens in a race for him; they shoved, blasted, tore, and flew, mobbing to see which group could reach them first to get the sought-after object.

Jesse's mind was a garbled mess. He heard Hallia repeating, *Give me the power source,* but he also heard a cacophony of other voices, as if he were listening in on an alien board meeting and they were all squabbling over stocks and earnings.

Once the three teens were all together, they stood shoulder to shoulder with Hayden and Kate shielding them from the coming attack.

What if he lifted the power source in the air? There was no time to debate the possible result. He lifted it and imagined the lights turning into beams that could strike the charging aliens. Nothing happened at first, except for the obvious strain Kate and Hayden were under.

Come on, come on.

The ship teetered above the water. Nothing broke through the barrier protecting the teens, and when some aliens tried to approach the ship, they burst into electrical currents and plunged into the water.

Did he do that?

"Good, die, you assholes!" Hayden screamed.

Two Belites charged the ship, crackled with fire, and shot back in tumbles across the ashy sky.

"Cease!" an alien voice shouted. "Cease! We have to negotiate with the Triumvirate! Cease!"

It was Hallia who spoke. The Shaaris halted here and there, but the Belites and Gelfs kept coming.

"Cease! They are our only way to end this! They have the power source! Don't you see?" Her voice echoed like thunder, and that must have been what average humans heard because they continued to run and crush each other, snaking routes into the city. Emergency teams raced to help wounded and put out fires. Hallia took her hands and made a fire ball the size of a tractor tire. She hurled it down the lake shore, and it landed miles away on a rocky part of the shore.

"That will keep everyone busy," she said. Her massive body hovered over them and dripped ooze from her left hip. Her cheeks were covered in charred marks that must have been burns. She took a capsule from her pocket and ate, and this sent her body into ripples until she was a liquid ball that rained a thin stream to Earth, re-forming into an average humanoid shape. Perhaps by assuming a vulnerable state she made the other groups pause. A Belite male Jesse recognized as the one with the Bull of Heaven yelled, "Halt!"

Then a red-haired Gelf with black eyes, muscled arms and legs but a shockingly pinkish baby-like face flew forward. "Enough," he said. He didn't need to shout.

"Thank you," Hallia said in a smooth voice. She was in first-rate diplomatic mode. Before she could protest, the well-built Gelf and the gold-haired Belite turned into liquid balls and re-formed next to her.

"Hello, Roland," she said to the Belite. "Nosh." She nodded to the baby-faced Gelf.

"Hallia," Roland said with a smirk, the same one he had used to taunt Hayden during the bull fight. Was that really only last Friday?

Nosh didn't say anything to Hallia.

"Release my Chimera," Nosh said to Hayden.

"No way."

"I'll tear you apart." His voice sounded like a roller truck smashing down wet asphalt.

"Bite me."

"My pleasure," Nosh said. His baby face twisted. The dichotomy of the soft pinkish-red skin and the horrible voice sent a shiver through Jesse.

"You know, I might take you seriously if you weren't the color of a jellybean," Hayden said.

Where did he get that kind of nerve?

"We'll include your Chimera in our discussion, agreed Nosh?" Hallia asked.

He blinked in her direction, and Hallia took that as an affirmative.

She clapped her hands together and started to approach the teens with a mother's adoring face. When she came to their force field, one neither Hayden nor Kate made any effort to remove, she waved her hand in an attempt to lower it herself. It didn't work.

"No matter, you three can stop now. You've done it. Now give me the power source, and everything can go back to how it was."

Both Roland and Nosh shouted, "No!" at her idea. Jesse's mind did a flip. Go back to how things were before last Friday? He longed for it, craved it, but he also knew that things would never go back to how they were. He and his friends had crossed over into new and uncharted territory. The looming alien ship was testament to this new reality.

"Things will never go back to how they were," Jesse said. "Send some Shaaris to rain on those fires you just made for fun, or we're done here."

She waved and three Shaaris sailed south. She threw up her hands and made another force field between their odd negotiation circle and the fleeing humans.

"Now, hand me the power source, Jesse."

"I thought we were negotiating, Hallia. Who says you get

it?" Roland said. Golden ripples waved down his face and arms.

"Roland," she answered in a clipped tone. Jesse didn't hear the rest; he had a surreal moment where he pictured her as a housewife from the 1950s, a Mrs. Cleaver or someone from one of those ancient shows, who said to her son, "Now Beaver." No one could make that shit up, he thought.

Focus! He clutched the power source tighter and concentrated on what his mind may be able to do with it while all the aliens conversed. He closed his eyes for a moment and saw a door, one of many on the side of the ship, yawning open. A metal bridge slid out from under it and stretched to shore. He pictured the three of them running across it and on to the ship. It closed.

Jesse opened his eyes. Kate whimpered; sweat ran down her face and neck. Hayden had one hand in a fist, locking the Chimera even tighter in the fire lasso's grip.

"Shaari defenses are weakening, your borders breached, even Gelfs can break through. Face it, Hallia, you're done. It's time for new gods for humanity!" Roland raised his hands in the air and the Belites hollered back.

Once the roar quieted, Hallia smiled. "Good try, Roland, but we both know this is one battle of many. We still control ninety percent of the Liquid Light. What do you really think you'll accomplish with this, this, ship," she said with a wave of her hand.

Were ships looked down upon on Terria? And they had one. Surely the Ancients saw this ship as an asset; otherwise why hide it for some human teens to find thousands of years in the future? No, he *knew* they had an asset, and he was damn sure he wasn't letting go of it.

The looming giants hovered above the discussion; each time a Belite floated closer, the other groups did the same, making a ceiling of terrible monsters bearing down on them. Some aliens grappled with steadying their beasts. The bulls snorted and shuffled their hooves as if stomping firm ground; the Chimera floundered in its fiery chain with each head shooting smoke and sparks until two Gelfs shoved something into each maw. The glorious Shaari horses whinnied and huffed, making Jesse think of ghost stories with headless horsemen in spooky woods. Despite the feeling that the entire halted battle scene was spilling over, not one rogue alien attacked Jesse and his friends.

On the ground Hallia put her hands to her slim hips and tossed her long hair back. Then she smiled at Hayden, cocking her head to one side.

Heads up, Jesse thought and directed the message to Hayden.

Got it. Hayden's fist remained clenched.

"Hayden, put your hands down. There's no need to fight this," she said.

"Oh I think there is," he said. "Have you noticed how many humans have died because you watery whack jobs are fighting over who gets to play god? You're a pretty twisted species as far as we see it, so no, we'll stand here as long as it takes. You need to go home. *Then* things will go back to how they were."

Hallia considered his words. Her eye twitched. Jesse thought he smelled a waft of flowers, a scent something like his mother's perfume. This was a mind game. He had to keep his hands on the power source. *Keep talking, Hayden,* he thought, and Jesse went back to picturing the ship opening for them.

"The boy's pluck is exactly what makes him a candidate to join us," Roland said. He directed his words to the largest Belite formation.

"Back off Bull Man, I remember you. Don't trust you as far as I can spit, which isn't far considering my mouth is full of ash."

A wave of discussion rolled through the Belite ranks.

Hallia walked the length of the outer rim of their force field. She accentuated her backside with a sweeping motion of her hips. She jutted her breasts out.

Hayden checked Hallia out for a second. It was just enough time for the Chimera to buck. The snake wiggled from the noose in that moment, but Hayden regained his concentration and tightened his grip again. The snake hissed like a burst tire when it was secured once again in the ring.

"I don't think so, Roland. We Shaaris have a soft spot for Hayden, especially me. He's mine." Her voice was liquid itself, clear and supple, like her body. Jesse felt his own groin stir, so he worried about Hayden. All of this, attraction, emotion, fear, and their physical bodies could make things happen. Hallia knew how to manipulate it all; Jesse sensed their shields weakening.

"You'll have none of us," Kate cried. Her voice cracked with strain, but there was so much genuine passion in it that all three alien representatives appeared more interested in her.

"This Kate?" Nosh asked and stepped toward them.

Kate shivered next to him, but she kept holding the orb.

"Yes, Nosh, but she's not for your kind," Hallia said.

"You don't know our kind you fucking Shaari bitch!" He threw his hand back and went to claw at her cheek, but she was too fast for him and the other Shaaris at the ready. Two silver-haired giants shot down and grabbed Nosh. They meant to pin him to the ground, but the Gelf thrashed and kicked until they held him by the wrists and elbows. Nosh's feet dangled fifty feet in the air. Hallia had sent a shield of some sort their way, and Jesse wondered if it was to shield Nosh from escape or to mask themselves even more from average humans.

Surprisingly no Gelfs moved to counterattack. Nosh stopped writhing because it was obvious he wasn't going anywhere.

"Enough of this nonsense. I can't believe you are even here," Hallia said with a shaky voice more from anger than fear.

"I'll be glad to rip your Liquid Light core wide open, straight up the middle," Nosh said while motioning his index finger in a vertical line. His black eyes stared her down.

Hallia blinked and turned from him.

"Don't walk away, Shaari. I got something for you," Nosh said in a sing-song voice.

Jesse shivered, and Kate made an uncomfortable squeak next to him.

But Nosh looked at the three teens instead of Hallia. Then he tossed back his head; three Gelfs ate something and became streaks of red light racing out of the atmosphere.

Hallia looked up. "Impressive, Nosh, you can tell your criminals to run away."

There was silence for two solid minutes, and it felt like an eternity.

Nosh spoke directly to the teens, "I'll take my Chimera back and that power source, too, boys." His face broke into a childish grin.

Jesse and Hayden glanced at each other, both unsure of what to make of his obvious confidence even though he was fettered by massive Shaaris.

Another red streak lit the sky, but this time the Gelfs were coming and not going. The three had returned with a protective bubble Jesse was getting accustomed to seeing. The Gelfs tossed the bubble back and forth until the person inside of it was visible from the ground.

When Jesse saw her, he shook with rage. The outline of her body came into view first, and then, just like when he saw his family safely sleeping on a bed, there was Sofia, the details of her, swaying inside the light red sheen. She looked either asleep or unconscious in a night shirt and black and purple underwear Jesse recognized. He could make out the shapely curves of her body. Her light brown skin glistened in the shimmery ball; her long waves of dark hair were tossed as she swung back and forth by the strong winds.

Jesse felt like he was going to be sick.

"Ya see, I have what humans call a bargaining chip," Nosh said.

CHAPTER TWENTY-FOUR
CHASE

There was no one, at first. There was not one animal, yet, and no bird, fish, or tree. There was no rock or forest, no canyon, no meadow.
There was sky separated from all things.
The face of the earth was invisible. There was nothing that could make a sound.
— "The First Creation," the Popul Vu of ancient Maya

Have you ever seen the stars? Unending, limitless flashes of light like stepping stones from one world to another? Have you ever found a path before you, one you didn't know existed, and then it surfaces, your ship, on a new horizon? Your path now is uncharted, your journey just beginning, and you must find a way. Because if you don't, there will be nothing but the stars, unending, limitless. Alone.

— From an Undetermined Text,
Jesse Woods, translator

"Put her down," Jesse shouted.

Nosh laughed; both Hallia and Roland approached the outer part of the shield protecting the teens from the aliens.

"Jesse, I'll help you get Sofia back, just give me the power source," Hallia said.

Don't! Hayden sent a message directly to Jesse's mind.

"Jesse, I'm a Belite. I'm closer to these Gelfs than Hallia is or any Shaari is for that matter. Let me help you," Roland said. A string of his spittle caught in the wind and spun off.

Nosh squirmed and laughed manically, and then he repeated, "We got the little boys now," over and over; each repetition got louder and shriller.

The only voice Jesse didn't hear was Kate's. She kept staring at Sofia with a pained expression: Her face was bright red, and lines of tears started down her cheeks, leaving wet streaks in the soot.

The Gelfs had formed two lines like it was a hostile square dance with Sofia drifting between them. It was clear the Gelfs controlled the bubble and were shielding any aliens from getting to it. Nosh was right; they had a major bargaining chip.

Jesse's rage melted into hopelessness in an instant. What was he supposed to do? He loved Sofia and it made him sick to see her in a position of danger all because of him, but he could not imagine what Nosh and the Gelfs would do if they had the power source and the ship. It seemed the ship was only coveted because it was linked to the power source. What if there was a weapon, something so strong that it could destroy Earth, on board that ship?

He realized he *had* smelled his mother's perfume earlier, but instead of some mind game of Hallia's, he suddenly knew that he had conjured the scent from his own mind. Just like his friends in this make-shift Triumvirate, his brain was channeling into new highways of abilities, whether from the alien "gifts" given from his ancestors, or his work at honing the skills, it was a fact. As that old rap song went by someone he couldn't even remember, "I got my mind on my money and my money on my mind."

We will save her, Jesse, I promise. Jesse turned to Kate and nodded. Her face broke into a reassuring smile, but tears streamed down her cheeks in earnest now. She muffled a sob. Jesse knew what to do.

Tunnel to ship. Now! He sent the message to Kate and Hayden. *One, two, thr—*

Hayden let go of the lasso and both he and Kate directed their protective measures to form a tunnel, much like the one they had done over Roosevelt Road. The switch was seamless, and the tunnel ran from where they were on the museum campus to the shoreline closest to the alien ship.

Chaos ensued above them. The Chimera bucked and set off on a rampage, butting the giant Shaaris and Belites, and then setting them on fire from each of its hideous mouths. A few Gelfs secured the bubble with Sofia, but both Shaaris and Belites tried to take control of it in order to manipulate the Triumvirate. Before Jesse knew it, both Hallia and Roland were enhanced again and racing their monstrous bodies along the tunnel to try to find a weakness. But just like the shield they had made during the negotiations, this one held the aliens off.

It must be the power source, Jesse thought. Then he pictured the bridge stretching from the ship to meet them at the shore. The three teens ran hard, each pumping their legs and holding their precious objects in their hands. Kate tripped on some rocks when they got to the lake shore and sent the orb aloft. Hayden caught it on its descent and tossed it back to Kate once she had regained her balance.

They reached the edge of the water. Jesse looked up and saw that the Gelfs had attacked the Shaaris with the Chimera's ferocity and had freed Nosh. He was enhanced again and floating just under Sofia's bubble with that same baby-faced smirk, like a toddler who got one over on his mom or dad. He broke free of the different skirmishes and approached the tunnel.

"She's a sweet one, Jesse. Won't be so sweet after Gelf initiation," Nosh said. He gave Hallia a swift shove as they floated over the teens like cartoon word bubbles.

"Now what?" Hayden asked. "Seemed like you had a plan."

"I do," Jesse said. He put Sofia out of his mind for the moment and pictured the ship bridge extending to where they were standing on the shore. The scene was so real in his mind he knew that if he opened his eyes it would be there.

Almost, a few seconds more.

He felt the ship's presence then, like warmth from a heater, and he heard a grinding of metal engines starting up, like a furnace kicking on in a silent house at night.

"You did it," Kate whispered, and Jesse opened his eyes. A silver walkway stretched from a door on the ship right up to the place where gentle waves lapped at the sandy stones.

"Let's go my Triumvirate friends." Hayden waved them on and then backed along the bridge for a few feet to watch the fuming aliens outside the tunnel. He flipped Hallia off and smacked his own backside with a big grin on his face.

Once all three had crossed the threshold, the walkway slid back toward the ship and the door hissed shut behind them. The thrashing of the outside battle was completely muffled.

"Battle stations, Han, Leia!" Hayden laughed nervously.

Jesse bent at the waist and took several long breaths to fight back the rising bile from his stomach. Gelf initiation! He hated to imagine what that entailed. He hoped Nosh was only baiting him, and they'd keep Sofia safely asleep and floating in the bubble. Until when? He had to get her back.

Jesse stood and scanned the room. Ancient Terrian writing covered the controls, but apparently Kate didn't need to read it because she had already slipped the orb into a reservoir, and it lit the main cabin with a multitude of blinking lights.

"Jesse, bring the power source too," she said. "I think it goes here." She pointed to another reservoir next to the slot for the orb; it was a perfect impression of the underside of the flower. He locked it into place and engines pulsed beneath them.

"Whoa, I guess we're leaving," Hayden said. "I don't want to be a naysayer, but do we have a plan here or are we winging it as usual."

"All I care about is getting Sofia away from the Gelfs." Jesse sat in one of three metallic chairs that were in front of the main control panel.

"I'm with you, bro."

"Me too," Kate said. She smiled briefly and reddened.

Nothing like a girlfriend captured by aliens and floating in her underwear in front of a new relationship to put up a wall of awkwardness.

He sighed and touched Kate's hand; a small pulse of heat ran up his arm. She pulled away a fraction and said, "Jesse, let's..." She trailed off for a moment. "I think we can drive this thing, at least I pictured myself doing it with your help. You're the one who can read this stuff."

"Yeah, let's do it. Shoot the fuckers apart," he said.

"Wait, I'm all for it, but what if we hit Sofia, and what'll happen to all the people down there?" Hayden said.

No one had an answer. Jesse stood and paced up and down

the main room, reading the Terrian text. "We have weapons, I say we use them, and fast. It's getting more heated out there."

"They can't get in though," Hayden said. "We can take a minute to cool down." He placed a gentle hand on Jesse's shoulder and guided him to the chair.

"Kate, try a practice shot far from where Sofia's floating," Hayden said.

"Which ones are the weapons, Jesse?" When he didn't answer because he was imagining blowing up Nosh and the other Gelfs, she repeated, "Jesse," with more urgency in her voice.

"Over there," he said pointing to green buttons. "Seems like they are ranked with gradations of power. Start with the lowest level on the bottom."

Kate took aim at a band of Belites and Shaaris engaged in a side battle of hand to hand combat; the Chimera writhed not far from them, grabbing Shaaris in its jaws and shooting fire at Belites.

Pop! The weapon, a bright flash of light and sound, released from beneath the ship and spun in a whirl over the lake and into the sky. Pop, and another pop! It exploded in the vicinity of the band of aliens, obliterating their gelatinous-liquid bodies and sending thick globs of rain into the water.

"Cool."

Jesse stood and clapped. "Do it again!"

"No, let's draw them off," Kate said. "They're going to be mad now. I don't want them to start killing other humans to get us to stop."

Jesse knew she was right, but he shook with the need to destroy them.

"How do we fly?" Hayden asked.

Jesse focused on the control panel. "Seems pretty straight

forward. These three buttons are for thrusters; this lever accelerates and provides lift; this seems to take us to faster-than-light speed, and wait a minute," he said. He touched one blue button gingerly and smiled at Kate and Hayden. "This one will cloak us."

"Awright, Triumvirate, let's give these motherfucking aliens a run for their money," Hayden said. He paced the cabin and slashed his dagger in the air. "How about we bring this war to their own turf."

"You mean go to Terria?" Kate said. "We don't know the way."

"I'd bet our navigator could figure it out given the time," he said. "But with the very angry aliens outside, I say we lead them to the edge of Earth's atmosphere, cloak, and follow the Gelfs to Terria, to rescue Sofia."

"Let's find Eruk and Palk too. We need to get them out of that ghetto," Kate said.

Jesse nodded. Then he could tear Nosh apart.

"Okay," Kate said. She pressed the buttons for thrusters, and the ship heaved and groaned. "Aah," she shouted, stood, and sat back down anxiously.

Jesse regained composure and focused on the tasks at hand. They both put their hands on the levers to accelerate, and the ship darted into the sky and hovered on the outskirts of the battle to get everyone's attention.

"Come and get us," Hayden whispered.

"Ready?" Kate asked.

"Yeah," the boys answered in unison.

"We're on our way," she said.

The ship lurched and sprang to life under their touch. It shot higher into the sky. Outside the eight-foot windows, the enhanced aliens swarmed and fought. Chicago passed beneath them. They rose higher and higher, and the Chicago shoreline was a war zone with smoke and smears of fire crackling up throughout the city. Countless pockmarks in the ground peppered the museum campus. After they were on the cusp of visual range, Jesse watched the swarms of humans scramble along the streets like ants in a colony.

All three alien groups had ceased fighting and waited in abeyance for the Triumvirate's next move.

"Hit it, Kate," Jesse said. She slapped at the acceleration control quickly, almost like she was afraid of changing her mind.

The ship knocked Hayden off his feet as it darted toward Earth's outer atmosphere.

"Whoo-hoo!" Hayden yelled. Kate kept her hand on the button and then hit the full reverse control when the Shaari border control came into view.

Hayden slid across the floor like a seal on ice. "What're you doing?" he asked.

"Cloak, cloak!" Kate shouted.

Jesse hit the cloak button, and the ship hissed.

"It says we're cloaked," he said. "Hopefully, the border aliens didn't see us and the ones on Earth will think we're long gone."

Numerous border Shaaris drifted back and forth. They held light lassos, battle daggers, and long lance-like weapons. Some rode horses or other half serpent, half bull beasts that Jesse hadn't seen before.

"We need to follow the Gelfs. Let's wait," Kate said.

Blue and gold streaks of light came from Earth. It was the Belites in their Liquid Light form. The colors snaked back and forth in front of the Shaari border control. The enhanced forms of the Shaaris on their beasts made a formidable line; their beasts hoofed the air. Quickly the blue and gold lights re-formed, one by one, into enhanced Belites, each one charging the border in a furious advance. Before long red lights came, the Gelfs, and some silver ones, the Shaaris, who took up arms with the border guards and tried to lasso as many Belites as possible with rings of light. Once any enhanced alien tore through the barrier, it ingested the Liquid Light once again and raced into outer space as smears of light. A few Shaaris managed to capture three Belites and one Gelf, but the rest broke through easily once the Chimera re-formed, hissing and spitting to clear a path. The Gelfs shoved the Liquid Light down its throats and the Chimera became a blur of red, and then Gelfs followed, escaping the outer atmosphere and flying home. They still had Sofia with them in her protective bubble.

"Follow them," Jesse said, and Kate pressed the faster-than-light speed controls controls. The ship kicked in pursuit, the red Gelf light a bloody trail.

Jesse clenched his fists and said, "We're going into the dragon's lair now y'all, and there's no turning back."

ABOUT THE AUTHOR

Jenny Benjamin is a former high school English teacher who served at-risk, inner-city students for thirteen years. She is also the author of the novel *This Most Amazing* (Armida Books), the poetry chapbook *More Than a Box of Crayons* (Finishing Line Press), and the poetry chapbook *Midway* (No Chair Press), which won second place in the 2017 No Chair Press contest. Her novel, *Heather Finch*, will be published by Running Wild Press in June 2022.

ACKNOWLEDGMENTS

This book would not have been possible without the support and guidance of many people. First, thank you to Ananke Press for taking a step in a new direction and publishing my young adult trilogy. A special thanks goes to Cate Hendrickson for sending the initial acceptance email that made me cry with joy and working so thoughtfully on the design and layout for Enhanced.

Thank you to my writing groups for your feedback on Enhanced. For my online children's writing group, a special thanks to Sandy Brehl, Christa von Zychlin, and Lori Kuhn. In addition, thank you to the fine writers in WG in the order of our shared history: Colleen Harryman, Angela Sorby, Monica Maniaci, Catherine Koons Hubbard, Melissa Schoeffel, Liana Odrcic, and Jennifer Dworschack-Kinter. Yes, Monica, there are aliens in these books, but they're humanoid aliens. In addition, I want to thank my brother-in-law Dan Gapinski for reading a version of the trilogy and being my best sci-fi fellow enthusiast.

Thank you to my dear friends who are really family: Ann Oldham and Aki Gamblin. Our deep discussions about science, myth, Star Trek, and the Lord of the Rings influenced me on cosmic and visceral levels because this book would not be here without you two.

Thank you to my NOVA family. Our shared love and experiences—the day-to-day magic making that happened at NOVA—created my main character: Jesse Woods. I love him like I love all of you. When I see you shine, my heart expands to interstellar proportions.

Thank you to my bff from five-years-old, Mandy Hatje, and her clan of wonder-boys: Joel, Jon, and Luke. I feel your support for my writing from across the state line.

Thank you to the Commune! You know who you are! We are a Court of Wonders, and we got this way through so much mundane daily grind accomplished with devotion and love. Without you, I would not be here writing this. Your support and love fill me up each day.

Thank you, Adam, for the quantum entanglement.

Always, always, thank you to Sophia, Maggie, and Ally Ruth. There is no way I could imagine other parts of the universe without having you.

Reading Questions for
ENHANCED

Chapters 1-2

1. What information do you learn about Jesse Woods in the first two chapters? Predict how you think Jesse will grow in the story.

2. What do you think about Jesse's feelings for Kate? Is he being unfair to his girlfriend Sofia?

Chapters 3-5

3. During the devastation of the tornado, which is really an alien battle, Jesse, Kate, and Hayden learn they are one of many Youth Triumvirates who carries the weight of the fate of humanity. What text-to-text connections can you make with this element of the story?

4. In what ways does Jesse emerge as the Youth Triumvirate leader in these chapters?

5. In what ways do the chapter quotations from other texts and the references about what Jesse has read in his AP class influence the overall story?

Chapters 6-8

6. In chapter 6, Hayden questions Jesse about his view about being stopped by police because of being Black. How and why has the worldview on this topic changed from 2012, when the novel is set, to today?

7. How do the Youth Triumvirate teens develop their skills in these chapters? What do their progress and learning methods reveal about them as characters?

8. What do you think about the character Hallia? Do you trust her? Why or why not?

Chapters 9-11

9. How has Jesse and Kate's relationship progressed? How is it tied to their powers?

10. Predict how Jesse's ability to read the ancient Terrian text could be beneficial.

11. What themes do you see emerging in the novel so far? What scenes in the book support your idea about a theme?

Chapters 12-14

12. What tensions build between Jesse and Hayden in these chapters? How do they resolve issues?

13. Revisit the idea of the Youth Triumvirate's emerging skills. What new developments occur in chapter 13? How might Jesse's abilities affect the dynamics among the three characters?

14. Jesse struggles with his homophobic feelings in chapter 14. Do you think he will grow as a character on this point? Why or why not?

Chapters 15-17

15. Discuss the changes in Jesse and Hayden's relationship. What scenes show the development of their friendship?

16. Jesse's thoughts often drift to his family as he and Kate and Hayden are walking toward Chicago. What do these reflections reveal about Jesse and his family?

17. What information does Jesse, Kate, and Hayden learn in these chapters that could save their lives and help them accomplish their quest?

Chapters 18-20

18. How do you view Kate as a character? How has her character changed or grown in your perception of her?

19. What do you find unexpected or surprising about the events in chapter 19 that take place at Union Station in Chicago?

20. What does the Chicago setting add to the mounting tension in these chapters?

Chapters 21-22

21. How do the action, Jesse's experiences, and the alien battle culminate in these chapters? Do any of the scenes connect with your own experiences, even though they are fantastical?

Chapters 23-24

22. Did you predict any of the outcomes with the power source or characters that occurred in these chapters? What do you think will happen in Book 2?

MORE FROM ANANKE PRESS

Jesus The Time Traveller
by Roberta-Leigh Boud

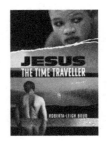

What would happen if Jesus were a time traveller, or a mad man, or both, and he chose to go and save the world because, even though he wasn't a god, and even though he was deluded, he felt that it was fundamentally the right thing to do?

The Witches Of Riegersburg
by Julie Anne Stratton

For the fans of *The DaVinci Code*—with three generations of extraordinary women keeping alive the ancient Goddess faith.

Print In The Snow
by E. V. Svetova

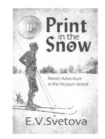

A down-to-earth teen girl must get back home from the Otherworld before the fairytale dream turns into a nightmare. Join the unlikely heroine on an adventure of a lifetime! Lush watercolor illustrations of cool characters, weird monsters, and spooky villains. Book I of *The Green Hills* trilogy.

Made in the USA
Las Vegas, NV
19 November 2021

34850032R00144